Cow Cookies

Cow Cookies

A Modern Western Mystery Novel

C. F. Button

Cow Cookies

Interior Design: Day to Day Enterprises
Cover Design by Janni Kerns

ISBN: 1-933155-00-0

Printed in the United States of America

10 9 8 7 6 5 4 3 2 1

Library of Congress Control Number: 2004097884

Published by Snakeweed Press
Baker City, Oregon

Dedicated to
All my friends who,
with their quick and Quixotic humor, have provided
the inspiration for these otherwise fictional characters.

Special thanks are due to my wife, Kata, for tolerating my
aberrant behavior
and to Charles Patterson, Jean Findley, Kathy Cushman, and Sue Badgley
for editing and encouragement.

Chapter One

The fan inside the dashboard reacted to the dust rising from the gravel road and clogging the air-conditioner filter by changing pitch. Within minutes the fan became intermittent, uttering a low, strangled growl. Heat welled up from the manual transmission and radiated through the windows from the bleached blue of the eastern Oregon desert sky. After several fruitless minutes of cursing and pounding on the dash, Tom opened the window, preferring clogged sinuses and the rime of dust on his glasses to smelling his own sweat. He sped up, hoping to leave the dust behind rather than breathe it, but like most SUVs, this one was a dust-sucker.

As it climbed, the road swung sharply left, then looped right through a cut in a huge rock outcrop. The Bronco skidded to the left. Unaccountably, four vehicles blocked the road. Tom recognized the sheriff's Tahoe, a state fuzz cruiser, Baker County's new ambulance, and an unmarked pickup with a gumball on the dash. Tom locked the brakes and skidded to a stop just in time. The dashboard let out a final agonized squeal and emitted a puff of smoke. The inside of the Bronco was suddenly filled with a foul odor, causing Tom to gag.

Fester Johnson's scowling face appeared from the cloud of dust thrown forward by Tom's locked brakes. Fes was a second-string "on-call" deputy and part-time rent-a-cop when highway construction companies wanted to discourage speeders. He saw the Department of Interior license plates, hitched up his pants, and tried to look larger and more intimidating than his paunch and 5 foot 8 height allowed. "Goin' a little fast on a blind curve, weren't yuh?" Considering Fes's personal dislike for Bureau of Land Management employees in general, and for Tom in particular, it was a mild rebuke.

"Nah, just hadn't been here in a while. Didn't know the washboard was quite that bad." The sheriff was visible in the background, talking to an ambulance attendant. Tom noticed the ropes trailing out from the truck down the steep slope. "What's the matter," he asked, "did someone go over the side?"

"When was the last time you were up here?" Fester knew Tom mostly did field work.

"Oh, about two weeks ago, Thursday. Didn't see anybody or any vehicles then. Usually don't." Tom hoped Fester wouldn't get a whiff of the dead fan. It would become a sore joke that would make the rounds of his low-life friends for months.

"Well, you can probably get around that cruiser. Just don't get in the way here."

Recognizing contempt in the dismissal, Tom jockeyed the Bronco past the maze. It occurred to him that nobody was likely to inform the BLM office of the wreck. The BLM law enforcement people would want to know when unprepared tourists took their nice sedan over a cliff. Instead of calling in, Tom left the radio mike on the dash until the incident was forgotten.

The sun began to sear his bald spot the instant he emerged from the Bronco. He jammed a worn straw hat on his head to resist the blast furnace breeze coming up the ridge. From a cardboard box on the back seat, he unfolded a National Forest map, covering the vinyl driver's seat and back, shading it from the sun. That would make it possible to sit when he returned. It gave him wry satisfaction to think that the Forest Service was doing something to save his ass.

Next he extracted a day pack, a hiking stick, and a topographic map, heavily marked in pencil and ink. Adjusting his sunglasses and hat to protect his eyes from the glaring sun, he set off to hike along Willow Creek, checking the survival of several hundred cottonwood cuttings. Months before, he had conned a crew of high-school students into a field trip to plant the cottonwood among the rock and cobble of the eroded banks. Then the landscape had been green with a brief flush of new growth and covered with bright, colorful wildflowers.

Now the grass was cured to a pale straw color, and the sagebrush had resumed its normal dusty gray appearance.

By noon he reached the creek and crouched in the shade of a dirt bluff long enough to eat a container of yogurt. There was a bitter smell in the air that made it seem unlikely the BLM had succeeded in keeping cattle out of the drainage during the summer. Six hours later he trudged out of the canyon, cursing the trespass cattle that had eaten all the cottonwood sprouts. Tom added another failure to his list. Odds were it would take several days before the owners would round up their animals. At this time of year ranchers were usually busy baling hay, or else trying to fix one of their old tractors so they could.

*

At 8:15 in the evening, Barney's Pub was reeking of smoke, sweat, and cheap cologne. The young cowboys were outnumbered by construction workers two to one, and women by men nearly five to one.

"Hey, Emma," Tom addressed the waitress, "looks like a tough night for the down and out. How about a porter and a chicken fajita salad?"

"We're out of porter. In fact, we're out of stout too. It's either Coors or Mud Hen brown on tap. How come you're in here tonight? I thought Thursday was your beer and grease night."

"No politics, please, give me a Mud Hen. It was a tough day. Don't feel like cooking beans."

"Yeah, it was a hot one. You look like you've been crawling in the dirt. Hope you weren't planning on picking up a hot date."

"I've been living clean for a year now. It may be time for a change, but I'll settle for a beer." In fact, it had been well over a year since Tom had been on a date. Reacting to his sense of rejection, he had gone through a period of intense social activity the first year after his divorce. All the women he had dated were recovering from their own marital disasters, and none were seriously interested in starting another. When he got the job transfer to Baker City, Tom had decided it was a good time to slow down.

Emma moved through the bar, scooping up empties and automatically refilling glasses, knowing the crowd was just starting to roll. Tom divided his attention between the large screen TV where the Atlanta Braves were apparently demonstrating professional spitting and the dark corner where the two best-looking women in the bar were posing for the appreciative crowd.

"Hey Tom, it's only Tuesday. You lost?" Bill Christen, the BLM hydrology technician, appeared grinning crookedly. "Oh, jeez, Man, sorry. You look like you need a beer. Who kicked the shit out of you?"

"Oh, I was trying to fix a cut fence up in that draw near Owl Spring, off Willow Creek. That was after I found a bunch of cows down in the canyon licking the dust off the rocks. The water is trickling under the rocks, so they were tracking back to the spring. It was churned to a stinking mudhole. Plus, the AC in my truck went down, so everything inside had about an inch of dust on it, including me."

"Smells like you brought more than mud back with you. Couldn't you hose off?" Bill noticed Tom's gaze drifting toward the corner, "Whadda ya think about them apples?"

"We could use some back-lighting. Maybe Emma would turn on the stage lights if we asked.... Didn't bother to go home to clean up. Just stopped in for a quick dinner. Saved myself the trouble."

While Tom and Bill were exchanging desultory comments on the Braves' batting, the stage lights came on in the corner. Jesse Jackson was setting up his drums early for the 10 o'clock set. He and Eddie Willings were the local talent for weeknight music if any was to be had in town. They played a mix of country, jazz, and blues. Jesse Jackson was a balding forty-ish, healthy and athletic, but with a pale pink complexion that would burn if it saw the sun. Because of that and the coincidental choice his parents had made with his name, he had forever been tagged with the nickname "Reverend." It had embarrassed him as a teenager, but was now a crowd-pleasing asset on stage. When he looked up from the cymbals and saw Tom, he made one quick adjustment, waved, and walked over.

"Hi, Thomas, how are you?"

Tom's salad arrived, smothered in fried onions and with a heap of guacamole. He set down his beer and gestured, "Hey, it doesn't get any better than this!"

"Are you kidding?" snorted Bill. "This is the high point in his life, Reverend. He comes in once a week, and then goes home after two beers. What kind of social life is that?" He looked back to the women in the corner, "You know, I don't think much of the one on the left, but that's looking like a pretty sharp pair on the right."

Jesse looked back over his shoulder. "Yeah, those are new. I picked them up over in Boise this week."

"Huh, what?" Bill looked puzzled for a moment. "Oh man! DRUMS! This guy thinks I'm talking about his goddamn drums!" He shuffled off for a better view of the women, leaving the Reverend looking wounded.

"Well, they are nice looking drums after all," Tom offered. "Just didn't see them in the glare."

Jesse decided to change the subject. "Did you hear about the body today?"

"No, I've never seen her before, and Bill didn't have time to tell me about her." Tom was not going to let the joke pass away that easily.

Flustered, Jesse checked over his shoulder again, as though someone might hear if Tom wasn't shouting. "They found a body south of town. I heard it was on BLM land."

"No, I didn't hear anything. Who was it?" Tom asked.

"They don't know yet. The critters had been at the body for a while."

"Oh, yum!" Tom replied, realizing his onions were getting cold. "Where was it?"

"A rancher was rounding up strays down in Cow Creek. He saw some color and a couple vultures halfway up the canyon side. When he checked, it turned out to be human." Jesse added, "Or at least it had been."

"Did they find a vehicle too?"

"No," said Jesse, "it looked like he was down there on foot."

"I might have seen the sheriff and his boys near there with an ambulance."

"What was going on?" Jesse pried.

"Nothing I could see," Tom replied. "Fester got huffy as usual. Ran me off. Keep your ears open."

"I always do. Are you interested for a particular reason other than that it happened on BLM land?"

"It was a long way from the highway to dump a body. There must have been something going on for someone to die out there alone without a vehicle nearby."

*

Wednesday morning the thermometer outside the window read over 65 degrees and was headed for the upper 80's by noon. Late August weather had held on into September, and was threatening to stick around until November.

Tom arrived at the office by 7:30. Since he had not logged on to his computer in three days, he had at least thirty e-mail messages waiting. He checked the senders and deleted all but one. That one was from his supervisor, explaining that the District was overspent on travel. The training session he had applied for was cancelled.

Since his supervisor occupied the desk immediately on the other side of the partition, Tom added to the general bedlam by talking loudly. "Hey, Vince, did you really think I was counting on going to Portland in September? Hell, I wrote that off last May when we sent the whole office to Ontario on per diem for the annual sputum awareness training. Besides, it was really important for the District Manager to go to Puerto Rico in February to recruit Hispanics for our workforce."

Bill Christen interjected from four cubicles away, "I can't believe they announced that in a staff meeting instead of trying to cover it up!"

"Hey, now, Georgette was really trying to do something good. You guys need to cut her some slack." Vince DeMarco was nothing if not charitable. He had inherited his mother's undying optimism as well. A third-generation Italian-American with an olive complexion, Vince was what passed for ethnic diversity on the BLM side of the building. While they had plenty of women in the professional workforce, racial diversity eluded the agency outside of major cities. The temporary employment of summer fire crews was all that kept the agency out of really hot water.

"Vince, use your brain," Tom scolded. "How many Puerto Ricans work for this outfit west of the Mississippi? Don't answer, 'cause you don't know any. Now, what is the Hispanic population around Vale and Ontario? Think any of their kids might want to go to college to get a decent paying job working close to home? How many Puerto Ricans want to come out and work in a stinking cow town like Vale?"

"Well, you don't know. Maybe a lot if they had the chance," Vince said defensively.

"So, did Georgette announce how many she recruited?" Vince didn't answer, so Tom decided to let up. "Is Randy in here yet?" Tom grabbed his coffee cup and headed down the hall, speaking louder for his voice to carry over the rat-warren of partitions. "Hey, Randy! You here yet?"

"Who wants to know? Don't come in here unless you've got good news. I'm taking my Employee Assistance Program training seriously." The voice behind the partition took on a pedantic simper.

"Start your day out right with pleasant tasks. Leave the oh-ner-us tasks for later when you are at your peak of energy. Come see me about 10 o'clock." Randy Bergen was Tom's role model for dealing with agency insanity. He was also the range conservationist who dealt directly with the ranchers about grazing allotments near Watchtower Mountain.

Tom leaned on Randy's desk and randomly punched keys on the keyboard to divert Randy's attention from the computer monitor. "Didn't you tell me there wouldn't be any cattle in Willow Creek pasture this year? I was in there yesterday, and I saw about 40 head. They wiped out my cottonwood planting. With this heat, they never get out of the bottom, not even to find some grass."

"Well, it was sure nice of you to provide a little garnish," Randy drawled. "There wasn't much down there but rock last time I looked. The permittees fixed the fence at the mouth of the canyon where it empties out to the Burnt River. They're not supposed to be in there."

"I thought maybe someone sub-leased the permit. There were three different brands, a mix of Herefords and Black Angus and one very weird Black Baldy. Oh, yeah, also the fence had been cut up by Owl Spring, so some of them might have come in from over the ridge."

"That whole country on the other side is dry this year, so they might have smelled the water and pushed the fence. What makes you think it was cut?" Randy asked.

"Only that you could see marks on the wire. That and the boot prints where somebody actually rolled the fence out of the way so the cows wouldn't trip on it."

"Isn't that a mile from the nearest road? Old Roy wouldn't have gone up there. He doesn't even get on a horse any more. Hemorrhoids got too bad." Randy smirked. "Let me see who's running cattle on the other side. What brands did you get?"

"There's an old trail near the upper end of the canyon, but it's washed out. You might be able to get there on a 4-wheeler, but I didn't see any sign of one. Here, I drew the brands." Tom handed Randy a folded page from his notebook. "One looks sort of like a circle with a line through it and a second mark below and to the left. Those were on the right shoulder. One was the P-square brand. The other looked like a big snake, and it went from the left hip all the way across the ribs and over the shoulder. If your daddy made a mark like that on you, he would have been in jail for the rest of his life. In Colorado, the ASPCA would have been after this guy."

Randy opened his brand book. “Don’t tell me about Colorado. Nobody but Californians live there anyway. Besides, unless you’ve been peeking over the stall in the men’s room, you don’t know what my daddy did to my ass when I was a kid. Here, look at this. Is this the brand?”

“It sort of looks like the circle and slash mark, but I couldn’t see the whole J there to the left. What about the snake?”

“That’s the Roberts bunch over on Little Crow Mountain. Their cows would have to cross a lot of country and at least three fences to get there.” Randy looked unhappy. “I don’t like the sound of this.”

“Well, they might want to check their cattle because there isn’t much forage left, and from the smell of things a couple miles downstream from Owl Spring, there’s at least one dead animal in the bottom of that deep cut.”

“Did you get the brand on that one?” Randy grinned.

“Oh, man, that baby was ripe. I didn’t even get close enough to see it. The wind was blowing up-canyon.”

“Well, you never know, it might have been lying on the wrong side anyway. I would have turned it over to check, though.”

“Don’t worry. It’ll be there for a while. You might want to wait for it to dry out,” Tom advised. “It gets lighter and easier to turn over that way. Most of the cows were headed downstream, but the ranchers might want to look around the spring too. I think there was something stinking out in the juniper on the ridge.”

“Thomas, Thomas,” Randy clucked, “try to maintain a proper sense of decorum, please. There is the sound of self-righteous glee in your voice. Those cows are somebody’s family!”

“Well, don’t bother to trespass them. If these guys are losing cattle, it’s going to cost more than we’ll ever charge them. Oh, I also heard somebody was rounding up cattle in Cow Creek yesterday and found a body.” Tom explained, “I mean a human body. You hear anything about that?

“Yeah,” Randy frowned. “Troy Grey found it. He called this morning to say he had cattle scattered all over the country. He thought somebody was cutting his fences too. Maybe the local kids have been making motorcycle raceways again.”

“Well, maybe one of them died. Except from what I heard, nobody saw a vehicle or a bike.” Tom probed, “Did Troy say anything about the body? Anybody he knew?”

“Troy said it was a stinker. The animals and flies messed it up too much to see who it was. He saw a ponytail, but he didn’t look too close once he saw the head. The body was too big to be a young kid."

"Seems awfully quiet in here for that kind of news to be going around," Tom noted. "Did you tell anybody?"

"Why? They'll find out soon enough. The silly bastards will probably hold a meeting to announce it. They won't know any more than I already told you, probably less. I'm going out to Dooley Mountain. Maybe I'll spot an elk I can go back and shoot later."

"Good idea unless you'd rather go out to Cow Creek with me and check fences," Tom invited.

"Hell no," Randy replied. "I know what you have in mind. Just because you like to play detective doesn't mean I have to get in trouble with you. If you were really smart, you'd let the cops figure it out without you. Nobody is going to appreciate you sticking your nose in."

Tom went back to his cubicle for his pack and canteens. "Hey, Vince, I'm headed out to Cow Creek. It'll be a short day. Back by six or so."

"OK, but call in on the radio by 4:30 to let somebody know when you're gonna get back for sure. And sign out on the board by the copy machine!"

"Yes, Mother."

"I'm serious! The ADM's warning us we've got to check in each day. Otherwise he's gonna send a helicopter after you, and you're gonna pay for it."

"Radios don't work when they're in your truck and you are two miles away in a canyon. I'll call you at home tonight if it makes you feel better." When Tom walked out of the air-conditioned building, the heat slammed him in the face. By the time he had walked two blocks to the warehouse compound, he was whistling and waving at the neighbors. He found the Bronco's air-conditioner was once again pushing out a faint stream of musty, cool air.

*

This time Tom took the blind curve on Watchtower Road slowly. There was another BLM rig already parked where the ambulance had been. He leaned out the window. "Hey Mary, can you back up and make room for another rig? Fester might come back and give me a ticket for blocking the road."

Mary Twil was a law enforcement ranger who worked out of the Vale District Office. She smiled and waved. Giving Tom barely enough room to squeeze the Bronco in front of her Dodge, she waited as he climbed out with his pack and arranged the map over the seat. "Hey, that's clever. Why don't you buy a real windshield sunscreen?"

"Vince told me I only got sixty bucks of procurement money this year, and I had to buy a book. Besides, they charge me two and a half bucks for each canteen I check out of the supply cache. The Forest Service gave me this map for free. See here? It's stamped Official Business Copy – Not for Resale."

Mary looked at Tom like he was a hopeless dog. "What are you doing here? Do you know anything about where they found the body yesterday?"

"Yeah, I nearly ran over Fester. He seemed to think he was going to protect the front of his truck with his body when I slid around that curve on the washboard."

"Oh, you were right here when they brought the body up?"

"Well, I didn't know there was a body. I saw some ropes tied off in Fes's truck and thrown over the side of the hill. I figured somebody lost a car over the edge, but he didn't bother to fill me in. He wanted me out of the way, so I went on around."

"Didn't you call in to the office?"

Tom had heard her gripe before about people not reporting accidents or potential crimes, so it seemed like the appropriate time for a lie. "Fes said something like they had already informed the Vale Office what was going on. By the time I got back to town, it seemed like it was old news."

"That jerk! I don't think he'd ever cooperate with BLM, and me being a woman only makes it that much worse." Mary looked at Tom suspiciously. "Nobody in the Baker Office seemed to know about it an hour ago when I called. How come you knew and nobody else did?"

"I heard it in the bar last night. Randy knew about it when I talked to him this morning. From what he said, it sounded like Troy Grey was the one who found the body when he was rounding up stray cattle."

"And you're right back out here before anybody knew enough to tell you to keep out of it," Mary said sourly. "You weren't planning on hunting around the accident scene, huh? See if you might find something interesting?"

Tom skirted the subject. "The cattle were supposed to have been out last May. Thought I'd go see how bad the riparian area got used, maybe take some pictures. Since Troy Grey found the body, and he was rounding up cows down below, this seemed like a good place to check."

"Yeah, right," Mary said skeptically.

"There's no yellow tape saying 'keep out.' Didn't really figure I'd pick around where they found the body though. The sheriff probably found everything and carried it out."

"Well, I did plan to check it out," Mary said. "If this turns into a liability suit, I want to know what it looks like. Maybe I can keep the DM from saying something to the newspaper that we have to explain later."

"Maybe Gilbert will write a press release quoting you so you can send it to your mother. 'Those must have been some mighty hungry coyotes,' BLM Law Enforcement Officer Mary Twil said today, 'they ate everything but the metal snaps off his suspenders.'" Tom looked at Mary and smiled. "Have you noticed how anybody Gilbert quotes sounds like they died in the fourth grade and were resurrected by Dr. Frankenstein?"

"Women have enough problems without Gilbert writing their material. All right, let's go. Where were they?"

"Look for a buffalo trail. The sheriff must weigh about 290 and wears cowboy boots. He probably slid halfway down to the creek. You got a walking stick?" Tom waved his.

"No, I prefer to keep my hands free."

"Maybe when you get to be my age you won't be so macho. You walk down enough hillsides and your knees will start to give out."

They started down into the canyon. Mary was being quiet, saving her breath for the climb back up. She thought Tom talked a lot older than he looked or acted.

A mild breeze was blowing from the north, deceptively masking the heat Tom knew awaited in the bottom of the canyon. "I know you have hair, but don't you have enough sense to wear a sun hat?" he asked. "The clouds won't build up 'til three or so. It's going to be hotter than it feels right now."

"Are you always this fussy?" Mary retorted. Their comfortable friendship was prone to teasing insults. Mary had dated Tom once after his divorce. Then she met Gabor Szabo, the love of her life. He was a Hungarian restaurant owner who enjoyed cooking for her at home too. Gabor was Mary's third husband. Tom had told her that law enforcement people were notoriously difficult to live with, and that she ought to regard Gabor as her last chance. Tom was not surprised that she didn't change her last name.

Mary stopped on a rock outcrop to look around. The brown and tan canyon slopes were dotted with gray sagebrush and a few small dark junipers. The creek bed in the bottom was white from dried mud and algae. Even with sunglasses, the sunlight was blinding.

Tom pointed. "Looks like they went down to that juniper over there."

"How do you tell that's their trail from here?" she asked skeptically.

"Because it looks fresh and it's going almost straight down slope. Cow trails pretty much go parallel to the contour except near water. They cut uphill a few feet at a time and level off to graze a bit before they climb more. Look at the grass near us. It hasn't been grazed in years."

Since Mary was still listening and evaluating the evidence, Tom decided to show off. "On the other hand, deer mostly go at an angle up or down slope. They have small feet and wouldn't leave a clear trail like that." After more than 20 years as a wildlife biologist, Tom's pronouncements still led too frequently to embarrassing exceptions. In this case, however, it was simple fact that few animals other than a stupid human would climb several hundred feet above the creek without a darn good reason.

When they got close enough to see boot prints, Mary was suitably appreciative. "For someone carrying around a Y chromosome, you actually have some useful attributes. Looks like they scuffed it up pretty well, but they didn't go any farther. He must have been lying about here." She stood looking up and down the slope. "Now what in the heck was he doing here and how did he get here without a car or a horse?"

"How do we know he didn't have a car that somebody else drove off, or for that matter, a horse that wandered off? In fact, how do 'we' know it was a he? I heard it was a chewed up body, period. You're the cop, what did the sheriff tell you?"

"He didn't," she replied. "The state police report said 'Officer Phillip Dolan assisted Sheriff Robert Greenwood in recovery of a body identified as a Caucasian male, age undetermined.' They have to get the coroner from Pendleton to perform the autopsy. I tried to call Dolan, but he was off duty. I guess they didn't see any sign of a vehicle, and nobody reported a horse."

"Well, I can see tracks of at least one horse over here. It must have been Troy when he came up to investigate. Looks like he might have gone down canyon to report it. There is a ranch house down where the creek hits the highway."

"Can you tell if there was more than one?"

"Do I look like Lieutenant Leaphorn? I'm a misplaced Midwestern white boy. I can track a Ford or a Camaro, maybe even a dirt bike, but horses have four feet, and for all we know, Troy was trailing a pack animal."

Mary looked frustrated and started eyeing the trail back up the slope. Tom suggested another thought. "You know, there's not much reason to be on this steep hill unless he had been down by the creek hiking, or was headed down. If you want to go with me while I take a look at the vegetation, we might see something."

"Like what?"

"Hell, I don't know. Maybe he was growing marijuana. No, that wouldn't make sense. Not enough water, plus the cows would like it better than my cottonwood trees."

The mention of drugs gave Mary an incentive. If she found something the sheriff had missed, it would give her leverage. "Any place he could hide a meth lab down there?"

"There's a spring surrounded by some big juniper about three quarters of a mile up the canyon. You could hide out until a cowboy rode through or the hunters came in during fall. Seems like there would be lots of easier places to hide something and be able to get away quicker if they needed to, though. It's a long way to carry anything."

"I guess the day is half shot anyway. If you're going down there, you might need me to carry you back out. Besides, you have a habit of finding interesting things in strange places."

Mary set out down the slope ahead of Tom. She went nearly straight down while he switch-backed, leaning heavily on his stick. When he rejoined her, he could see she was watching and evaluating his careful movements.

"When you get old, the downhill is tougher than the uphill," he reassured her. To prove his point, he set off along the dry creek bed at a good pace. Twenty minutes later they arrived at a grove of juniper. Several had trunks that were more than a foot in diameter and gnarled branches reaching out nearly twenty feet. The shade looked welcoming, but the odor of fresh cow dung was serious. The spring was trampled and muddy. Tom crouched on his heels in the shade and eased a canteen from his pack.

"Good Lord," said Mary. "This is the only shade for miles, and it's full of cow shit! You can't even sit down without having some in your lap." She tried to kick some cow pies away from the trunk of the largest tree, but found them a little too fresh for kicking. "Gross!" She scraped the toe of her boot on the peeling bark. "I hate cows! Don't laugh, you creep, you hate them, too."

"I do get tired of squatting on my haunches instead of being able to sit down in some nice clean grass," he agreed, "but I wish people would quit telling me what I think. Drink some water and let's head on back. I've seen enough."

"How many cattle were in here?" she fumed.

"Probably not many and they might not have been here long. The grass in the creek bed downstream wasn't mowed. Most of the cattle sign is right here next to the spring. Maybe it was too hot and they didn't feel like moving. If they were Troy's cows, he keeps track of them. He wouldn't let them wander off for too long before he noticed."

Carefully stepping around the stinking mud, Mary approached the spring source. "Hey, look at all this trash. Plastic all over the place! Maybe somebody was carrying chemicals. No, actually it looks like a bunch of milk jugs with the tops cut off. There is some dried brown crud, but it doesn't smell right. It smells sweet."

Tom thought of meth-amphetamine labs, as he stood watching carefully, wondering how he was going to pick up her body and get out without breathing some poisonous chemical if she dropped over. He guessed Mary weighed almost as much as he did. Gabor had been feeding her too well. It would be a long climb out of the canyon. He blanched when she stuck her finger into the sludge in one container and held it to her nose.

She smiled, "Molasses!"

"No, DUMB!" he yelled. "What the hell are you doing? Don't you go through six training sessions every year about sticking your head into barrels of toxic crap? Don't pick that junk up."

"It's only trash," she sighed. "Meth paraphernalia is a little more distinctive these days." She started picking up the pieces of jugs and stacking them, one inside the other.

"Oh, sure! Are you gonna carry that out of here? If some asshole brought it here, why don't we leave it for him to pick up, chemicals and all? Mary, you don't know what was in it, even if it does smell like molasses!"

"Oh, all right. Calm down." She set the stack of milk jugs down, looking puzzled. "Where are the tops with the handles?"

"What?" He was beginning to think there was a serious defect in her second X chromosome.

"Somebody cut the tops off all these jugs. Where are the tops and handles?"

"Maybe he brought them here the same way you were going to carry them out, stacked like bowls. Then he mixed his chemicals and served molasses cookies to the cows! Maybe it was an insecticide or a wormer. Let the toxic waste squad clean it up. You can absorb it through your skin. Let's get out of here before you drop dead. Maybe that's what happened to him."

Mary reached for the radio on her belt and thumbed the mike. Naturally, it was dead silent. She adjusted the squelch until it let out a loud squeal, backed it off slightly and thumbed the mike again. Again it failed to hit a repeater. She knew what the problem was. Nobody could hear the radio now unless they were in a line of sight.

They walked back to the trees. Tom picked up his empty canteen, put it in his pack, and pulled out another to slip into a belt pouch. Mary was again kicking in the needle duff under the tree. "OK, we've got about a 40 minute hike out before you can call anybody, so let's get going."

She stooped to pick up a piece of paper, "Poison."

"Oh, now you're worried about poison? That looks like an envelope."

"It says 'POISON,'" she explained, holding it out.

"Now you have me worried!" He took the envelope and turned it over. "POISON" was all it said. On the flip side, it had a plastic window and a post office box return address. "It was probably from a bill. No name."

Mary poured the last of her canteen over her hands and wiped them on her jeans. Without further words, Tom started back. Breaking out of the edge of the juniper, the canyon slope looked impossibly high and steep. He saw a flash of light at the rim. Mary saw it, too.

"That looks like one of our rigs," she said. The light moved and disappeared.

"We parked on the other side of the cutbank. You can see a truck moving on the road at the rim. That's why our body decided to climb out. If we angle up from here, it's about a mile to the road. If we walk all the way down the canyon to the highway, it's closer to three."

They started a straight path to the rim, Tom in the lead, climbing continuously at a gentle angle. He aimed toward the point where they had observed the vehicle. Halfway up the slope he unexpectedly found a small belt pack. "Look at this. We must be right on the body's trail." He saw two water bottles on the ground a few yards down slope. Tom handed the pack to Mary, then retrieved the bottles. She watched the plastic bottles in his hand as he climbed back up.

"These are empty. You need some water?"

"You have an extra canteen?"

It was Tom's turn to sigh. The macho people always carried too little water. Tom never left his truck without three quarts in his pack. He took it off and sat down. "So you gonna open the pack? Maybe he left us a candy bar."

She did. Inside the pack were a couple empty plastic bags, a plastic trowel, a wallet, and a form letter from a group of lawyers asking "Dear Jerry" to send money to help sue somebody. Inside the wallet were six dollars and a driver's license with a picture of Jerry Skinner, Baker City resident and citizen of moderately clean repute.

"Well, now there are only five."

"Five what?" Mary cooperatively played straight-man.

"Five environmentalists." Tom took a swig from his second canteen and passed the third to Mary. "I met Jerry last spring when we gave a public tour of a forestry project. He was real proud to tell me there were only six active environmentalists in all of eastern Oregon. He was going to protest our environmental assessment if we planned to cut any big trees."

"He won't be protesting much of anything now."

"Well, this is strange," Tom mused. "He retired from an art gallery business several years ago. Drugs don't seem too likely to be in his retirement portfolio. Besides that, Jerry was a tree man. I can't see him wasting time down here worrying about a creek that hasn't held a trout in fifty years."

An echo of voices came from above. Several figures were working their way down from the rim toward the lone tree where the body had presumably been found. "Looks like they were anticipating your demise, Mary," he said sarcastically. "Help is on the way."

She looked at him more resentfully than he expected so soon after giving her his third canteen. She picked up the empty water bottles, put them back in Jerry's pack, and stalked up the hill. Tom finished his water, knowing there was more waiting in a cooler in his truck. Then he followed her to the tree.

As Tom approached, he saw Fester Johnson watching him with his hands on his hips and a sour look on his face. "Hey, Fes, did Mary tell you she figured out who your body was?"

"Since when did you graduate into a cop?"

"Not my idea of a good time. Mary thought it was convenient to drag me along."

"I thought it was clear you should stay out of the way here."

"Didn't see any 'keep out' signs. Besides, I was working down there, not here. This is Mary's gig."

"Let him up here, Fes. I've got some questions to ask him." The sheriff's bulk appeared through the sagebrush.

Fester moved out of the way, but just barely. Tom had to breathe Fester's aura and push through a bit of brush to avoid kissing his belly. Tom remembered an old adage that a short man with an attitude will rarely pass up an opportunity to use a hill to good advantage.

"Mary said you found that pack. You know Jerry Skinner?"

"I met him last spring on a project tour farther up the mountain. Other than that, I didn't know him."

"You have any idea why he was out here?" the sheriff asked.

"No, but Mary found some odd trash down in the canyon and a note that might have been his. Something about poison."

"You have any reason to think he might have been working with chemicals down there?"

"I have no idea why he would be down there."

"He was studying up on the BLM? Thinking of causing a fuss about something?"

"You're talking to the wrong man. I have no way of knowing what he was up to." Behind the sheriff, Tom could see a state cop and a plainclothesman with a camera. The plainclothesman had his hands in his pockets, looking bored. The state cop was holding Jerry's pack. The wallet had gone into a plastic bag and the envelope with "POISON" into another. "Something odd going on?"

"What got you interested in coming back here? Fes did say you went by yesterday."

"Our range con told me there had been some cattle in the canyon. They weren't supposed to be there since last May, so I thought we ought to assess the damage."

"Mary says you thought somebody might be growing marijuana down there, that right?"

"We were guessing why someone might be in the canyon. The thought crossed my mind, but it didn't really make sense."

"Why not? Kinda lonely down there, don't you think?"

"Well, there isn't much traffic in the summer, but there isn't much water to grow crops either."

"Does it take much water, growin' marijuana?"

This line of questioning was getting real uncomfortable, as was the fact that Tom was the only one answering and everybody else was listening. "It grows wild in the Midwest. That's in about 20 inches of rainfall. We get maybe 4 inches here all spring and summer in a good year."

The sheriff looked down the canyon. “That’s a lot of country. Pretty good work finding that little-bitty pack out there.” He left that one hanging, but there was a big question behind it.

“We pretty much took a straight line up from that turn in the canyon. We were in a bit of a hurry after Mary found that note. It looks like maybe Jerry did the same.”

The sheriff looked at Mary as if for confirmation, then back at Tom. “You figure he left a note about poison and then walked back up here?”

“Maybe. Otherwise someone else had to leave the note. It had been trampled in the dirt under the trees. Troy Grey was down there. Maybe he has another explanation.”

“If John Doe does turn out to be Jerry, why were you in a hurry? After all, he is dead.”

“Mary found some jugs with sludge in them. I thought we might have been exposed to something, especially after seeing the note.” Tom noticed Mary absent-mindedly wiping her hand on her pants again. “After all, John Doe didn’t make it up to the top.”

That was enough to sound like sass to Fester, who rose to the bait. “That sounds like bullshit to me. You don’t think anybody sick from poison would come up here.”

The sarcastic note in Tom’s remark had not escaped Sheriff Greenwood either, but he was not one to get irritated when it didn’t suit his purpose. He grunted and looked quizzically at Mary. She nodded. “You look pretty healthy to me, both of you.”

Something in Fester’s outburst struck Tom as both sincere and odd. Fes seemed certain that Jerry had not been running for help from poison. It seemed like a reasonable guess to Tom. Fester walked over to look at the note in the evidence bag. From the look on his face, he did not find it relevant. He handed it back to the state cop.

“Mary, are you thinking it was a meth lab or something?” The sheriff’s brain was still cooking. He was not going to pass judgment quickly.

She hesitated, thinking, “No. I admit I wondered when I found that envelope, but it smelled like molasses and nothing really looked like drug trash. Tom thought it might be a wormer. Now that I think about it, the jugs were all placed in the brush where they wouldn’t get kicked over, but where a cow could get its head in to feed. It looked like they had been feeding out of them. Maybe it was only a mineral supplement.”

“That would fit the molasses smell,” said the sheriff. “An old cow will eat anything with molasses on it.” Like most members of the county's reigning political class, he spoke from the experience of being raised in a ranching family. "I think we're about done here." He looked morosely uphill and started climbing slowly.

Tom grumbled to Mary, "Well, what the hell explains why Jerry wrote that note?"

Fester, who had sneaked up close enough to hear his thoughts, sneered, "What makes you so sure Jerry wrote that note? It looks like it could have been lying out there for months. Looks like it got wet. It hasn't rained since early June."

"Good observation, Fes. Except a cow could have pissed on it yesterday," Tom retorted. The sheriff looked back with a smile, now willing to enjoy a moment of low humor at the expense of his deputy. Tom used his walking stick to good advantage climbing the slope. Well above the others, Tom turned around and yelled back, "Besides, Mary told me the address on the envelope is the same one on the form letter inside the pack." Four cops converged on the pack. The state cop reached inside and gingerly removed the letter. Mary waited on the hillside just above them. Tom thought she was probably figuring out how to explain why she hadn't called that particular item to their attention.

By the time Mary reached the road, Tom was halfway through another quart of water, savoring the cold of melting ice. He usually put two frozen canteens in his lunch cooler, leaving them to enjoy at day's end. It took the sheriff another five minutes to arrive at the top. Fester was diplomatically behind him. Mary had opened the back door of her fancy extra-cab pickup to reach a dusty four-quart canteen under the seat. Wiping dust from the neck, she turned the canteen up and grimaced from the taste of warm, stale water aged for months in aluminum and plastic. Tom wandered over.

"You ever notice that brown slime on the plastic of those canteens? Rub your finger inside the neck and you'll see it come off. They tested some old canteens like that to see if the aluminum content would give people Alzheimer's, but what they found was the sewage sludge fungus that grew in the stale water absorbed it all, so they're basically safe."

"Tom, you are so full of shit you don't have to worry about sewage sludge. You think you left me in it deep with those guys down there, but I came out smelling like a rose. Here comes Greenwood. Don't cross me."

As the sheriff approached, he said to Mary, "I guess it was a good thing you came out to check on things today. We probably wouldn't have found that hip-pack without you. I guess we should have called you to say we were coming back out ourselves, but it was kind of a late start. We didn't get the coroner's report until nearly noon."

"That's all right. We were already down in the canyon by then. We probably couldn't have been contacted by radio." Mary was also playing the diplomat. "What happened? How did he die?"

Sheriff Greenwood glanced at Tom, then back to Mary. "Looks like he ran out of water. I'll see that you get a copy of the coroner's report. Once you've read it, you might want to give me a call."

Tom recognized he was being cut out. He interjected, "You know I had to apologize to Mary because I didn't radio in yesterday to tell her something was up. I got the impression that Fes had already taken care of the protocol. You know, notifying the BLM law enforcement about an incident on BLM land."

Fester had moved closer and heard his name coming from Tom. He bristled, "We don't have to call in the BLM."

"Well," said Sheriff Greenwood, demonstrating more diplomacy, "we do have a cooperative agreement, Fes. You should have reminded dispatch to let BLM know what was going on. Picking up bodies isn't anybody's favorite chore, though. Guess we had a lot on our minds yesterday, and it got overlooked. We'll try to do better next time, won't we?"

Fes looked like he had swallowed a cat. "Yeah, sure" he mumbled, and left to go find some water.

While Fes was still in earshot, the sheriff said, "Some of us are a bit old-fashioned. We're not used to a woman cop figuring out things we didn't. Good thing I didn't look at that letter, or I would have felt dumb not seeing how the address matched the envelope."

When Fester had moved out of hearing range, Tom said, "A man thinking of running for public office ought to develop the skill of eating humble pie graciously. Fes should know there are women running ranches in this county who won't put up with a man who can't accept strong women."

Sheriff Greenwood, widely known to be planning on two more terms as sheriff before he retired, raised an eyebrow. "Now that's a fact! Well, I'd better get on down the road." He stalked toward his Tahoe looking like a gunslinger about to draw.

"Damn!" said Tom. "Did you see that eyebrow raise his hat? I thought it was going to fly off backward."

"Tom, you are a nasty skunk. Where did you hear that Fester was thinking of running?"

"Man, I would really like to be able to grow eyebrows like that. I could comb them back over the top of my head to cover my bald spot."

"Did you make that up? You did, didn't you? God, you are a nasty, nasty, low-down. Ooooee! I would not want to be in Fester's shoes for the next month."

"Make what up? Did you ever know a Neanderthal like Fes who didn't dream of taking power in the sheriff's office? I bet he's been scouting the staff to see who will support him. If not this election, then next time around."

"Well, if he ever gets to be sheriff, you better plan on retiring in another state. Another county won't be far enough." She got in her truck and pulled off in a cloud of dust. To get back to Vale, she had almost an hour more to drive than Tom did.

Tom waited for the dust to settle and the air-conditioning to cool the vehicle. Thumbing the mike, he said, "Hello Mother, this is Tom. I'm coming home now." He knew Mary would appreciate the humor. No doubt she was the only one still near a radio to hear it.

Chapter 2

Thursday morning started with a glorious sunrise enhanced by the smoke of range and forest fires on the Idaho side of the Snake River. The mountaintops to the west were still reflecting the orange glow as Tom finished his second cup of coffee. Scrub, a part Australian shepherd, part accident mutt, was lying on the kitchen floor panting heavily. They had come back from a four-mile run before the sun had time to heat the pavement.

"You are hoping to stay inside with the AC on today, aren't you?" he said to Scrub, who perked up her ears. "Well, I'm not going to be out late, so maybe that's OK. Just don't get used to it." Their home didn't have much for shade in the yard. Tom had planted trees, but Scrub would be long gone before they got big enough to provide real shade. The grass was barely surviving despite frequent and heavy watering. The reflected glare from the glass door had definitely killed a large patch. Staring at it, he decided to plant paving stones there next weekend.

He went to the office, planning to put in a short day and head for the mountains that afternoon. A note on his desk warned him to wait for Vince's arrival before going to the field. The computer sounded like a coffee grinder warming up when he logged on to write up his field notes.

Vince showed up a few minutes before 8, looking sleepy. "Hey, you're here. How come you didn't call me last night? Lucky for you I saw your name scratched off the sign-out board when I came in to check."

"Yeah, I didn't want to interrupt your dinner and figured signing back in would do. I think the dog chewed through the phone wire at home."

Vince looked dubious, but didn't want to call Tom a liar. "Well, I wanted to talk to you because I got a call from the Washington Department of Wildlife up at Chief Joseph Wildlife Area yesterday. You know those cows they found floating in the Snake River near Lewiston last spring? Well, they think they floated out of Joseph Canyon because they found some more dead ones in the Wildlife Area."

"I thought we didn't have an allotment on that ground. Don't we have an agreement with the Fish and Game folks to manage the BLM with the state land for wildlife? Do they know whose animals they were?"

"Kathy is checking with Hillman and the Froth's because they run some stock near there," said Vince, "but nobody reported any missing cattle."

Tom shook his head. "Didn't anybody bother to get a brand, or were they too far gone for that? Nobody is going to tell us about missing cattle unless someone is rustling."

"No, the Fish and Game flew over in a helicopter. I think it was too steep and rocky to land. There's no road close, either. Since you like to hike so much and you are the wildlife biologist, I thought you should be the one to go figure out what happened. After all, it is a wildlife area."

"Are you in a hurry Vince? It takes about six hours to get to the mouth of the canyon, and another six to drive back. Some day you'll have to explain to me why the Spokane office gave us control of southeast Washington. I'll probably have to stay overnight up at Lewiston. Maybe I should go next week. How far up the canyon are they?"

"Uh, I guess I forgot to ask exactly."

"OK, but you better figure on next week being a real short one for me. I'll have my forty hours in at 1:30 this afternoon. I'll call the Chief Joe and ask. Maybe it would be closer to hike down from the rim somewhere along Highway 3." Tom had stopped donating extra hours to the agency years before. Overtime pay was a fantasy and the system of flexible hours and banking "compensatory" time-off had its limits. As a supervisor, Vince was usually flexible on adjusting work schedules off the books.

The refuge manager told Tom the carcasses had been on a gravelly flat in Joseph Canyon about two miles up from the access road. The pilot didn't figure dead cows were part of his mission except to complain to BLM. The refuge manager had never heard of anyone identifying the cattle that had floated down the Snake River during the spring floods. He assumed that some ranch operator with a winter feedlot had pushed the earlier carcasses down to the bank where the river would take care of the problem. It was a local tradition. He didn't have any idea if these animals were related.

Tom decided to take his own pickup truck for the trip so he could take Scrub along. The BLM office was traditionally lax about a lot of personal behavior and appearances, but somebody in the Washington D. C. office had decreed years before that dogs were a liability and therefore forbidden in government vehicles. Vince did not allow exceptions.

He stopped at his house to pack an overnight bag, extra food, and camping gear in case he decided to spend the weekend in the mountains before returning. He opened the windows on the shell so Scrub could get some cool air riding in the back. She had forever been banished to the back of the pickup after once nearly causing a wreck by climbing into his lap when the noise of passing over a cattleguard spooked her.

The drive was uneventful and depressing. Tom made the mistake of driving through Walla Walla instead of going northeast through Enterprise. The surrounding agricultural lands were carved from the fertile Palouse prairie over a hundred years ago. Soil conservation district signs announced the latest federal subsidy programs to save the soil next to fields gashed by last spring's rains. Knapweed and yellow star-thistle lined the roads in every patch of waste ground left unplowed. Farther east, where the ground became too miserable for wheat, the cattle and horses hunted among the cobble of the dry, gullied creek beds for the last sprigs of grass. Entering the strip development at the west edge of Clarkston was actually a relief. It was like arriving on Mars, an alien environment, instead of an open sore defacing the landscape.

Since the travel budget was shot, Tom drove past several high-priced motels in Clarkston, crossed the Snake River into Idaho, and checked in to an obscure motel hidden behind a truck plaza in Lewiston. He had found it the previous year when all the other motels in both towns were booked. As long as he kept the windows closed and ran the air-conditioner, he could sleep through most of the truck traffic until 4:30 in the morning when things really got busy. It wasn't much, but there was a small refrigerator with a freezer in each room. He put two canteens in the freezer and went out for supper.

As he crossed the Clearwater River, he saw a sign announcing a wildlife refuge and stopped to let Scrub take a break. The sign said the refuge was funded with federal dollars. The refuge appeared to be a riprap rock channel bank with a road on top. The only wildlife was a pair of mallards out on the open river. Unable to find any grass to pee on, Scrub settled for the road. She carefully picked her way down the boulders to the river for a swim. When she emerged, they walked toward the Potlatch pulp mill until she dried out. Back in the truck, she settled down on his backpack as he closed the tailgate. She grinned happily. "You are a lot more forgiving than I am, Scrub. I'd appreciate it if you would get the hell off my pack!" When he parked near Lewiston's gentrified, old city center, she lifted her head off the sleeping bag and barked a few times to complain of being abandoned.

Crenshaw's Grill was overflowing with young, working singles taking advantage of the extended happy hour at the bar. As he looked in the doorway, Tom reflected that the price of heavy breathing would be an intense dose of second-hand smoke, so he turned away. Down the street he found a Mexican restaurant populated by young families and older people in business attire.

The waiter seated him in the center of the half-filled room near a sprinkling water fountain. Ordinarily a small table in the corner would have felt more comfortable, but at least the noise of the fountain drowned out the whining of a three-year old at a nearby table. The only Mexican beer on the menu was Corona. Tom settled for water. While eating chips with thin salsa and waiting for the burrito verde to come, he amused himself by counting coins lying in the fountain. There was about enough within reach to buy a six-pack of cheap beer, but not enough to risk the embarrassment of being caught fishing.

The burrito was hot but otherwise unremarkable. The green chili sauce was geared to the palates of folk who had never lived in the Southwest. He picked up the salsa bowl and tipped it over the rice and beans. The cheese started to remind him of the probable condition of his arteries. He watched traffic out on the street instead of the food.

When the family with the kid left, two women in neat business suits took their table. The younger one provided an interesting alternative to watching cars. The older woman had dark black hair with no trace of the gray that obviously should have been there. Her makeup looked unhealthy beige compared to the dark burgundy of her suit. Tom tried not to be obvious about studying her companion's legs. Before long it occurred to him that the older woman was making far too much eye contact for a disinterested stranger. He finished his glass of water and headed for the cash register.

The lapse of happy hour had not put a dent in the singles crowd at Crenshaw's Grill. People were standing in the doorway. Tom considered going in to have a beer, but the cloud of smoke at the door was too much. Besides, all the women looked like recent high school graduates. With that depressing thought, he drove back to the motel. At 8 P.M. when the air temperatures had finally cooled enough to believe it was September, he put the leash on Scrub and went for a long run.

A little after midnight a semi parked outside with its refrigeration unit left pumping loudly until 4 A.M. when it pulled out. At 5 o'clock, the water pipes were whining and the occupants of the next room started thumping luggage against the wall, signaling the beginning of another day. The difficult part about being an early-riser in Lewiston was finding a restaurant open before 6:30. Scrub helped waste time by wandering through some weedy fields near the motel.

An hour south of Clarkston the road along the Snake River turned up the Grande Ronde River canyon. After two and a half miles it crossed a bridge to the south side of the river, dropped over a small ridge, and entered the combined drainage of Joseph Creek and Cottonwood Creek. About three miles farther there was an unmarked trail that led through a corral to a small parking area and access trail into Joseph Canyon itself.

Tom was always awed by the geologic majesty of Joseph Canyon. Two thousand feet above them, the canyon rims were more than two miles apart, but the flat terrain in the canyon bottom was only 300 feet wide. Upstream, the bottom narrowed to as little as 50 feet. The canyon slopes are a series of broken, stair-step cliffs carved from the Grande Ronde basalt flows, thousands of cubic miles of lava that flowed from the earth's crust on top of thousands of cubic miles of the Imnaha basalt flows. The geology book he had read said those series of flows caused the continental crust to sink beneath their weight. That caused all of eastern Washington to drop below the surrounding landscape, shifting all the rivers in the region through its basin. Now the Grande Ronde and Joseph Creek both flow northeast to the Snake, which drains north to the Columbia, which cuts through the basin on its way out to the Pacific Ocean.

By 8:30 A.M., Scrub and Tom were happily walking up the trail, which within a half mile, broke up into a number of game trails, leading up and down the slopes between the cliffs and loose gravel. At times their path would pinch down to a narrow ledge over a forty-foot sheer drop into the rocky creek bed. In spring the creek slammed from side to side of the channel, undercutting the cliffs and creating deep holes filled with boulders. In late summer it was possible to walk up parts of the creek if you didn't mind wading the rest, but hopping from boulder to boulder and walking on rough cobble was hell on knees.

Tom also knew the creek changed unpredictably. A deep, fast hole between rocky cliffs made wading too dangerous. He would be forced to crawl on his hands and knees through the alder, hawthorn, and poison ivy to get out of the channel. That meant risking a face-to-face confrontation with a bear in the dense brush or getting bitten by one of the many rattlesnakes that inhabited the shade by the water. The fresh bear sign along the trails indicated they were picking fruit from the hawthorn that day.

Tom decided it was safer to crawl from ledge to ledge above the creek. His hiking stick became a liability. He needed both hands to hold onto rocks to keep from falling. Scrub compounded the problem by alternately getting in the way and climbing above him, kicking down rocks. Tom envied her low center of gravity and four feet, although the crumbling rock once nearly caused her to take a long dive into the creek.

The going was painfully slow. It took four hours to find the first dead cow. By Tom's interpretation of the map, it was considerably farther up the canyon than the pilot had reported. The body had lodged against some white alder on a small gravel bar. There was nothing distinctive about it, not even the smell. Between the coyotes and insects, it had been cleaned up pretty well. The hide was torn and shrunken from drying, but still mostly intact around the bones. It was not branded on the upper side, but Tom thought he would check around more before trying to turn it over.

Another quarter mile upstream on a broad gravel fan at the mouth of a small tributary, a clump of tall white alders spread along the creek bank. Several dark shapes lay underneath the trees, and two of these, with their right hips to the sky, bore a lazy horseshoe brand. Tom decided the cattle might have come down the north side where there was at least one fairly prominent game trail. Why they had come down was another question. It didn't look like the slopes were grazed. In fact, the shoreline shrubs didn't look browsed either, which made him think the cattle hadn't spent much time alive on the gravel bar.

Three of the four carcasses were well above the high water mark. Only one looked like it was partly below the flood line, and sure enough, the hair on the head and neck looked like it had been soaked and dried. There was mud and sand in the ear. Tom checked the others and found nothing similar.

"Well now, this looks like a puzzle," Tom mused. Scrub decided she liked the puzzle and stayed to roll around on it while Tom retreated to a smooth boulder by the creek to have lunch. "If you find anything fresh, you're going to swim back and then run behind the truck on the way home, you know!" he yelled. She grinned at him from on top of the cow's hollow rib cage. She tried a tentative chew on the ear, but then disappeared off to the other side. Tom finished his yogurt and opened a bag of fig cookies. Scrub heard the wrapper pop and came running. She was still wet from diving in the creek, and covered with sand. "Hey, glad you decided to wash for lunch. Want a cookie?" She sat patiently while Tom ate his, then took the offered one from his hand. "Disgust! You should have brushed your teeth too! Get away." She backed off and lay down, hoping for a second treat. When it didn't come, she stretched out and arched her back, rubbing her head backward in the sand.

Tom took his camera and walked back to the dead animals. "You know, it looks like they were stretching out their backs, too. Rigor mortis does funny things. I've never seen anything quite like it. This cow was kicking so much gravel she was practically digging her own grave." He looked for bullet holes or other unnatural signs, but he didn't see any. To turn over one of the dead animals, he got a dead alder and used it with a rock fulcrum. "No wounds. Had to be damn healthy to get down here, all of them. Didn't drown. Didn't eat everything in sight." Scrub seemed to look admiringly at him for his deductive skills. "Well? What else, eh?"

They walked back and forth across the gravel bar. "I don't see much but thin cow shit. Were they eating spring-green grass? If they were, they got it all. None here now." Scrub was not interested in dry manure. She only appreciated the fresh green kind that set off her gold eyes and dried hard on the long hair around her ears. Tom picked up a piece of manure and looked at it closely, but he couldn't make out anything except a few dried seed hulls.

At the top of the gravel fan, Scrub was sniffing something that looked white. Tom picked up the bottom half of a plastic bucket. "Can you believe it? Some slob hunter carried this in here and left it." Littering offended his sensibilities, particularly here. Joseph Canyon was more wild than most of the wilderness areas in the continental U. S., and without the designation. The bucket was well above the flood line and had to have been brought in from downstream and dropped there. Then he spotted a second bucket a few feet away in the brush. "Probably rode in on a horse with all kinds of crap." Tom nested the dirty buckets in a plastic trash bag and put them in his pack. "Come on, let's get out of here." Scrub was getting too interested in another one of the dead cows.

They picked their way through the ledges and cliffs, sometimes following their trail in, and sometimes trying a path that looked easier. Occasionally they hit a dead end and had to go backwards. Tom stopped to rest. His legs were shaking from the constant exertion of scrambling on loose rock. "You'd have to be a maniac to ride a horse in here! It's bad enough on foot. Bringing a pack-horse would be suicide." Scrub braced her back legs against him to keep from sliding downhill. They were less than half way out, and the sun was behind the canyon rim. The down-canyon breeze felt cool as it dried the sweat out of his shirt. "I think we spent too much time back there, Scrub. It won't be fun if we have to spend the night on a ledge."

He maneuvered another hundred yards along the ledge around a bend. There was a short stretch of sandy floodplain on their side of the creek, and they happily took advantage of it. There he found a third bucket, apparently washed downstream where it had lodged in the alder. This one was entire, with a handle and a piece of rope tied to it. Scrub sniffed at it and tentatively licked the inside. "Get out of that," Tom scolded. It would not fit in his pack, even nested with the other pieces. "Why in the hell would anybody carry a bunch of buckets in here?" he muttered. "There's no way they would have walked a horse up that rocky creek bed either. It would break a leg in the boulders." He tied it to the outside of his pack, knowing he couldn't climb the slopes with both hands occupied. Then deciding to sacrifice his walking stick to appease the river gods, he left it propped against a boulder the size of a mini-van. The next spring floods would take it.

When they made it back to the truck, Scrub's feet were bleeding from her scuffing on rocks and jumping in and out of the creek all day. She was too tired to jump up on the tailgate and growled at the indignity of being lifted. "Don't you growl at me! I'm in charge here. You are the subservient and grateful dog." She flopped down on his backpack again. He stacked the buckets from the pack inside the whole one, then re-wrapped them in the plastic bag so Scrub wouldn't try to lick the scummy contents. "To hell with adventure. Let's really go home."

He thought about the buckets on the long drive home. A camper or backpacker would carry a lightweight, collapsible vinyl bucket, not three large, inefficient paint buckets. They must have had a specific purpose. It could have been a coincidence that two had turned up at the same spot as the cattle. Tom didn't have a good explanation for the cattle deaths either. Their appearance had been as odd as the unlikely chance that several would die together at once without a visible cause. He considered and dismissed the thought that lightning might have struck them. The canyon walls would have caught any lightning.

When they got home, Scrub collapsed next to the bed as soon as Tom let her in the house. He stayed awake long enough to have a beer and a bagel with cheese.

*

Scrub's snoring woke Tom about 7 A.M. on Saturday. He was surprised he slept past first light, but it took three cups of coffee before he could think about breakfast. The grapefruit was good enough to eat two. The fourth cup of coffee went slower, lasting through a bowl of cereal. Thinking about fishing, Tom checked Scrub's feet, but the pads looked ragged. "You better stay here out of the water for today." Lying calmly beside the table, she didn't look interested in a major outing anyway.

Going through the garage, Tom stepped around a tablesaw and two bookcases under construction, pulled his fishing gear off a shelf, and went outside where the truck was bleaching in the hot sun. The fishing gear went into the back of the truck. He removed the garbage sack, dropping it into the nearly empty rolling garbage bin. On second thought he leaned into the bin to grab the bag and empty it for re-use. As Tom pulled his head out and lifted the bag, he saw his neighbor, a comfortably retired naval officer, watching curiously. Tom waved. "Just practicing for retirement." The neighbor disappeared without response. Apparently he had little sense of humor.

One of the buckets was thoroughly stuck to the bag. Some of the sludge had liquefied and congealed again. Shaking the bag to dislodge the crud released a shower of little brown pellets onto the concrete driveway. Looking at them up close, they were obviously seeds of some sort, mostly cracked and split. The sludge in the bucket was full of little lumps, identical seeds. Tom put several that appeared whole into a flowerpot. He emptied the last canteen from the previous day onto the pot and went inside to call Randy Bergen.

The phone lifted on the third ring. "Randy, this is Tom. Sorry to bother you on the weekend, but I was hoping you might be able to help me."

"Uh—uh, bud. You are on your own this time. I spent your bail on a new set of tires."

"Nothing that drastic. I was hoping you might either know Troy Grey's number or could tell me if he's the one listed over in Richland or in Weiser."

"I don't think he's going to post your bail either. You got anything else to talk to him about?"

"Well, I had a couple questions, like whether he knew anything about a feed supplement down in Cow Creek, and maybe he could fill me in about his fence problems. Didn't you say Cow Creek wasn't his allotment?"

"It's not his, and neither is Willow Creek. He found two of his cows down there, but I don't think he wants to talk to you right now unless it's to cuss you out."

"What's the problem? I didn't cut the fences. Those were my cottonwoods they ate, and we were only asking them to get their cows out, right? You didn't threaten to trespass him, did you?"

"No, it's not my problem, Thomas, it's yours. Troy said he rode up Willow Creek on Thursday. He says you set some sharp sticks at the top and bottom end of that headcut pointed so a cow could get in, but would stab herself if she tried to get out. There were half a dozen dead ones in there. By the time he was done, he'd found ten. He was going to call the other ranchers to go look. I'm surprised you haven't been lynched yet."

"I don't have a clue what he's talking about. I pruned those cuttings off flat about five inches above the gravel. Even if they got kicked out, they wouldn't stab anything. I walked the whole way from Owl Spring down to within fifty yards of that headcut, and nothing looked like a pungi-stick. Hell, it was hard to find any of my cuttings left that hadn't been completely eaten off."

"Well, there's gonna be some fur comin' off your ass on Monday, if you live that long. There's something wrong going on, 'cause Troy said all four of the animals he had loose in Cow Creek were sick and two died when he tried to push them out. They didn't even make it down to that old road or he would have left them there and gone to get a trailer."

"What was wrong with them? Mary Twil and I both walked that drainage. We saw where his cows had been, but we didn't see any sharp sticks there either."

"I don't know, but you're the only one who's been down either canyon in two years except for the permittees. You better have some good pictures of what your plantings looked like when you left."

"You want photographs, I put about sixty on the computer before I went to Joseph Canyon. But unless I was blind, they won't show any dead cows or stakes. Guess I should have walked down to the headcut after all. Crap. So much for fishing today."

"Maybe if I was you, Thomas, I would go fishing and get the hell out of town. Maybe you ought to see what the fishing is like down in Argentina right now."

"Thanks, Randy. Have a good weekend." His thought process diverted, Tom forgot about the seeds in the bucket.

Lynching aside, Tom thought it prudent to take Scrub and his camping gear, just in case Randy was right about someone raising hell in his direction. Fester Johnson would probably jump at the opportunity to take up a portion of Tom's weekend. He threw some food into a cooler and loaded Scrub into the truck. They headed south out of town.

*

Two hours later he parked in a well-used, hunters' camp in one of the thickest patches of old-growth juniper on Watchtower Mountain. Scrub was excited as ever by the prospect of exploring. Tom checked the pads of her feet again and decided she would be all right as long as he could keep her out of water. He sat on the tailgate and spooned yogurt from a container while Scrub wandered back and forth whining, hoping to get Tom moving. She brought three different sticks to his feet. "You're going to get enough exercise without playing fetch. Why don't you find me a new walking stick?" He checked his map once before starting off, then shouldered the pack and headed down the ridge to the east. They entered the headwaters of Willow Creek near Owl Spring.

Tom walked the fence line where he had observed the break. He could see a fresh set of horse tracks, probably from Troy Grey, but he could not find any sign of motorcycle or ATV tracks from earlier that week. The boot tracks he had seen near the cut wire were cleated similar to his own hiking boots, not smooth-soled, pointy-toed cowboy boots. By now the tracks were mostly obscured by the wind, but he found one from which he could sketch the pattern of the lugs. He checked to make sure it was not his own print and then photographed it for good measure. "You know, Scrub, I'm getting paranoid in my old age. Now I have to collect evidence to protect myself from taking someone else's rap."

As he headed down the wash, Scrub streaked by, swiping his pant leg with foul mud. "Great! You sleep outside the tent tonight, you nitwit!" he grumbled. As he walked, he kept a close watch for any sharp sticks along the creek that Troy might have considered threatening. Other than one attempt to interest Tom in a sagebrush branch, not even Scrub found any. A jackrabbit flushed from beneath a sagebrush, enticing Scrub into a long run. After that, she settled into a slow pace, staying close and looking wistfully at the water bottle on his belt.

When the breeze brought Tom the smell of rotting flesh in the wash ahead, he called Scrub back. Tom tipped his canteen over her mouth and she lapped at the falling trickle of water. He clipped on her leash and tied her to a sagebrush. Taking the camera and a notebook, he set his pack down to show he was coming back. He growled, "Stay here and keep out of trouble."

The headcut began abruptly in the channel below a ledge of ancient marine shale. The banks became vertical, broken only in a few spots where cattle walking up the bottom had managed to scale their way out over the years. Most of the channel from this point on was twenty feet below the old floodplain. Once the water managed to cut through the soft shale, the erosion would continue upstream unless enough vegetation was restored to hold the soil. Tom reflected that it was unlikely the BLM would manage to repair the stream in the next few years unless some environmentalist sued them to remove grazing for good. And that probably won't happen until after I retire, he thought.

He started down the steep bank, slipped, and as he fell, grasped a branch over his head. Rather than stop his descent, it pulled out from the bank, throwing him completely off balance. Ruefully he looked at the stick, observing that it was cut on both ends, not broken or uprooted. It was neatly shaved to a strong but very sharp point on one end. "Well, now, I guess this was what Troy was talking about," he said to himself. "What was it doing up there?"

He carried the stick back up the crumbling dirt chute, and found it fit snugly into a hole in the bank. Fully inserted, its sharp end aimed at his chest, and blocked his path out. "Hmm. I suppose a cow could stab itself with that." Careful to maintain his balance this time, he threw it into the creek bed before easing his way to the bottom of the gully. He picked up the spear and moved downstream, using it as a walking stick.

The smell of rotting flesh became overpowering as Tom approached a Hereford, its belly with a gaping hole where the coyotes had been at it. With his eyes watering, Tom held his breath and examined the carcass. He ran downstream a few yards when he had to breathe, but the air there was nearly as bad. He remembered that a similar smell had filled the Bronco when he had encountered Fes Johnson on Tuesday. Skinner's body must have been close, he thought. It didn't improve his opinion of the deputy. Fes had been too busy being self-important to get sick.

Holding his breath again, he inspected the hide near the dead cow's head and chest. This process he repeated six more times for the other animals in the bottom of the draw. Along the way he pulled four more sharpened sticks from the banks, each blocking a potential way out. He could clearly see his own boot prints in the loose dirt, but didn't see any tracks indicating that the cattle had tried to get out past the spears. Farther down where the walls of the narrow gully were still completely vertical, he found a barricade of eight spears across the bottom, pointing upstream. Tom sat down to rest and make some notes.

He finished a canteen of water and set his notebook aside. "It does look like someone was making a trap. It worked too, didn't it?" He photographed the barricade from upstream and from the side, then took close-ups of the spears. They were arranged so the shafts of three pairs converged in "V" shapes with the points narrowly separated. The other two pointed straight upstream between the angled shafts. All had rocks placed around the base to steady and reinforce the shafts. He pulled them out and placed them in a pile at the edge of the channel before turning back upstream.

This time, Tom photographed the head, chest, and flanks of each cow as he passed. He found a recently dead coyote lying in the rock with its mouth contorted as if the coyote had died in agony. "Troy caught you scavenging on his buddies, eh?" The coyote was bloated, but less fragrant than the cattle.

Tom used the stick to turn the coyote over. "Damn! No holes in you either." Pulling a knife from his hip pocket, he slid the blade through the animal's paunch, held back the skin, and slit the stomach. He backed off a few feet, took another breath, and went back for a closer inspection. It looked like the coyote had eaten entrails for its last meal. Tom had often seen how coyotes took a road-killed deer apart. Efficient scavengers, coyotes usually ate the fatty tissue around the anus and the organs from the body cavity first. Intestines or stomachs with partially-digested food were a real prize for them.

Tom returned to the carcass of the nearest cow. Its paunch was open, so he stooped to look inside. Nearly all the intestines and part of the stomach had been removed. A few feet away from the carcass he saw a root lying on a flat rock. He looked around. The down-cut channel was as barren as he had remembered it, bare dirt and cobble. "Where did that root come from? It seems a little out of place." Other than a stunted Scotch thistle growing on the collapsing bank, there was nothing of any substance in sight. He pulled up the thistle and compared its base to the root on the rock. They were clearly different. "Enough!" Tom rose and marched up the gully, stopping only to photograph the last cow and several more spears that he pulled out of the bank near the top of the cut.

Scrub was waiting quietly in the afternoon shade of the sagebrush. Tom unsnapped her leash and untied it from the brush. He found a plastic bag in his pack and filled it from his canteen, holding it open while Scrub drank her fill. At the head of the drainage Tom skirted away from Owl Spring out to the cluster of junipers where he had seen the shadow of another carcass. Again, he tied Scrub to keep her out of the way while he took more photographs. As he got closer, he could see there were two dead cows. He stepped around the bodies, looking for signs of injury. What he found was another root, lying on a flat slab of rock. It appeared the same as the one in the wash bottom. Without touching the root with his bare hand, he wrapped a plastic bag around it and put it in his pack.

He kept Scrub on the leash until they were well away from the last carcasses. Back at the truck Scrub walked expectantly to the tailgate, planning to hop in and sleep. "No, not this time. We're staying here." He lowered the tailgate and climbed in by himself, shifting equipment and supplies so they could be easily reached while setting up camp.

After he filled Scrub's dish and poured her some water, he set up his tent while the sky was still light. He heated water on his camp stove, then poured that into a plastic solar shower bag and hung it on a branch of a juniper. He found a flat slab of rock and placed it under the shower bag, and then set his old tennis shoes next to that. Then he stripped and showered. Scrub decided to check out the heap of clothes on the ground. "Get away from those! I may burn them." As Tom started a pot of rice cooking, he noticed the evening breeze was definitely getting cool. "I am going to appreciate that tent tonight. Don't forget you're sleeping outside."

Tom sliced vegetables into the simmering rice, then cut off several wafers of jalapeno jack cheese from a two pound loaf. As he waited for the rice to finish, he ate a bagel with a couple pieces of the cheese. Tom broke more cheese into small pieces over the hot rice and tossed Scrub the last piece. She swallowed it quickly, then looked surprised. "It may clog your arteries, but it will burn out your worms," Tom told her. He made a half-hearted effort to clean the pan before he stumbled to bed in the dark.

He woke to the chatter of birds at 5:45 A.M. By the time the coffee was perking, he had the tent disassembled and sat down with a bowl of granola. Scrub was once again full of life and waited anxiously for Tom to finish packing. "Don't get in a hurry. This is a two cup pot," he warned her, "and I'm going to relax and drink them both." Despite this, he had his second cup in hand as he started the truck down the mountain. He parked at the same spot where he and Mary Twil had stopped earlier in the week. Scrub barked continuously until Tom opened the tailgate. He got out the recycled garbage bag and some rubber gloves from his camp box and shoved them into his pack. "OK, less than two miles down and back, get it?" On second thought he added, "And stay away from dead things!"

An hour and a half later, they returned from the spring with the plastic rubbish he had earlier scolded Mary to leave behind. Tom considered getting out the dog brush, but decided Scrub had rubbed off most of the mud on the sagebrush and grass during the return climb. They were home before noon.

Chapter 3

Tom fished a cup of yogurt, an apple, and a beer from the refrigerator. He found his address book and then called Mary Twil at her home. Someone picked up the phone. "Hey, Mary, hello, this is Tom up in Baker." An accented male voice responded, but Tom didn't catch exactly what he said. "Whoops, sorry! Hi, Gabor. Is Mary available? This is Tom Krueger. I work for BLM up in Baker City."

"Hello."

"Mary, Tom here. I've been out of town for several days. I was wondering if the coroner report shed any light on Skinner's note."

She hesitated, "No, I guess it didn't."

"What? Did they test his blood?"

"Umm... Tom, I can't talk about details. This whole thing is still under investigation."

"Well, are you on this? Is anybody looking at the poison angle?"

"Tom, it's not my case. The sheriff has the note. They know about it."

"Well, for Christ's sake, do you know anything? Do you have anything to say about it? Are you at least asking them to check into the chemistry?"

"Tom, for the last time, IT IS NOT MY CASE! I can't ask them to do anything."

"OK, suppose he was involved in a federal crime and that somehow, something happened, and that led to his death. Then, couldn't you ask them to check his blood chemistry?"

"What federal crime? Now what have you got?"

"Call this a wild-ass theory. Let's say he was out there with the intent to poison some cows, and maybe he was exposed to the poison himself. We need to know."

"Number one, in a case of death due to unknown causes, the coroner routinely analyzes the blood. Number two, he didn't die from poison. Number three, why would he leave a note warning the cows about poison?"

"Mary, that note is driving me crazy. I don't have the answer. It makes no sense no matter which way I try to look at it. How do you know he didn't die from poison?"

"Shit! I shouldn't have said that. Do you have any idea what a coroner does? They don't only check the blood, they check between his toes to see if he's been shooting up drugs in private. They dissect the body. There isn't anything they can't find!"

"Look, you've known me for three years. I'm on your side, Mary! Now, how the hell do we know he wasn't poisoned?"

"Oh hell... All right. He died from dehydration. That's it. That's what the report said."

"Dehydration? That's stupid. See what comes from not carrying enough water?" He paused to think. "Mary, that is bizarre! This was a college-educated environmentalist. He was hiking miles from anywhere, all by himself, in the desert, with that crummy little belt pack and only a couple small water bottles. I met this guy before. He may have been naïve, but he sure wasn't stupid. He was experienced in the woods. We found his note at a spring! It was muddy, but he could have gone to the source and strained it. He traveled less than a mile from water before he died!"

"There were complications. He had a wound in his back."

"Oh, now that's different. But wouldn't that be called something else? I mean loss of blood, not dehydration? No wonder Fes thought poison was a stupid idea."

Mary hedged, "I guess it didn't look like he bled that much. It was a tiny wound. They didn't catch it when they picked up the body the first day. The coroner found it."

"Well, I cut myself all the time, but a little bleeding doesn't make me forget I'm thirsty. It takes a lot to die from dehydration."

"I know that. Maybe it was a complicating factor, like maybe he was hurting and confused, so he got lost or wasn't thinking straight, so he forgot about water."

"No way. His water bottles were empty." He paused again, thinking. "It has to relate to something else out there. We are missing the link."

"Link to what, Tom? Cattle poisoning? What is going on out there?"

"I was wondering about what possible connection there might be between a series of odd cattle deaths. Vince just had me check a report of some dead cows up at Joseph Canyon. It was really strange. I couldn't see anything that would have caused it, but there were some buckets that had some dried brown crud in them like those plastic jugs in Cow Canyon."

"Forget the toxic waste theory," Mary said. "Besides, that's pretty far away, Tom."

"Yes, and it happened quite a while ago. But there was something closer. The day before you and I hiked down Cow Canyon, I found some trespass cattle in Willow Creek. I only saw live ones, but I could smell something dead below where I stopped. There was a couple more at the head of the drainage. Also, the fence had been cut. The same rancher who found Jerry Skinner rode down Willow Creek on Thursday. He said he found ten dead cows. Some of them were his. I went back yesterday and found nine. It looked like someone set some spears in the bank of a draw and on the bottom to trap the cows in. If one tried to get out, it would have shoved the spear into its own chest."

"I didn't see anything like that in Cow Creek. You think Skinner could have fallen on one of those spears? How far away is this?"

"Almost three miles as the crow flies, and Jerry didn't look like a crow to me. I don't think he got it there."

"Did you look at the points? Were they whittled?"

"These were big sticks shaved down to a point. The smallest was three quarters of an inch in diameter. If a cow is going to impale itself, it has to be on something stout. Only none had any blood on them. It didn't look like there had been any struggle to get out. I found these odd roots in the wash. They were totally out of place. I was starting to think Jerry might have been involved in spreading some poison, but it doesn't sound like he got exposed to any. Maybe it is just a series of coincidences. There could be another explanation. Maybe the cows died from dehydration."

"You sound glum, Tom."

"Yeah, I think my fancy theory just went down the tubes. For a while there, I was beginning to construct a real spider web."

"Wait a minute. Ten dead cows and a trap set with spears still sounds like eco-sabotage to me. You better get me a report tomorrow. Maybe I can clear my calendar and come up to investigate it this week."

"Yeah, sure. I probably need to look at my notes and stuff. Maybe I can do that tomorrow."

"Hey, buck up. Maybe you can be a hero to the locals. If we bust some eco-saboteurs for killing cattle, you might get your name in the papers."

"Mary, unlike you, I never come up smelling like a rose. Every time I get involved in somebody else's business, I have to take a bath."

✯

Monday started with a surprise at the office. When Tom sat down at his computer at seven, Vince walked in with a worried look on his face. "Uh, Tom, you weren't planning on going to the field today, were you? I need you to stick around in the office. Umm, we have a meeting, and we need you to be there. Rich is in another meeting right now, but when he gets out, we...uh, something came up, and umm, maybe you can help us."

"Gosh, Vince, it must be important. Are your kids gonna be OK? Are they going to get to school on time without you?"

"Uh, umm, oh yeah. Uh, yeah it's kind of important. I think we'll need you there."

"No problem. I was about to download some pictures of dead cows off my camera for you guys to look at. Hey, see that? How do you like my new walking stick? I busted the sharp point off so I wouldn't hurt myself, you know. Somebody left it out in Willow Creek, and I found it when I fell on my ass."

"Oh!" Vince's eyes widened. "Um, yeah. Uh, I've got to go, but we'll want to talk about this later." He backed out.

Tom connected the camera to his computer. After only a year with the new-fangled digital, he was already accustomed to thinking that downloading photos was a slow process. However, it took only twenty minutes, compared to a week to develop film prints. He picked up his coffee cup and walked down the hall. There was a murmur of voices from behind the panels.

"Hey, Randy, you got a hot date in there?" He stuck his head into Randy's cubicle. "Oops, wrong thing to say. Sorry, Alice, I didn't mean to insult your taste in men." Alice Straw, one of the other two range cons in the office, glowered at him. "You two are being awfully quiet in here. Anything going on today I should know about?"

"Well, the lynch mob is here, but they're still talking to Rich, and Mary Twil showed up, so you might have a chance of living to see due process in action."

"Aside from you," said Tom, feeling his blood pressure rising, "is anybody in this office really dumb enough to think I set up that mess in Willow Creek?"

"Tom, boy, don't ask if we got dumb. Ask if we got any smart." Randy drawled. "The cowboys are pissed and blaming environmentalists in general. The sheriff is asking questions. Rich and Vince are scared somebody is going to make them look bad, and you walk in here every day looking like Cactus Ed and talking like Ed Abbey. You keep telling people our creeks look like shit just because they look like shit. You need to learn some diplomacy around the office. Be more like me."

"Hoo!" Tom laughed. "Well, thanks for keeping this in the proper perspective." He looked at his empty cup. "Think I'll go see if Bill finished washing his socks in that big urn."

Sipping the foul brew, he sat down at his desk again. The camera was still downloading, so he pulled his notebook out of his pack. The plastic bag holding the odd root caught his eye. He tossed that on the other table near a microscope, then opened his map and laid it on top of the pile of books and papers on his desk. He started typing, trying to think of the particular details that Mary would want to see in the report. Who, What, and Where, the words surfaced from his memory. "How about just what and where? Let's not talk about who until somebody else shows up in this picture," he mumbled to himself.

After a while, he checked the results of downloading and unhooked the camera. He set the software to view the photos as a slideshow. He clicked through the images one by one. The first twelve were from Joseph Creek up in Washington, so he moved those to a separate directory. Thirty-eight were from Willow Creek, and the last two were of the plastic trash he had picked up from Cow Creek. He put those in a separate directory folder also. Then he copied the thirty-eight photos to the shared network drive so Mary Twil would have access to them.

When Mary tapped him on the shoulder, he nearly dropped his coffee. "Damn! Man, I need to put a rear-view mirror on this computer."

"You working on that report?"

Tom brought the notes up on the screen. "Here's a pretty good start. I figured maybe we should talk about it, and then I can flesh out anything else that might be useful."

"I think you better write down everything you can think of, then we'll talk. Greenwood might want to be there too. He knows you called me yesterday."

"Anybody nervous about me finding out more than I know already?" he asked rhetorically. He heard voices in the hall. "Is that meeting over? Probably mine is next. Excuse me, I've got to go to the boy's room." On his way down the hall, Tom looked back to notice that Mary checked both directions before stepping out of his cubicle. "Oh, good, I love being a leper."

He stood in the foyer and waited for the ranchers to come out toward the public parking lot in front. As expected, they stopped to visit the restroom, including one he recognized as Troy Grey. Tom followed them in. There is a cultural taboo against talking in a men's restroom unless you make a joke but Tom didn't want to pass up this opportunity. "Whoa! Full house," Tom cracked. That broke the ice.

Troy looked over and grinned. "I'm gittin' too old to pass up a bathroom any more. I was squirming like a kid in church before that meetin' was over."

"Know what you mean. Our staff meetings last so long I'm ready to split a gut. Next time I'm going to hold up my hand and ask to go potty!"

At the sinks Tom got to the point. "You're Troy Grey, aren't you? Don't know if you remember me. I'm Tom Krueger. I'm the one who asked Randy to let you and the others know there were some animals in trouble down in Willow Creek."

"Yeah, I remember you. I asked you about that patch of weeds on my ground over by the Snake River."

"Yes. Well, last Tuesday I didn't have time to check things out, and Randy told me what you found, so I went back Saturday to take some photos for evidence." Tom held the door to the hall open for Troy.

Troy looked interested. "They got you working on Saturday? Are you a cop?" They stepped aside for the last rancher who came out of the bathroom.

"No, I simply felt stupid that I was so close and didn't go look the first time. Only problem was I would have been walking out in the dark if I'd stayed any longer." Tom noticed Vince coming up the hall and waving to get his attention.

"I thought I remembered you was the biologist or somethin'. I should have known you weren't a cop. You ain't wearin' the uniform." Troy grinned. "And you ain't near as pretty as that young gal back there neither."

Tom laughed, "Now that's a fact. Before you go though, I wanted to ask, Randy said you told him there were ten dead cows in Willow Creek. I only found nine. Where was the other one?" He waved back at Vince and nodded.

"I think I counted seven down in that deep gully. That was the damnedest thing I ever saw. Some son-of-a-bitch put these sharp sticks a-pointin' where a cow would run into 'em and stab herself. Excuse my language. Then there was one up on the hill there by a spring, and there was two up in the cedar near the head of the crick."

"OK, I missed one by the spring. Are you talking about Owl Spring?"

"No, this one's up on the hill between Willow Crick and Deer Crick."

"Were spears set for traps up there too?"

"No, now I don't know what killed that one for sure, but there she was, dropped deader than hell. Her legs were just folded right under her. Maybe she'd been shot, but if she was, she fell on that side."

"Did you see any blood?" Tom could see Vince was nervously trying to decide whether to approach closer or retreat.

"No, no I didn't. It's a mystery to me."

"What the heck is going on?" Tom thought for a minute. "Did you see anything odd like plastic buckets or milk jugs, or anything else that seemed out of place?"

"No, but there was a pile of branches where somebody cut down some bushes."

"Oh, now, that's interesting. Could you tell what was cut down? Maybe it was either chokecherry or serviceberry." Vince was now hovering and listening closely.

"It could have been either. I'm not sure which it was. The leaves were mostly shriveled up."

"Did you notice if the cow had been eating the branches or leaves?"

"Naw," Troy looked like he was losing interest.

"Well, if it was chokecherry, she might have been poisoned. There are cyanide compounds in the leaves and shoots."

"I'll be damned. No, I didn't look. I've seen my cows eat chokecherry before though, and they weren't poisoned."

"I think the leaves and shoots have to be stressed, like with frost, before the cyanide gets concentrated. Maybe it works if you cut the branch off. Did the leaves look about this long?" Tom held his fingers about three inches apart.

"Yeah, I think so. Was that chokecherry?"

"Probably. Serviceberry leaves are kind of round, with little teeth at the end, and only an inch long."

"No, they were longer, and kind of pointed."

"I'd bet on it then, chokecherry for sure. One last thing, Randy said your stock in Cow Creek were sick when you found them. A couple died, right? Did you find any spears down there?"

"No. Those cows were just plain sick like they ate something bad. They didn't want to get up at all. They were weak and kind of stumblin' along. Then they put their heads down and got to shakin', and collapsed, and just wouldn't go no farther. The two I got out I put in a trailer. When I got 'em home, I put 'em in the shed and give 'em some clean grain and a little hay. I think they're gonna be OK."

"You don't know of anybody setting out a feed supplement or a liquid wormer out there, do you?"

"No, it's not my ground." Disgust and anger showed on Troy's face. "Somebody cut my damn fences. Prob'ly that damned environmentalist. I found his body. Serves him right," he fumed. "Now I got animals scattered all over the country. Willow Crick ain't in my allotment either."

"Well, I hope we get this all figured out. Thanks for your help, Troy." They shook hands, and Tom watched the wiry, bow-legged, old cowboy go out to a beat-up pickup with a stock rack on the bed. Tom shook his head in wonder, "I hope I'm in that good of shape when I'm eighty years old."

"What was that all about?"

"Oh, not much, Vince. He just needed to vent a little. Troy and me are getting to be good old buddies. We've had some pretty good conversations about riparian ecology and noxious weeds, all kind of things. Sometimes he unloads a little of life's burdens. You know, I think he's sweet on Mary Twil."

"Well, come on. Rich is waiting to have a meeting about what happened out in Willow Creek and we need you there." Vince led the way down the hall. "What were you saying about pictures?" he asked turning around. "I mean earlier this morning. Did you get some photos when you were out there last week?"

"Yeah," Tom replied, "I took shots of different sections of the creek bed where we planted those cottonwoods. It didn't look like any survived. Got some shots of brands on the trespass cows too. A bunch of them ran all the way down the canyon in front of me."

"Uh, you didn't see any dead cows?"

Tom was deliberately obscure. "Not last Tuesday. I could smell something dead a long way off with the breeze blowing up canyon. Didn't go check on it, though. I did tell Randy to call the ranchers about the stray cows."

Tom entered the door of the "Lodgepole" meeting room which Rich Moeller, the BLM Field Office Manager, had commandeered for the day. Tom thought it was a grand title for a long, narrow room too large to be a coffin, but too ill-shaped to be useful for much else. Rich was sitting at the end of the table near the door next to Sheriff Greenwood.

Tom smiled and nodded. "Sheriff. Morning, Rich, sorry to keep you waiting. Troy stopped to bend my ear. I didn't want to be impolite." Randy Bergen, Gilbert Dawson, Associate District Manager Bob Dodd, and Mary Twil were seated around the other end of the table. Since nobody could get between the sheriff's bulk and the wall to the empty chairs on his side, Tom and Vince walked around Rich and took the two open chairs opposite the sheriff.

The silence hung heavy for a moment. Then Gilbert decided to facilitate. "Rich, since we have some new faces in here, maybe we should go around the table and introduce ourselves again." Tom thought Gilbert liked the word "Officer" in his Public Affairs Officer title.

Rich, on the other hand, considered himself to be a no-nonsense decision-maker. Trained in the science of forest economics, he had spent most of his career as a timber manager in western Oregon, converting 400-year-old forests into tree farms managed on a 60-year rotation. When timber harvests slowed in the 80s decade, he jumped into managing people instead. "Maybe that's not necessary. Tom?"

"I know everybody here. I think they all know me." Tom looked around. Everyone nodded. Randy shielded his face from the sheriff and Rich and demonstrated that he could roll one eye independently of the other. Gilbert straightened the notepaper on his clipboard and examined his day-planner. Tom looked at the ceiling and breathed slowly and deeply to keep from laughing.

"Right. Then let's get down to business." Rich paused for a moment, at a loss for what to say. "Hmm, Vince, why don't you bring Tom up to speed on what we heard this morning?"

"Uh, um, well, we just heard from several of our permittees, and uh, they lost some cattle in Willow Creek." Glancing over at Sheriff Greenwood, Vince continued, "I don't want to go into details, but it looks like we have a case of environmental sabotage." He looked back to Rich Miller, hoping that introduction was sufficient. Apparently, it wasn't, since Rich remained silent and stone-faced. "Uh, well, Tom's been working in that area, so maybe he ought to tell us what he knows."

Tom looked at Rich for acknowledgment that it was his turn, feeling the heat of suppressed anger in Rich's stare. Rich grunted, and Tom made a show of consulting his little notebook. "Let's see. All right, it was Tuesday I went out to Willow Creek to check on those cottonwoods we planted last April with the high school kids."

Rich interrupted "Seems to me we're wasting a lot of time on these kind of projects. Why were you going out there again?" He glared at Vince for allowing Tom way too much freedom.

"We do have a history of starting projects and then walking away from them," Tom nodded. "But in theory we're supposed to go back and evaluate what we did and decide whether to do more of the same or change the procedure, or maybe even give up. So, that's what I was doing. If we want to fix any of our streams, it's going to take at least several years of planting and controlling the livestock."

"The local newspaper gave us a nice little article with a couple of photos on that project," Gilbert interrupted. "Any time you get kids involved, the paper sells to their parents. It's good community relations. Actually, Tom, you did a good job on that one, but you should have been wearing a BLM uniform in that photo," Gilbert added petulantly.

Rich turned his glare on Gilbert. "Let's get back on track. Tom?"

"Not much to tell that day. I came down the creek. I saw about forty cattle with three or four different brands. They were bunching up and running ahead of me down canyon the way cattle usually do. It looked like all but two or three of the cottonwood had been browsed back to the ground. We'll probably need to fix the fences and try planting again. From the looks of things, I would say the cows had been in there several days, maybe a week." Tom paused to look at his notebook. "The water was mostly running under the rocks, only a couple spots where you could see water. Owl Spring trough was empty, and the cattle were watering from that seep around the spring-box and the spillage out of the pipeline. Also, the fence was cut above the spring."

"So the trough was sabotaged, too?" Vince asked.

"No, just standard neglect. It hasn't been maintained in years. Probably the pipe got exposed by erosion and froze. The exclosure fence around the springbox is long gone. Anyway, I let Randy know about it the next day. Gave him the brands and told him to call the ranchers because it smelled like there were a couple of dead animals."

"You didn't see them? You didn't go look?" Rich asked angrily. "Seems to me that was your job. They're a hell of a lot more important than some damn cottonwoods."

Tom shrugged. "I knew about where they were. I thought I'd report it before some more starved to death or died of thirst. As it was, I didn't get back much before eight. Vince would have been sending out a helicopter if I hadn't come back. He's a stickler about this safety stuff."

Vince's eyes had opened wide at the mention of his name. He relaxed a bit and nodded, appreciative of having the ADM present to hear this affirmation of his devotion to duty. Rich knew better. Randy tucked both feet up on his chair and rolled his eyes to signify the bullshit level was getting too deep.

"Why didn't you radio in and stay longer?" Rich demanded.

"Number one, the office was already closed when I got close enough upwind of the first one to smell it. Actually, it isn't that unusual to find a dead cow, especially in a drought year, so it didn't occur to me that I needed to go look."

"Not even with the fence cut!" Rich snorted incredulously.

"That was two miles back upstream. Found that on my way out, and I had to go out of my way to check the spring. Besides, it occurred to me that somebody other than an environmentalist might cut a fence in a drought year." Tom looked at the sheriff. "It makes it handier for the cows to find some water and feed."

The idea surprised no one, but Rich didn't like the implications. "Don't be making accusations unless you've got some proof." Tom's impertinence was more than Rich could bear. His volume switch was creeping up uncontrollably. "Now, what the hell were you doing out there Saturday?"

"Well, you know how excitable Randy is. He gave me the impression Troy thought my cottonwood cuttings were sticking up like pungi stakes and might hurt something. I thought I'd better see if some of the kids had cut them off wrong or left some big ones where they might cause a problem. That did seem like my responsibility."

"Who said you could work on Saturday?" Rich threw a venomous glance at Vince, who looked like a cornered rabbit facing a Rottweiler. Then he turned back to Tom, "Who told you it was your damn job to investigate a crime?"

Tom raised his voice a notch in response. "As far as I knew, there wasn't any crime except someone cutting a fence, and nobody but me gets very upset about that. It wasn't until I found the spear trap that I got the idea there was something else going on."

"Well," Rich snarled, "how do we know you weren't out there destroying evidence? You and your tree-hugger buddy. We're going to look into that." He turned to Vince. "I want you to write this guy up for misuse of a government vehicle and working unauthorized hours. Give him two weeks off without pay and confine his work to the office after that until the investigation is over."

Tom boiled over. "Vince isn't stupid enough to invite a grievance. I went out there in my own truck, on my own time. There's nothing on my timesheet about Saturday."

"Claudel knew he should have fired you ten years ago!" Rich pointed his thick finger at Vince. "You put that clown on a short leash."

"All right," said Bob Dodd, deciding to exert his authority. "I think we could all use some time to cool off a bit and think clearly. Tom, I understand you were writing up a report for Mary on what you saw, right?"

Tom nodded. The permanent sunburn on his neck was indistinguishable from the heat in his face. He was half-crouched, ready to leap at Rich.

Bob continued, "Then I suggest you finish that this morning and take the rest of the day off on my say so. You plan on staying around the office the next few days in case Mary has any more questions for you." He looked around at the others. "Sheriff, we'll make sure you get a copy of Tom's report this afternoon. Everybody else, keep this to yourselves. If you get any calls asking about it, you refer them to my office." As they filed out of the room, he put a hand to Rich's shoulder to calm him and spoke softly with a low, sympathetic chuckle.

Back at his cubicle, Tom was thinking about kicking in the screen of his computer when Vince, followed closely by Randy, crowded in.

"Wow, Man, that was tense. I'm sorry. I didn't know Rich was going to lose it like that."

Tom sighed heavily. "It's all right, Vince. Probably if either one of us had said anything more, it would have been worse than it was."

"Who was he talking about, that Claudel?" Vince asked.

Randy laughed, "Claudel was Tom's best buddy ever in the whole BLM."

"Yeah, we would have gladly died together, just as long as each of us had our fingers wrapped around the other one's throat," Tom shook his head. "Claudel was my boss in Phoenix, another old west-side Oregon forester like Rich. Odds are that he and Rich know each other from the good old days." He shook his head. "Some things never change."

"Piss on him, Tom. Rich don't have no more brains than Claudel did," Randy said. "I guess there is someone in this office dumb enough to think you were involved. So what did you find out? Was Troy right? Did Skinner do all this?"

"Vince, did you ever wonder how a big-city Jewish boy with a master's degree in Agronomy came to speak like a hick from West Texas? I believe Randy could run for Governor."

"Yeah," Vince agreed, "I don't think the Bureau would have hired him to kick cow turds if he didn't do something to dumb down." He was happy to have someone else be the butt of Tom's humor for the moment.

Mary Twil peeked in. "It reminds me of a coyote that rolls around in fresh manure for camouflage," she said. "How about you guys let Tom finish his report. I can't believe you're wasting time when you could be off for the day, Tom."

"Good point. Clear out." Tom spun his chair toward the computer. "You can stay, Mary. Here, read this and ask questions. If I missed anything, I can fill it in." He started typing. "I need to make a small change based on what Troy told me this morning."

"How's that?"

"I think Troy found the source of the spears used in the trap. Here." Tom handed her the stick he had brought back. "This is one of them. I broke the sharp tip off so I wouldn't stab myself. Ten to one it's chokecherry."

"It could be. So?"

"Randy sent me in there afraid it was my cottonwood. It isn't. It's heavy and solid for something that small in diameter. The bark is different."

"Is this going somewhere?"

"Time estimates, for one thing. I guessed the cows had been there between four days and a week." Tom pulled a knife from his hip pocket and peeled a strip of bark from both ends. "This end was drying in the sun." She looked at it. "This end was stuck in the dirt bank, protected from drying much." He saw her blank response. "The cambium layer is still green and soft. At the dry end, the bark is stiff. The cambium is already brown. Troy said the leaves on the cut branches were shriveled, but he could still tell how long they were and what the tips looked like. It sounded like chokecherry."

"What's your point, Tom?"

"A week at most, that's when the trap was set. I told Randy I found tracks at the fence where it had been cut. That was on Tuesday. By Saturday they were mostly erased by the wind. That was four days difference. By the way, I got a photograph of a lugged boot print at the fenceline. It wasn't mine."

"So, Skinner could have done it. Is that what you mean?"

"The last time I believed in coincidence was when my marriage was breaking up." He hesitated. "But the fact is we don't know what Skinner was doing out there. I think he was involved somehow, but he wasn't alone, not even the day he died."

"OK, Leaphorn, I thought you couldn't read tracks. How do you know he wasn't alone?"

"For one thing, I'd bet he was too experienced to be out there with less than two quarts of water. He either had a vehicle near enough to reach, or expected someone to pick him up. His partners either bailed out on him or ran off with his vehicle. Abandoning somebody in the desert might qualify for manslaughter. By the way, did anybody look for Skinner's vehicle?"

"I'm not giving you any more details, Tom. You are not a cop. Got that? Greenwood will be talking to you again. It's his case. If I give you anything, I will be in deep doo-doo. He's sharp."

"All right, it's not that important anyway. Most likely the partners covered their tracks and are long gone."

"Another guess?"

"Mary, whoever planned this is smart, not some dip-wah tree-hugger fresh out of school. They knew they could walk in with nothing more than a machete and find the materials to make spears. They picked the perfect spot. The walls of that wash are so steep it took less than twenty spears to close the escape paths. One person could have carried them tied in a bundle. All this happened within a mile of the road at the bottom end of the wash. Then they walked upstream two more miles and cut the fence right where there was a little water to draw cattle in. Afterwards, the cattle trapped themselves looking for water or feed in the bottom. The saboteurs were already gone. If Troy hadn't gone in there for a few more days, Lord knows how many more animals would have been trapped and died."

"So they walked back down to their truck? Maybe."

"Or they had parked another mile up the ridge, like where I parked in the trees Saturday. It wasn't too far from where the fence had been cut, and it's a good place to hide a truck."

"You know, I wouldn't speculate too loud, Tom. There aren't many people around that want to think about walking miles in rough country carrying a load of branches on their back. Rich might think you were bragging about being smart, too."

"Good point. OK, look at these photos." He brought the camera software back up. "Here's how they set the spears at the downstream end. It reminds me of a big game pass-through on a fence, one-way. An animal can get in by pushing the spears apart, but the points are too threatening from the other side. Here's a close-up of the point. See how it is shaved to a sharp triangle? Simple and quick."

"Were any of the tips broken off?"

"Not that I saw. These were designed for one purpose, stabbing anything clumsy that wanted out. Here's one stuck in the top of the bank. If you try to climb up this chute, you get it in the chest." He clicked through the slide show, the photos alternating from head and chest shots of the dead cows to a wide-angle full side shot and occasionally another spear. "I've put all these on the shared network drive where you can get at them. I suggest you copy them to your own drive and directory, then delete them off the network. I'll keep the originals here as a back-up."

The photo of the dead coyote came up. Mary grimaced, "Gruesome! I suppose somebody shot it."

"That's what I thought at first too, but there was no bullet hole and no blood. The cows weren't bloody either except where the coyotes chewed through, and not much there. The blood settled before the coyotes got started." Tom clicked through the rest of the series quickly. "I photographed all but a couple of the spears. You can see there wasn't any blood on their points either."

"Well, like you said when you called me Sunday, they could have died from dehydration. I suppose if they were in there for several days, that would be enough time."

"Yeah, it would. They need about seven or eight gallons of water each day."

Mary stared at the computer screen. "Can you blow those up any more? I mean can you tell if the points were all the same? Were any whittled sharp and thin so they might have broken off at the tip?"

"I could enlarge the photos if you want, but I looked close watching for blood. If any were broken, you could have seen the fibers. After all, the wood was drying, not brittle. They were just sharp enough to puncture your skin if you pushed against them. If you whittled them thinner, it might puncture easier, but a broken off splinter wouldn't kill a cow, and they might spook and run by." Tom was puzzled by Mary's scrutiny of the points. "Well, I'm out of here unless you have questions. I'll print a couple copies now so you can take one to Greenwood. If you want me later, you can either find me at Barney's Pub or at home."

"Here, take your munchies with you." Laughing, she picked a plastic bag off the table next to her and tossed it to Tom. "Looks like your cookies melted in the sun."

"Yuck. That's a root I collected. I used the bag to give Scrub some water." He opened the bag and left it to dry. "See you later." On the way out, he invited Randy to drop by Barney's at office closing time.

Chapter 4

When Tom walked into the bar at 3:30 P.M., Randy was already there, sequestered with Jesse Jackson at a small table near the empty stage. He took a mug of stout from Emma and went over.

"I figured you'd be here in your cups a long time ago," Randy drawled. "Me and the Reverend already finished our first platter of nachos. Why don't you go order some more before you sit down?"

Tom sat first, waited for Emma to look their way, and signaled for a new plate. Emma nodded and spoke to the kitchen help.

"Now, how come she looks after you so good? I've been trying to catch her eye for the last ten minutes."

"I think he brings out the mother instinct in women," Jesse chuckled. "They all think he's shy and helpless."

"Did you invite her home tonight, Randy? Could be a reason she's ignoring you," Tom responded. "Any further drama at the office after I left?"

"No high drama like you and Rich pulling knives, but Rev' could be right about the women. Must have been three of 'em mooning around asking about you. It was starting to sound like a soap opera," Randy complained. "I had to get out of there."

"Did you have a fight with your boss?" Jesse was collecting fodder for the rumor mill.

"Not really. The dumb shit all but accused me of killing cows with Jerry Skinner. Or maybe it was killing Jerry. He'd like to fire me, but he can't figure out the right excuse."

Jesse's eyes opened wide. "Jerry was killing cows? That sounds like a good way to get yourself killed."

"Somebody has been killing cows. Skinner's body wasn't all that far away from the action. Revenge killing is something I hadn't thought of, but the cattle problem was discovered after the body."

"Well, I heard yesterday that Jerry had been murdered. They found a bullet in his back." Jesse sat back in anticipation of a satisfying reaction.

Randy whistled in appreciation, "Could be...Tom, what are you thinking?"

Tom was thinking that bullet wounds drain lots of blood, and the cause of death wouldn't be dehydration. He wondered if he had missed something in the conversation with Mary or if Jesse's source had misinterpreted something. "I've never seen Troy with a gun. If he shot someone, though, it would be right between the eyes, not in the back." Tom paused. "Randy, you were in the meeting with the ranchers this morning. Is it likely that any of them were out on horseback in Cow Creek within a few days before Skinner's body was found?"

"Not likely. Nobody knew they had cattle missing except Troy, and that was because he was checking fences. The others were either farming or working day jobs in town."

Emma delivered a platter of cheese nachos and left quickly.

"Thank you," Tom spoke loudly to her retreating back. She waved without looking.

Reverend, have you heard any rumors of Jerry having problems with friends or hanging out with any strangers or tough characters lately?" Tom thought a friend might make a mistake and leave someone stranded, but if the Reverend was hearing rumors of murder, that added a new and more serious wrinkle. Maybe the wound had been more serious than Mary had let on.

"Not anything unusual. He was always going off fishing or hunting or hiking with somebody, though. He knew people from all over the country. He would go out on organized trips with people from the Sierra Club, or Trout Unlimited, groups like that."

Tom risked giving out a little information in exchange for an opinion. "How well did you know him? Would he be dumb enough to be out in the middle of Cow Creek carrying only two little water bottles, with no vehicle nearby?"

"He was more the sportsman type than I am," Jesse admitted. "That doesn't sound like Jerry. He was real organized. If that's all he had, he was probably expecting someone to pick him up."

Tom agreed. The question was who had abandoned Skinner when he needed help, and what piece of information would turn an accident into a murder. "You know, the possibility of murder makes this a more interesting challenge. It's not like someone is going to feel guilty about leaving the guy out there and then confessing they made an unfortunate mistake. Let's say we rule out revenge for the cows as a motive for now. The other most likely motives are money, women, argument with a friend, or involvement in something illegal that went sour. Which would it be?"

Jesse had some useful information. "He wasn't rich, but he had enough money to live comfortably. He didn't ask me to pay him for being my fishing guide. From what he said, I don't think he charged anybody else either. Money wasn't an issue for him. He had an old Land Cruiser and a small house, all paid off. He lived cheap and was proud of it."

Tom asked, "What about his friends?"

Jesse considered, "The ones I know about are pretty low key people, nonviolent ex-hippies. Most of his environmentalist friends are from John Day or Bend. I haven't heard much about women. I think Jerry was divorced a long time ago."

"How would you go about meeting some of those people Jerry used to hike with? I mean suppose I wanted to go hiking someplace in Washington. Do they have something like a ride-share system for backpackers?"

Emma returned, "How you guys doing? You want a refill, Reverend?" He nodded and handed her his empty.

"I'll take another pale ale, Darlin'," Randy drawled. "I was thinking about joining one of those clubs. Only, I like the idea of bicycles. I might meet some babe with strong legs."

"Have you ever thought about becoming an Internet predator, Randy? You might have better luck." Emma blew him a kiss and left.

"The best advice always comes from women, Randy. You can take it to the bank." Tom grinned and stuffed his mouth with a wad of cheese nachos.

"Oh, yeah? It's a good thing we can report you're getting your ration of junk food. Alice says you're carrying the health food shit too far. Says you've got some kind of ginseng root lying on your desk." Randy looked knowingly at Jesse before delivering the punch-line. "I told her it's supposed to cure impotency better'n Viagra. She damn near had a hemorrhage!"

Jesse guffawed in appreciation, dripping cheese in his lap. Randy added, "Then I asked if she had sneaked a piece of it, cause it was known to cause all kinds of bizarre side effects in women, going well beyond prodigious and indiscriminate sexual acts with men in uniform. Whooee! Damned if she didn't dump her recycling box on me! I nearly died right there."

When he could take a sip of beer without choking, Tom said, "I wonder if her reaction had anything to do with seeing you wear an official uniform last month."

"I think it had something to do with Alice being in denial."

"Isn't she going through a divorce?" Jesse had a pipeline to all the town's gossip.

"It seems to be in the water at all federal buildings these days," Tom sighed. "From what she said, there's a chance her husband might pull his head out and repair the damage. I wouldn't count on it, though."

"You got an interest, Tom?" Jesse was prepared to spread that rumor too.

"No way. No office romance, ever. Can't say I'm ready to start over either. If Alice does break up with George, I bet it'll be a year or two before she calms down again."

Emma reappeared on her rounds. "Anybody ready for another?" Only Tom's glass was low, but he declined. She put a hand on his shoulder, "When you start looking, Hon, I know a couple women who could use a decent man." She winked and walked back to the bar.

Randy fumed, "Now, who the hell elected you to be the one decent man in this stinking little town?"

"Oh, I don't know about that. The Reverend here always seems to be shaking women off his arm. There must be something going on."

Bill Christen sat down at the table uninvited. "What's going on boys? Hey, Tom, I heard you got Rich on your ass again. Heard you were out messing around where they found Jerry Skinner. You must be dumb to keep looking for trouble."

"That might explain a lot of my problems," Tom replied. "Maybe you could keep me from hanging. Know anybody who might have wanted to kill Skinner?"

Bill laughed, “Hell, he was an environmentalist commie! I would have killed him. Half the people in the county would have killed him.”

“He’s been living here, making noise for a long, long time,” Randy said. “How come you didn’t kill him last time you had an argument with him here at the bar?”

“Ah, I’m not serious,” Bill apologized. “Poor bastard. He was a pain in the ass, that’s all. Nobody took him that seriously.”

Tom kidded Bill along, “He didn’t steal your girlfriend, did he?”

“You’re a real smartass, you know that?” Bill shot back. “Women were the only thing he and you and I had in common. None of us got laid in the last year.”

“Then I take it you didn’t dump him out in the desert so you could get his wife.”

“Shit.” Bill scowled. “You think any woman would stay with a guy like that? As far as I know, he never was married. You never know. He might have been, but he was in here a lot trying to pick up the same women I was hitting on. He never got anywhere that I saw.”

Tom finished his beer. “Have fun. I’m going home to feed my dog.” Tom walked home slowly, thinking about murder and what reasons anybody might have had to put an untimely end to Jerry Skinner’s life.

*

Scrub was lying in the shade of the wooden fence, on top of a bed of iris that Tom had planted. “You are as bad as a damn cow,” he told her, looking at the broken leaves. “I hope you didn’t eat them too. Those things will make you sick, you know.” Apparently Scrub did know. She ate the quack grass and would eat any vegetable from the garden as long as she knew Tom might otherwise cook it or put it in a salad. But she never nibbled anything in the Iris or Lily families except onions and garlic. Tom had put a fence around the garden to prevent her forays.

He let Scrub in to the house and measured out two cups of food into her dish. Then he pulled a large container of frozen vegetable stew from the freezer. “Looks like it’s tirne for you to cook something again, Scrub. We need to get a bigger pot.” For good measure, he also brought out the final remains of a thirty-pound turkey he had cooked around Easter. He broke a portion of the turkey into small chunks and added them to the frozen stew in a cast iron pot and set it on the stove to thaw.

Scrub finished licking her bowl, belched, and looked hopefully up at Tom. "That's it. The vet said you have to lose weight. He wants to see your ribs again." Tom sniffed something. "Is that you or did we forget to take out the garbage?" The smell was strongest near the sink. He took the paper grocery bag out of the trash container and carried it outside. Remembering the trash in the back of his truck, he lifted out the bag full of plastic debris. Another small shower of seeds fell on the concrete driveway.

When he looked closely, he saw seeds were stuck to the plastic with the brown grunge that had come from the buckets at Joseph Creek. He set the bag back in the truck, bending down to pick up a few of the seeds. They looked the same as those he had thrown in the flowerpot. Expecting nothing, he checked the pot anyway. One seedling had sprouted. It had a small three-parted leaf above the cotyledons. He examined the seeds in his hand. "Seed coats are mostly cracked. Now, why the heck is that?" Looking at the oddly familiar seedling, he noted it looked like a legume, and the seeds in his hand looked like tiny beans. "Some sort of feed?"

He opened the door to the house. "Scrub, do you want to come to the office with me?" She bounded out to the back of the pickup. But instead of opening the tailgate, Tom opened the door. "Why don't you ride up front this time?"

At 6 P.M., the office was empty. Tom whispered to Scrub as they entered, "You keep quiet and stay close. Otherwise you don't get any quality conversation this evening." To be cautious, he donned latex gloves. He cleared a place next to his microscope and carefully spread the top of the garbage bag on the microscope platform. Scrub decided to lie down in the corner. "If any of this drops on the floor, don't eat it."

As he looked through the microscope, he used a scalpel to scrape seeds and dried grunge onto the glass plate. He adjusted the light. "This could be nothing but dried root-beer. It looks like crystalline sugar in it." Scrub looked on unimpressed. "Those are definitely legume seeds. The seed coat is very hard. That's why they crack them, so they can be digested." Scrub sighed. "What do you know?" Tom scowled at her.

Carefully, he opened the bag over the trashcan, being sure that all the spilled seeds went into the can. He removed the plastic milk jug pieces, and set those on the table. Slowly he turned the bag inside out, examining everything clinging to the surface. Then he returned to the milk jugs, scraping bits of the contents out on to the microscope plate.

"Ah-hah! Seeds again! Only this time we've got a mix. This one's a legume, different species though. This one's an umbel." He looked at Scrub. "For you, that means it's in the same group as carrots and celery." Scrub lifted an ear. "Yeah, sounds like food, but don't eat. Some are good, some are bad." He pushed the bits of rubbish around on the microscope plate and continued to enumerate his findings. "Another legume, this one looks like a lupine seed. You know those flowers I planted in the front yard? Still looks like it was coated in something. Mary could have been right about molasses. It smells like burning caramel with this hot light. These look like grass seeds of some kind. They all have a black fungus."

Tom used tweezers to grasp a piece of the chaff. "Now this is different. It looks like some kind of leathery old shrub leaf. The upper surface is dark green, almost shiny. The bottom side is lighter, and the margin is rolled. If it's a huckleberry or a rhododendron, it's not the kind of thing you would expect to find in a feed supplement."

He looked in the remainder of the milk jugs, where he found a couple larger pieces of debris. "These look definitive, Scrub." He crushed the dried flowers, spilling seeds onto the microscope. "Awfully tiny seeds. It reminds me of a columbine." He reached for a book on the shelf and opened it to the pages describing columbines. "I do not want to spend hours looking through the pictures, Scrub. Any bright ideas?" Tom flipped a few pages, looking at the illustrations. "Oh, it might be a Delphinium...larkspur." Tom interpreted the look on Scrub's face as approval.

"Back to weaving spider webs. Who's going to believe this?" He looked around and seized the bag and root from his desk. Look at this! Water and dried crud make molasses. It smells like molasses!" He used the scalpel to split the broken stalk and root. "Hollow stem, no, there's a cross membrane. What do they call that? Fat root. Bunch of cross membranes in there too." He slid the root under the microscope. "Nothing much. Looks like gummy crap on the outside."

Tom had no luck in calling Randy, so he looked at the phone directory and dialed Alice Straw. A man's voice answered. "Hello, George? This is Tom Krueger from the office. Is Alice home?"

"Just a minute." Muffled voices muttered unintelligibly.

"Hello?"

"Alice, this is Tom. Hope I'm not interrupting your dinner."

"No."

"I have an odd question for you. What kind of seeds might be in a horse or cattle feed other than wheat or oats or barley? Is there some kind of legume, something that has three leaflets?"

"Alfalfa and clover have three leaflets, Tom. You know that." Her voice sounded strangled.

Tom looked at the phone. "Oh, no, I don't mean the actual leaf, just the seed, and all one kind. It looks like a bean seed about half the size of a fat sweet pea. It's not alfalfa seed. This was in a bucket with some kind of brown sludge, maybe molasses. I also found another odd mix that has small legume seeds and a lot of other stuff. There is something that looks like some kind of umbel, but it's bigger than a carrot seed."

"Tom, I can't think of any. Maybe somebody might put beans in a feed, but not for horses. Maybe you've got pig or chicken feed, I don't know. Is that all?"

Her voice sounded very odd, almost like she was having trouble breathing. Tom noticed the root lying next to the microscope. "Alice, that root in the bag on my desk.... You didn't eat a piece of it, did you?"

"You Goddamned men! You are all crazy!" She slammed down the phone.

"Oh shit. She was choking, Scrub! She doesn't even know what's wrong." He redialed, letting it ring "Come on, George! Do something right!"

The phone lifted "Hello?"

"George, Alice didn't understand me. I think she might be poisoned."

"This isn't George. I'm her neighbor. What are you talking about?"

"It sounded like she was having trouble breathing, even choking. I think she might have eaten a piece of a root from my desk, and I have a bad feeling it was poisonous."

"Who is this?"

"Tom, Tom Krueger from her office. I'm serious. This is not a joke."

"Alice is not feeling well right now, but she hasn't been poisoned."

"Look, can you let me speak to George, please, or Alice. Let me explain to them."

"George is not here. Alice does not want to talk to you."

"Look, do I have to call 911? Ask her if she touched or ate anything from that bag on my desk. For God's sake, I can hear her choking in the background."

"Listen, Nitwit. She's crying. George beat her up. With any luck, he's in jail now."

"Oh." Tom listened to the dead silence following the slam.

He stacked the jug bottoms together, slipping them into a paper grocery sack from a bundle he used to collect grass and wildflower seeds. He repeated the process with the odd root, then the plastic sack from Joseph Creek, stapling them shut and labeling each one "evidence – do not open." Then he shoved them inside the herbarium cabinet and closed the metal door.

He sat down at the computer to send Mary Twil an e-mail message. "Let her call me in the morning. I'm in enough trouble," he muttered as the e-mail program opened, showing him a list of over twenty messages that had arrived in two days. "Look at this crap, Scrub. These dumb-asses are in love with the Internet. I could die and go to hell, and they would keep sending e-mail here forever. Not one of them would even know I hadn't opened their stupid messages. Computers were supposed to make us more efficient. Now we use our time to empty out the garbage."

He typed slowly, organizing his thoughts and trying to remember details of what he had observed at Joseph Creek and Cow Creek. Then he tried to hypothesize a connection between those incidents and the Willow Creek livestock deaths. After fifteen minutes of typing, Tom crumpled onto the keyboard. Without lifting his head, he looked back at Scrub. "Do you have any idea how stupid this would sound to another human being? There are too many missing pieces. Hell, what if somebody believed even part of it. Those damn buckets in our trash bin would look like I did this." He deleted the message without sending it, then deleted all of his incoming e-mail. "I used to like computers, Scrub, but that was before e-mail. Before the Internet...." Mouse poised over the "log-off" icon, he hesitated. "Emma, you may have been giving the right advice to the wrong chump." He looked in the phone book for Jerry Skinner's address, then logged off the computer, and dropped Scrub off at home before going off to investigate.

*

As Bill had suggested, Jerry Skinner had lived alone. Tom parked on Cherry Street, walked around the block, and entered an alleyway. He climbed the fence and approached the darkened house. The back porch was enclosed and screened. Tom poked his pocketknife through the screen door and lifted the hook from the catch. The ill-fitting back door to the old house had an antiquated lock that had not even been used. Inside Tom found a computer in a spare upstairs bedroom. Tom drew the curtain over the window, turned on a small light, and went to work.

In contrast to the lack of security to the house, the computer booted to a password screen that Tom could not bypass. Tom looked for a crib-sheet with passwords, but found none. As he stared at the screen, he thought of all the clichés about poorly chosen passwords. "I don't even know when his birthday was."

In fact, he didn't know anything about Jerry Skinner except that he was now an ex-tree-hugger who had held to the party line that any tree over twenty inches in diameter was sacred. Tom thought of their conversations that day when he had tried to explain forest ecology and justify cutting some big trees. Although Skinner understood forest science, he had simply chosen to throw science away and replace it with the eco-political mantra.

"And he was awfully proud to be one of the chosen few on our side of the mountains...." Tom remembered Jerry's boasting words, "one of six active environmentalists in all of eastern Oregon." Tom consecutively typed 1of6, oneofsix, Oneofsix, OneofSix, 1ofsix, and successfully, 1ofSix. The hard drive started grinding. "I love hunches that work," he muttered. While the software loaded, he whistled "Luck Be A Lady Tonight," recently performed by the local high school theater group, now stuck in his memory.

Tom removed a scrap of paper from the wastebasket, writing down a number of e-mail addresses, and website addresses from the history log of Jerry's Internet software. He looked for downloaded documents, finding a series of environmental treatises, opinion pages, and saved chat-room discussions. He found a clean diskette in a box and copied a number of the documents. Jerry was not as careful about deleting old messages in his "sent" box as he was the "in-box." One indicated Jerry had planned to pick up Joshua Freeborn at the bus station the Saturday morning before his body was found. A second confirmed the pick-up time. Tom re-checked the history log, "Looks like Jerry was home Thursday and Friday night, but he never got back on the computer after that."

Tom shut off the machine and wiped the keys and mouse with his handkerchief. He also dusted the lamp and wiped the doorknob on his way out. "Joshua Freeborn sounds like a made-up name. Might as well be Cactus Ed."

When he returned to the office twenty minutes later, he went into Rich Moeller's office and reached behind the monitor for a well-thumbed, yellow sticky-note. He returned to his own desk, closed the window blind, and logged back on to the computer system.

Tom decided that Jerry Skinner had belonged to a million environmental organizations. Their websites all seemed to link back and forth. Quite a number linked to topical discussions for activists on chat-line bulletin boards. Tom really liked the international site for the "Earth Rites" group. The diatribes they posted indicated there were some seriously disturbed people on their membership lists. Some seemed to be recruiting others for activities that would clearly be illegal. In his searching, Tom found Joshua Freeborn posting messages that made fun of people's stupidity. Joshua lectured them on how and why they would be caught and prosecuted. He also had some very incisive analyses of effective tactics and causes of social change.

"This guy would make a good lawyer, either that or a military planner." The more he checked, the more sites he found where Joshua had left traces. National groups, state and local, sub-committees of environmental groups, all were on his shopping list. "He does favor the ones that sue people or stage protests." Tom found a short biographical byline that said Joshua lived in southwest Colorado near Cortez.

There were also a number of links to ride-share boards, and some that had their own system of contacting people who wanted to join outdoor activities and environmental issues education. Tom found Joshua had contacts in at least six other states besides Oregon. "Sucker does a lot of traveling. It must be nice to have so much free time. Wonder what he does for a living."

Tom spent the rest of the night hunched over the computer keyboard, finally returning home at 6 A.M. He let Scrub out into the back yard. The last thing he did before passing out was to leave a message for Vince, saying he had a terrible hangover and would be taking a day to sleep it off. At 2:30 in the afternoon the air conditioning kicked on, waking him from a fitful sleep. He showered to clear his head. While he ate a late lunch, he decided he would have to go visit Joshua Freeborn. He found his address book and dialed an old friend from Colorado.

The phone rolled over to an answering machine. Before the automated voice was done, a live voice interrupted, "Hello."

"Rita, hello. This is Tom Kreuger."

Rita Cooper had been one of the first women to break into the traditional man's role of game warden for the Colorado Division of Wildlife. Starting in Cortez, she had endured the chauvinism of her male counterparts and the belligerent disbelief of the largely male hunting public she policed. There she had met and occasionally worked with Tom in his capacity as a wildlife biologist, and had become friends with Tom and his wife Vickie. Her husband, Robert, had flirted with Vickie, and pronounced Tom "anti-social," a final condemnation. Rita enjoyed being around them for the sake of their environmentalist politics.

Tom had found the reaction of the men predictable. Rita was a very pretty, small blonde, and he had a hard time not being protective when they worked together. When they had once entered a hunters' camp together, he sat in the truck hoping the shotgun on the rack behind his head was loaded, watching Rita give four big Texans a lecture and a citation for the camp-meat doe they had taken illegally. Then he helped her load the deer into the back of the truck. For good measure, she confiscated the rifle of the guilty hunter. Tom never looked at her quite the same way again.

After four years of busting poachers and confiscating guns from drunken men, Rita was transferred to Denver, where her duties revolved around public education and trapping problem raccoons out of garages. The transfer had been unwelcome. It took another seven years to get a rural enforcement assignment again.

In Denver she supported her husband through a master's degree in psychology. After graduation he promptly began an affair with a blonde undergraduate. Rita believed her husband selected the younger woman deliberately because her age, use of make-up, and choice of clothes would better enhance his status and image. Her divorce became final three years before she left Denver.

Since then, she had come to recognize the approach of a status-conscious man looking for a blonde. All too frequently, she found herself getting angry at self-deceiving men who were attracted by her looks and independence, yet could not accept the risks she took, nor the schedule she worked. Usually, her relationships broke up when her boyfriends discovered they would have to cook for themselves for weeks on end. As her friends married, divorced, remarried, and broke up again, Rita kept on the sidelines.

Two years before, she had received Christmas cards from both Tom and his wife, each in their own way announcing their divorce. She offered sympathy to both and guarded congratulations to Vickie for having found her "center" and her new vibrant love. Rita was not entirely surprised to continue to receive letters from Tom every few months. Occasionally on weekends or evenings they had exchanged phone calls. He had been depressed, reaching out to old friends for support. She was a good counselor, experienced at helping friends recover from the shock of being jilted.

"Tom! How are you?"

"Oh, I'm doing pretty well, how about you? It's a shock to actually catch you at home during daylight."

Rita explained, "I took a few days off before the deer season. I was overdue to get a few things done around home. Are you at work?"

"No, I've been working long hours and decided to take the day off. It felt so good I started thinking about taking a vacation."

"Good for you. Where are you going?" she asked.

"Actually, I was thinking of going out to the canyon country by Cortez again. There's a guy who lives in that area I'd like to meet. Plus, it would be good to get away from here and do some hiking." Tom was nervous about asking, "I wondered if you might be interested in doing some hiking out there."

"When are you going? Once the hunting season starts, I won't get a break for a long time."

"I know this is real short notice, but I was thinking of getting out of here tomorrow or the next day. It would take me most of a couple days to get over there. Could you meet me for the weekend?"

"I could probably extend my leave that long. Yes, let's do it. But how would your friend feel about having me along?" Rita wondered if she would be completing a foursome.

"Oh, don't worry about that. I don't even know the guy yet. I was going to try to set up a meeting. He can wait until after the weekend."

"So, who is this guy?" she asked. "What is the meeting about?" Tom heard Rita almost laugh. He figured it must have sounded like he had created an excuse to call her on short notice.

"He appears to be a friend of Jerry Skinner, a guy I knew up here. They were doing some environmental activity networking. Jerry had an accident and died recently. I wanted to talk to Joshua to see if he knew anything about what Skinner was doing when he died."

"Oh, does Joshua have a last name?"

"Yeah," Tom replied, "and it's a strange one. Freeborn—Joshua Freeborn. According to the note I found, he lives in McElmo Canyon west of Cortez. Ever hear of him?"

Rita's voice went flat, "Tom, this guy is something of a weird character. I checked him out once on some drug rumors. Are you sticking your nose into somebody's business again?"

"Oh, boy, I hope not!" Tom lied. "As far as I know, they were only writing each other, sending e-mail back and forth, that kind of thing. Jerry had his accident out on BLM land. By coincidence it was fairly close to where some fences were cut. Jerry was a well-known local environmentalist, so it was easy for folks to blame him for the fences." Tom paused, "I figured it was too much of a long-shot for you to know Joshua. You think maybe he's dangerous?"

"He had no record. It looked like he had a rich father. The place in McElmo was bought outright with money from a trust fund out of New Mexico. Joshua moved in a couple years after you moved to Phoenix. If the rumors are true, his only friends are some rough characters."

At 6 P.M., Tom went back and spent the night on the computer again. He searched for more traces of Joshua and tried unsuccessfully to find a regular pattern of communications with other particular environmental activists that might indicate close connections. Then he spent some time searching databases for references on poisonous plants. Before he left the office at 6 A.M., he filled out a leave request form, and a hand-written note in an envelope labeled "confidential" for Vince. He caught Randy coming in to the office. "Good timing, Randy! Here, sign this leave slip. You're my acting supervisor because Vince isn't up yet. I've got an emergency situation here."

"Wait a minute! Just what kind of crap is this? You gonna get me in trouble?"

"Nah. Tell them I said it was an emergency. See this envelope? It says 'Confidential,' only for Vince's eyes. It explains everything. Just put it in Vince's mailbox."

Chapter 5

Wednesday morning Vince was looking forward to giving Tom a hard time about the hangover. Tuesday afternoon, he had rehearsed his lines. When he saw that Tom was not at his desk, Vince checked to make sure he hadn't gone out to the field. Then he sorted e-mail for half an hour before checking his box in the mailroom. He found Tom's note and the leave slip.

At 9 A.M., Rich called Vince into his office. "All right, I've got that scrawny bastard now. I just got a call from the Vale District Office. They checked the activity on the computer system and found out Tom was in the office the last two nights visiting a bunch of websites and chat-rooms for environmental radicals."

"Uh, are you sure? He wasn't feeling so good yesterday. He left me a message that he was taking the day off. I didn't think he came in at all."

"No, not while the office was open. He came in at night and used the computer all night to communicate with his buddies! They were probably figuring out their next attack. We've got him for misuse of government equipment. We're gonna give him thirty days off without pay. But first you tell him not to leave the office. We're gonna have Mary Twil look at the records and get the goods on him. Maybe he broke some laws, and we can throw his ass in jail."

"Uh, gee, Rich. Uh, he hasn't come in to the office yet today. I mean he left me a leave slip and a note. He says he's checking in to a treatment center."

"What? You get him in here. Call him. Tell him he can't take leave."

"Uh, what if he's already gone? I mean, Randy signed the leave slip because he was acting supervisor, and Tom said it was an emergency, and he wouldn't explain it to Randy. He left me a confidential note."

"Goddamn it! Call him now. Cancel his leave. Get him in here!"

Vince scuttled back to his desk. He was saying a prayer and cursing Tom's name while the phone rang. When it picked up, he decided to play it cool. "Hey, Tom, what is this about a hangover? Randy says you must be a real pansy, because you only had one beer before you left the bar the other day. He had a different explanation about where you were all night."

"I'll bet he did. Well, Vince, the truth is that I'm a problem drinker. I went home and drank two bottles of wine and most of a fifth of whiskey. Then I slapped my dog silly. I've decided to turn myself in, so I'm off to the treatment center."

"You couldn't have been too sick yesterday. Somebody was monitoring the computer network. They said you were on the computer all night! Are you turning into a computer nerd?"

"Who was on the computer all night, Vince? What computer?"

"Your computer, Man! Come on, you know they can record everything you do on your computer. That's how they catch people looking at porn sites. They said your computer was going all night. It doesn't look good. Rich wants you to come in to talk about it. I'm supposed to cancel your leave."

"Look, Vince, here's what you need to do. Now, write this down. First step is call Buck down in Vale. Tell him to check the log-in and password that idiot used on my computer, because you don't really think I was well enough to come in. I'll bet somebody unauthorized was using it. They probably used Rich's log-in and password. You know, the one he keeps taped to the back of his computer monitor?"

"Holy shit, Tom! You didn't!"

"No, I didn't. That's step one. Keep writing. Step Two is to calm down. The record will show it wasn't me. Whoever it was just used my computer. Hell, have them check the keys for fingerprints. That's it! Call Mary and tell her somebody broke into my computer. Have her confiscate the keyboard and check it. Make sure nobody touches it. Step Three is to tell Rich you missed me. I left before you called."

"Tom, they'll know. I've got to cancel your leave."

"They don't tap our phones yet, Vince. Step Four is stay quiet and act helpless. Nobody would ever suspect. This will work out for the best."

"Come on, Tom, are you serious? I mean...nobody's ever seen you have more than two beers. You can't be serious."

"Vince, you know I'm a vet, right? Did I ever tell you I worked for the post office for three years, too? Ask Randy. He'll tell you I'm crazier than bug shit. That episode with Rich really set me off. I have some serious violent tendencies I've got to work out. You can't get me in there with that fat slob again. It could get really bad."

"Well, I don't know. I guess if you're serious, you've got to do it, Man. We can hold the fort without you for a while. Where are you going to be? Do they have a treatment center in Boise?"

"Look, Vince, this is a serious personal issue, you understand? If you start something going around, it could screw up my career, maybe even my personal life. I'm going someplace where I won't run into anybody that folks here know. I'll be out of contact, except you can call my sister in Florida."

"Well, what if Sheriff Greenwood or Mary Twil needs to get hold of you? It kind of makes Rich look right about you being involved if you leave town right now, you know?"

"Read the rules, Vince. I don't have to reveal where I'm going. You can tell Rich I'm going for treatment and counseling, but no medical stuff on the record. I'll take my vacation time and use up my comp time and credit hours. Whatever it takes. I should be back before I have to use any sick leave. Screw everybody. If they have a problem, they can send a warrant to my sister. I wrote my report. I'm out of it. I figured I would take up writing while I was in the treatment center. Maybe ease the stress before I blow up."

"Yeah, I guess that's right. You need to worry about yourself now. Uh, where can I find the rules? I mean, I don't want to screw up and violate the rules on privacy, and I know Rich is going to be on my back."

"Ask Sheri in Admin. She can probably recite the manual numbers by heart."

After hanging up the phone, Vince scurried over to Randy's cubicle. "Uh, Randy, have you heard any more from Alice? Is she doing OK?"

"Nah, nothing more than you. I think she's just bruised and shook like she said. She told Sheri that she was going to come in next Monday."

"Uh, gee, I hope she's OK. Do you think I ought to call her at home? Maybe she needs something from the store."

"No, I wouldn't do that if I were you, Vince. Alice is a little sour on men in general right now. I already called her. She wasn't in such bad shape that she couldn't give me living hell. Sounded kinda like Tom stepped in it, calling her up, not long after her husband walked out. I shared a little joke with Tom at the bar, and he must have thought it was damn funny because he called her to pick on her some more. Just bad timing. It's kinda like the story of my life, only this time it was Tom."

"Uh, oh. OK. I guess Tom isn't coming in for a while either. He's going to take some time off."

"Don't tell me. Did he find himself a woman? I did sign the leave slip, remember? But he didn't tell me what was in the note."

"Oh, yeah. Uh, I mean no. It didn't really sound like that. He may have been more upset than I thought. About what happened in that meeting Monday with Rich, you know."

"He seemed distracted. Wasn't paying attention to the ball game at the bar. Probably needed some time off."

"Uh, yeah. Um, I guess he and you are pretty good buddies. He said you know how he is and all. You know he was in Vietnam?"

"Oh, yeah!" Randy nodded wisely, wide-eyed.

"Yeah, I guess he can be pretty excitable at times, you know. Yeah, he told me about all the times when he was working at the post office too."

"No shit? Did he tell you about getting pushed out the door there for raping his supervisor?"

"Oh my God! Uh, well, he didn't say too much about that. Oh my, was she OK?"

"You mean he raped a woman, too? I only heard about the guy. Twice his size, he swears to it. Hit him in the head with a trash can, then after that.... Well, the only good thing you can say is that it was over quick."

Vince was suddenly convinced Randy was pulling his leg. "Oh, you guys! You don't give anybody a break, not even each other."

"Oh yeah? I'll bet he didn't tell you what he did to that lieutenant, did he?"

"No, I guess not." Vince was no longer certain, and he looked worried. "What happened?"

"If he hasn't told you himself, I'm not at liberty to say. But if you see that red creeping up from his neck to his sideburns, don't let the bastard get you in a corner."

Vince hurried back to his desk, sorry he had checked out the facts. When Rich Moeller called to ask about Tom's whereabouts, Vince walked to Rich's office and closed the door.

An hour later, Randy was puzzling over a new and peculiar piece of e-mail he had received. Given the content and the odd return address, he presumed it was from Tom. "Leptodactylon!" he sniffed. "Sounds like some kind of damn dinosaur." The message asked him to search out other possible cases of livestock being poisoned by weeds or other instances of more obvious sabotage. Randy carefully worded a message of his own, sending it out to a number of personal contacts working on the range staffs of different BLM districts in different states. His ploy was to pretend he was doing a preliminary query for a graduate student. He sent a reply to Leptodactylon, forwarded a copy of his other messages, and added, "If I do your research, you owe me a beer. If I get results, you owe me a six-pack." Then he deleted the original copy of each of his outgoing messages. "Big brother ain't gonna back these babies up!"

Mary Twil had received her own e-mail message, this one from "tkreug824." Following his suggestion, she had asked Sheriff Greenwood to check the Safeway parking lot for Jerry Skinner's truck. As predicted, they found it with a "For Sale" sign in the window. Now she wanted to find out how Tom had managed to give her that lead. She tried calling Tom, then Vince, then Rich Moeller, and then the receptionist. Sheri forwarded her call to Randy, and when Randy answered his phone, she didn't waste any time. "Randy, where is everybody? Sheri says Tom hasn't come into the office in two days, and Vince doesn't answer his phone."

"Vince is off somewhere having a good cry. Did you try calling Rich? He might have a notion where Tom is."

"Yes, I tried his office too. No answer. You mean to tell me you don't have any idea where Tom is?"

"He and I don't sleep together."

"That is probably the only good decision he has made lately," she said. "Thanks anyway."

Fifteen minutes later, as Randy put away the file he had been updating and was starting out the door, Sheri paged him to pick up his telephone. "Hello, this is Randy."

"What is this crap about Tom raping somebody at the post office?"

"Oh, hello, Mary! Gosh, it's been a long time since we had a good talk. How have you been?"

"Randy, no bullshit now. Rich and Vince said you gave them a line about Tom having a violent history. There's nothing on his record. What do you know?"

"Is that what Vince was worried about? He came over this morning hinting to me about Tom and him talking about Vietnam. It sounded like he wanted to hear something. He was fishin'. Vince said Tom was real excitable, you know, kind of like he was dangerous."

"And you said...?"

"Well, I might have embellished on the truth a bit, just to set the hook. I'm sure Tom must have said something with the 'F' word about this one old supervisor, so maybe I got it mixed up. I figured if Tom wanted Vince to think he was crazy, there must be a reason. He did tell me once it could be real useful to have folks think that."

"Has he been in contact with you? Do you have any idea where he is now?"

"Not a clue. If he's on the run, he's not going to come see me. Is he in big trouble?"

"No, but he's on the edge. He's got a halfway legitimate reason to take off, and Sheri said you signed his request for leave. She put it in the files already, so she won't let them take it back."

"I'll tell her to hide it good so they can't. More'n likely she's already figured that out."

"Damn it, Randy. I think Tom's still working this case. He sent me an e-mail saying we'd find Skinner's Land Cruiser at the Safeway. Now, how the hell did he know that?"

"Well, it's a pretty good place if you don't want it found right away. Lots of folks put a "For Sale" sign on their cars and leave them out by the street for a week at a time. Probably nobody would notice."

"So, whoever took Skinner's Land Cruiser knew that. We're probably looking for a local."

"Maybe. On the other hand, anybody passing through would see all those cars and trucks lined up, so it might give them the idea. They could probably hitch a ride to Boise. You guys figuring Skinner was involved in our livestock case?"

Mary ignored the question. "Hitchhikers get noticed. Nobody knew this truck was hot for several days. It would make more sense for an out-of-towner to drive it to Boise and leave it at the airport. Give me a good reason why Tom might leave town."

"Don't ask me to read his mind. I figured he was hanging out with a woman and was too bashful to share. If he's working the case like you say, then he must figure he's got a lead somewhere. Sounds like he's still giving you whatever he finds out. Hell, if he's been in touch with you, he don't need to check in with me."

"I probably shouldn't have told you that lead came from Tom. Rich told him to turn the case over to me and sit tight. Greenwood would be pissed. Don't spread it around."

"Discretion is my mother's maiden name," said Randy. "I won't tell a soul. Oh, one other thing I just thought of, Mary. The Safeway is only three blocks from the bus station."

Chapter 6

At Twin Falls, Tom gassed the truck and turned south, breezing past the obscene collection of RVs and trailers corralled around the casino town of Jackpot. Somehow it seemed fitting that the criminally sinful culture of Nevada would prey on the hypocritical elements of the culture of Idaho.

Nearly forty miles farther on he took a side road where the crumbling pavement attested to the low volume of traffic. He stopped to let Scrub out and collected a cup of yogurt and an apple from the cooler in back. They walked up a hill covered with stunted sagebrush and shadscale until Tom found a good view of the Humboldt Mountains thirty miles to the south. Scrub explored quietly while Tom ate. He carried his trash back to the truck, then called Scrub to follow him on a rambling walk around the hill while he stretched his legs and loosened the muscles in his lower back.

Tom kept his eyes mostly on the ground, noting the crisply dried leaves of the brush that cracked and fell if touched and the predominance of low-growing, grazing resistant species of grass. Three-awn and Sandberg bluegrass covered the rocky hillside. It was rare to see a bit of Indian ricegrass or needlegrass. He stopped to pick up an interesting piece of rhyolite with a bit of jasper in it. "We've found our treasure. It's time to get on," he said to Scrub. The rock went into an empty plastic bucket stored by the wheel well. Scrub sniffed curiously. "No molasses in that bucket, just dust and dirt."

They returned to Highway 93, bypassing Interstate 80 at Wells, and finally turned off at a sign for the Ruby Lake Wildlife Refuge. A vehicle came down the road in the opposite direction. Tom pulled over to let the dust settle, then continued until he found an unmarked two-track wandering off to the north. The afternoon light was waning, so he followed the track until it was swallowed in a patch of juniper.

Scrub started barking the instant the truck stopped. Tom let her out and settled back into the driver's seat with a canteen of water, leaving the door open and windows rolled down. Scrub was soon back, whining at Tom to go for a walk. "You know, you can go find something to chase by yourself. I'm trying to decide if this is where I want to camp. Now, shut up and go away." After a couple more unsuccessful attempts, she wandered off. Tom closed his eyes and listened.

A Townsend's solitaire fluttered nearby and in the distance, a dove cried for the end of day. Somewhere, a jet created a faint, annoying buzz, but Tom knew there was nowhere to escape that noise for long. He made his decision to break out the tent and cook dinner.

Scrub came back while Tom was heating the frozen bean soup and eating the last of the salad he had cleaned out of the refrigerator at home. She pushed her head against the mosquito netting of the tent door. "It's zipped, dummy. You don't go in until I do, and then only if you don't have something nasty behind your ears." He sliced a bagel and cheese, tearing off a small chunk of the bread for her. She clacked her teeth at him until he tossed it. "That is wolf behavior, most unbecoming in a civilized creature bred to protect sheep. Your bowl is over there under the tree." He pointed, but she only watched his hand. "Also, you are a lot less bright than your predecessor." Eventually when he finished the soup, she found her bowl without help.

The temperature dropped rapidly as the sun set. Tom put on a jacket so he could continue to sit in the ragged lawn chair and watch the stars. Scrub lay nervously by the door of the tent. "Nights like this, I wish you'd learn to sleep without walls around you." They had tried camping without a tent, but being a light sleeper did not mesh with a dog that stirred nervously at every noise.

He got a wool cap from his duffel bag and a spare tarp from the back of the truck. After spreading the tarp by the tent, he unzipped the door, allowing Scrub to go in, but he pulled his sleeping bag and pad out. She looked confused as he re-zipped the door. "OK, I'm going to be right here. You're safe. Relax and get some sleep." Scrub slept with her nose at the door, while Tom, stirring only to assess the flutter of a small owl and listen to the occasional coyote, slept soundly until first light.

Without exiting the sleeping bag, Tom lit the one-burner stove and placed the prepared coffeepot on it. He pulled cold clothes from under his head into the sleeping bag and mostly assembled himself before stepping out. Warning Scrub not to kick over the coffee, he unzipped the tent. They both stumbled out of camp to relieve themselves. "Crummy road maps don't show BLM land, Scrub. We're so close to Forest Service land I don't know if we're pissing on the Forest Service or BLM. It's a sad state of affairs." An hour later they were back in the truck, continuing south to Ely and turning east on Highway 50.

As they entered Utah and passed through the Confusion Mountain Range and Sevier Desert, the scenery became even more parched than in Nevada. Even the saltbush looked as if it had given up and died from the extended summer heat. Tom refilled the gas tank and his water jugs at Salina. Mountains surrounded the town, and the forests looked deceptively green from a distance. Tom suspected they would be crawling with escapees from Salt Lake and Provo. On I-70 south of the Coal Cliffs he spotted a gate in the highway fence and a dirt path that led through familiar eroded sandstone into small canyons with patches of juniper and pinyon pine.

Three miles from the interstate, they made an early camp. Tom filled a solar shower bag and set it on the hood of the truck to gather heat while he took Scrub for a climb in the general direction of Hondo Arch. By 5 P.M. they were back at the truck. Tom added a couple small pieces of petrified wood to his rock collection in the bucket, then looked for tracks that might have passed on the dirt road in the hours since he had arrived. Seeing none, he decided the site was suitably private and began unloading gear. Finding a flat stone to use for a bath mat, he hung the solar shower bag from the limb of a pinyon over the stone and took his shower. After slipping into clean shorts, he opened a container of salsa and a bag of chips, fished a beer from the ice water in the cooler, and settled into the lawn chair in the shade.

"This is the life, Scrub. I'm sure looking forward to retirement. I may not make it another ten years, though." She came to sit next to the bag of chips. He dipped one in the salsa and offered it to her. "I'm warning you, there's tomato in this stuff." She sniffed tentatively, then took it without licking his fingers. "You're getting used to hot stuff, aren't you?"

As he watched the changing light on the red sandstone bluffs around him, he studied his maps of southwest Colorado. "By the way, we have another short day tomorrow, and we are going to have company at camp. Someone you've never met before. Be on your best behavior, no flatulence, no jamming your bony head in her crotch." Scrub looked dubious. "You'll like her all right. Just don't get in a fight with her dog. He's big enough to rip your head off."

An hour later as the rice was cooking, a twenty-four foot long RV came tooling down the dirt track. Tom stood glaring with his hands on his hips, ready to pack up camp and leave immediately. "How in the hell did he get that piece of trash through those washes?" Luckily the RV passed without slowing. "Keep going, Turkey. There's a state park about twenty miles down the road. I don't want to hear your damn generator. Don't forget to turn left at Albuquerque." The RV obediently disappeared.

They saw no other signs of human folly until they returned to I-70 the following morning. Tom topped off the gas in Moab, purchased fresh vegetables and salsa from a grocery store, and stopped at an espresso shop for coffee. He thought the young woman brewing the coffee was attractive except for the patch of hair missing from the side of her scalp, her heavy purple mascara, the rhinestone stud and silver ring in her nose, and nail polish the color of dried blood. When she wished him a nice day, he noticed at least two tongue piercings. He handed the free biscotti sample to Scrub. "I'm having second thoughts about the coffee, too."

Back on the road, he sipped the coffee tentatively. "Not bad. At least it's not Starbuck's." Rural development was creeping out between Moab and Monticello. An occasional new house was dropped on a patch of scraped, raw red earth, and the owners were busily watering bluegrass lawns and spruce trees in the gaping holes between the drought-tolerant pinyon and juniper.

By comparison, the twenty-six mile stretch between Monticello and Dove Creek appeared to have been frozen in time for the last fifteen years. There was a new gas station and convenience store in Dove Creek that had probably earned its owners the enmity of half the town. Tom considered stopping to buy a forty-pound sack of the local specialty—dried pinto beans—but decided to wait until he was headed home.

At Pleasant View he doubled back on a dirt road toward Utah and Hovenweep. The countryside was pocked with ruins, mostly never seen by tourists. Nearly all the ruins had been vandalized by locals who sold trinkets on the black market. Development of the oil fields had brought outsiders in to plunder, but the new exploration roads had only accelerated the process, not created it.

Fifteen years before, Tom had camped near Sand Canyon. He had been unable to find a place to pitch a tent without moving Anasazi potsherds out of the way. It was impossible to avoid crushing the clay pieces without carefully watching the placement of each step in the red dust. When he had returned to that site alone a year ago, it took nearly an hour of intense searching to find a single fragment of pottery. Forty acres had been picked clean. Uncounted millions of potsherds had disappeared into shoebox collections to be left in attics, and eventually thrown away by the parents of bored children. For Tom it destroyed the romantic history of a half-millenium of human occupation that had lain intact another 800 years before modern civilization arrived. Tom had vowed he would never go back there again.

He found the trail he wanted, turned, and drove several more miles past isolated ruins. A huge sheet of bedrock sandstone lay exposed where he could overlook the transition from pinyon-juniper woodland to the salt-desert scrub that marked the edge of modern-day Indian Territory. He parked well back from the edge, let Scrub out, and went to sit with his feet dangling out over the cliff. When Scrub rejoined him, he told her, "This is home base for a while."

Chapter 7

Friday morning, at about the time Tom broke camp in Utah, Randy Bergen was clearing a number of e-mail messages off his computer, including three he had forwarded on to the peculiar pseudonym. Before leaving to check a couple grazing allotments, Randy stopped in the administrative staff area. "Polly, I was looking for a book in the library stacks, but it's gone. Anybody check out a book or two lately?"

"No, I don't think anybody has checked out a book in two years. I think if they want a book, they just take it until they're done."

"Hmm. Well, I don't suppose you've noticed anybody looking through the books in the range section?"

Polly shook her head. "I've got a couple paperbacks if you need something to read."

Randy persisted, "I'm looking for some old reference books, mostly about weeds."

Tongue in cheek, Polly said, "I've got a dictionary. There are probably some weeds in there. We got rid of the kids' old encyclopedias though."

"Thank you, no. My mom bought a set of those encyclopedias when I was a kid, too. They were way over my head. And the problem with dictionaries is, I've got to have somebody tell me how to spell. Hell, I might have to ask one of the Forest Service employees. That would be too embarrassing."

"Maybe you should ask Jeff," Polly offered helpfully. "He's the weeds guru now."

"He's worse than me. If it's not a picture book, he won't turn a page."

But he did head back to the corner where Jeff McGuire hid out. Randy doubted Jeff even knew where the office books were stored. Jeff had started out as a range technician during the Kennedy administration, became a fire chaser for twenty years, and diverted into weed control when it looked like that was the next big pot of budget money. He was able to get a grade increase to GS-9 and was angling for another increase without ever having moved in twenty-seven years. Randy looked into Jeff's cubicle, surprising him into dropping his hunting gear catalog. "Jeff, you don't have any of the poisonous range plant books out of the library, do you?"

"You got some weeds causing a problem?"

"No, I'm just trying to find a couple books. Got a school kid who wants to do a paper or something." Randy waited a minute for the question to sink in, then prompted, "Books? From our library?"

"No, I've got some brochures. There's this little pocket booklet 'Weeds of Idaho.' That's a good one, but I've only got two left. If he wants to come in to look at one while I'm here, that's OK, but I don't want to loan it out. Tom has the big book, Weeds of the West. Keeps it on the shelf over his desk with all that botany shit. Mostly we only got five or six weeds that matter anyway. They're all in this little book."

"Yeah, thanks. I'll check Tom's stuff."

Randy walked down the long hall. The half-empty bookrack over Tom's desk told him he had guessed right. "Hey, Vince, did Tom tell you when he was coming back? Looks like he took a lot of reading material."

"No, not exactly. He had a hundred and sixty hours on his leave slip, but I think he's going to come back sooner if he got things worked out."

"That's four weeks! Guess I didn't look close enough when I signed the leave slip. Damn, where is he going, Australia?"

"He said it was personal. He didn't want it spread around where he was going." Vince felt like rubbing it in that he knew something Randy didn't.

"Oh, so maybe he is sneaking off with a woman after all."

Bill Christen stuck his head out of his cubicle, "I think he's taking a busman's holiday."

Randy looked over his shoulder, "What does that mean? He was goin' on a bus?"

"I saw him outside the grocery store Tuesday, looking at an old Land Cruiser," said Bill. "What for, I don't know. Said he was going on vacation. He had a box full of botany books on the front seat of his truck. His stupid dog was going crazy trying to get out through the window of the shell. The guy's sick. I think he spends all his time studying plants and talking to his damn dog."

"He told me he was going to do some writing," said Vince. "Maybe he's going to do something on his wildflower garden."

"Yeah, so why did he have all his camping gear in the back of his truck?" asked Bill. "I'm telling you, he's gonna be out in the middle of the damn desert somewhere keying out plants. He's a crazy bastard. He ain't normal."

"How in hell is he going to get his e-mail then?" Randy wondered aloud.

Vince and Bill roared with laughter.

Chapter 8

Rita was looking forward to her last weekend off. Deer season would begin the next weekend. She would be on patrol during the week to catch the hunters who couldn't wait that long. There would be no chance to rest again until mid-December.

Ordinarily she would have been helping another "District Wildlife Manager" check licenses of bird hunters near Alamosa or Monte Vista, but the call inviting her to scramble around the canyon country west of Cortez had caused her to make excuses. She was happy to find that Tom was still excited about the remote mesas and sandstone canyons. She was also curious about the vague description of his plans to meet Joshua Freeborn and mystified by his request to intercept and bring along e-mail messages.

Wondering if she still remembered how to get to the place Tom had described, Rita followed the track beyond the ruins and avoided a turn that wandered off in the wrong direction. Her growling stomach reminded her that Tom was supposed to have dinner ready when she arrived. When she topped the last ridge beyond the stunted trees, she saw Tom's truck parked ahead, half-hidden and blending darkly into a juniper. She watched him guide his dog into the back of his pickup and close the shell. Then he turned and waved. The sound of barking roused Rogue from the back of her truck. When she stopped, he leaped out, and, not waiting for permission, investigated Tom. Then he inspected the green truck where the volume of barking was getting louder.

"Hello, Tom, it's good to see you," she said, hugging him. "You're looking healthy. Rogue, behave yourself!"

Tom laughed. "If the worst he does is piss on my tires, we'll get along OK. I'd tell my dog to shut up, but she won't listen. She might tear the back of the truck up if I don't let her out soon. Maybe you can hold Rogue until they get the preliminaries over with? I'll put Scrub on a leash to keep her under control."

The dogs sniffed each other briefly until Scrub decided Rita was of more interest. Rogue was definitely more interested in Scrub. Tom advised him, "She's fixed and she gets snappy, boy. Doesn't like dogs worth a darn." Once Rogue got a whiff of the food, he decided it was more interesting. "Oh, yes," said Tom. "The food is almost ready. Would you like a beer?"

"That sounds good. I have the e-mail you asked about. I printed it out." She walked back to retrieve it from her truck. "Couldn't help but read it, so you've got to explain it to me. What in the world are you up to now?"

"Maybe I need to read it first, to figure it out myself." He handed her a beer and placed a bag of chips and bowl of salsa between the two lawn chairs he had set out earlier. "Partly, I may try to meet that guy I talked to you about and thought that it might be possible to scout his property with a telescope from the tops of one of these mesas. Partly I'm trying to find some puzzle pieces to fill in the holes in a wild theory."

"And the puzzle has to do with livestock eating poisonous weeds? How does this relate to Joshua Freeborn?" Rita's curiosity was aroused, but she was also irritated that she had been invited out to a weekend of spying.

"The puzzle has to do with some dead cows up in my country. At least one incident looks like real deliberate eco-sabotage. There is enough evidence to hint at a connection and maybe a conspiracy if the sheriff looks close enough. Too many people need someone to blame. Sooner or later, even the people who blame Jerry Skinner will figure out he wouldn't have been out there alone without transportation. Everyone is going to start looking for another easy target. That means someone local who might be too vocal about mismanaged grazing, like me. The connection between Skinner and Joshua is a pretty tenuous stretch, but it's a maybe. So far, I'm the only one who sees the possibilities and I can't explain it all without causing myself some other trouble.

"Besides," Tom added, "you know I can't let a puzzle slip through my fingers without putting the pieces together. That's what makes life interesting. It will probably take me the better part of a month to figure this out. That's about how much time I put on my leave slip."

"Whoa, wait a minute! You only invited me to do a little hiking, not help you investigate a crime for a month. I have two days, then I head back to Pagosa."

"Oh, no, I didn't mean we should waste this weekend. I was thinking of hiking the canyons over by Monument Valley if you were interested in that. This goofy idea may never get anywhere. It can wait until Monday." He began to dish out rice and vegetables. "I found some good bagels at the store in Moab. If you want to slice up some of this pepperjack cheese, you can either put it on the bagel or in your rice, or both, I guess."

"That sounds good. Did you have any particular canyons in mind?"

"I was looking at a couple that drain all the way to the Colorado River. The map shows some ruin locations and petroglyphs along the way. It's all probably dry right down to the Colorado though, so you'd have to pack plenty of water for a good day hike."

They spent the waning hours of the evening looking at maps and talking about the turns in their lives over the last eight years. Tom was surprised to find himself feeling so comfortable with her. She was a bit too pretty for him, he thought. As the light faded, Scrub started acting anxious. "I think I'll put her in the back of the truck and put my sleeping bag under that juniper. It doesn't look like it's going to rain." Tom wandered off to brush his teeth.

When he returned, he found Rita already in her bag right next to his. He was feeling uncomfortably conspicuous as he tried to sit half in his sleeping bag and slip off his jeans. Snuggling down into his bag against the chill of the night he quietly said, "Good night." She rolled over and kissed him lightly. He fell asleep feeling warm and happy.

They were both up at daylight, downing coffee and cold cereal before loading into Tom's truck and making their way over to Utah. They decided to hike John's Canyon and look at petroglyphs and ruins. Despite the dirt road in the canyon, they hiked all day without seeing another human being. The dogs happily chased lizards, and Scrub once spotted a rabbit, but lost it among the crumbled ledges almost as soon as they started running. Tom and Rita speculated on the meaning of the petroglyphs, finally deciding one meant "eat deer, not lizards," and the rest were symbols of clan titles. They laughed and talked all day. With the drainage being completely dry, they had to share their water with the dogs. They walked back with empty canteens in the late afternoon.

✯

Checking the topographic maps, Rita found a likely camping spot at the end of an old oil exploration road. They parked Tom's truck at a rusted dry-well marker and carried the cooler and kitchen gear out to a sandstone rim overlooking the Monument Valley. Tom started cutting vegetables into a soup pot while Rita went back for a second load of gear. When she returned, she asked, "Do you mind if I set up your tent? It got a little cold with the breeze last night. I only brought my light-weight bag."

"Yeah, go ahead. My bag is probably a little warmer than yours. I do a lot of camping on the rivers in April, so I got a three-season bag." He adjusted the camp stove to a low flame and walked back to the truck for more gear. He removed a large water jug and a couple of lawn chairs. Returning to the rim he set those in the kitchen area. "Where did you put my pad and bag? I ought to set them up before dark."

"They're in the tent. I unrolled your pad already."

"Oh, thanks." As he opened a bottle of wine, he muttered, "I can handle this without making a fool of myself."

"That soup smells really good! How can I help?"

"Um, I guess relax and have some chips and salsa. It'll be a few minutes before the carrots and potatoes are ready. We've also got bagels and cheese. Not exactly French bread, but...."

"Hey, we're camping, right?" She sank into a chair with a sigh and lifted a cup of wine from the cooler lid. "Cheers. Umm, this is great. What is it?"

"The Poles are dumping cheap burgundy on the world market again. It has a good flavor, but any more than two glasses and I get a headache. Watch out for sulfites."

"Sounds like good advice." They halted conversation to scoop salsa and watch the sun's last rays paint the sandstone desert below.

Suddenly the sun slipped below the horizon and the gold and orange rock seemed to melt into shaded browns and purples. "Wow, that was gorgeous!"

"Yeah. I enjoy the changes in the shadows after sunset almost as much. You don't have to be awed." He ladled out a couple bowls of soup, and they ate in silence except to point out features of the swirling shadows of dark pastel. A saw-whet owl called in the distance as darkness hid the last rocks. Scrub moved in to lie at Tom's feet, keeping a wary eye open.

"So what did you have in mind for tomorrow?" she asked.

"More of the same, I guess. I'm enjoying the respite from thinking about all the world's problems. How about going over to Owl Canyon? No roads down in there."

"Sounds good. That soup is great. Any more left?"

"Enough for another bowl for each of us. Do you want some cheese for protein?"

"I was going to ask, Tom. Have you turned vegetarian?"

"No, it's just simpler to camp without meat. Don't have to worry about it spoiling." He cut a couple slabs of cheese from a block and split a bagel.

"Thanks." She paused. "Tell me more about your mysterious case of sabotage."

"Not much to tell. Somebody put some sharpened sticks around a steep wash to trap cattle. At least ten died. Folks seemed to think that the cattle stumbled into the spear-points trying to get out. But I saw no blood or stab wounds, and no pools of dried blood. Maybe there was a little blood around the mouth and nose. I took photos of the spears and checked them. The tips were white, not even dirty, let alone stained with blood. The rancher who found them went looking for his cattle only a couple days after they turned up missing. They definitely didn't starve and probably didn't die of thirst either. It looked like they simply dropped and went to sleep."

"You looked for bullet wounds and shells?"

"No holes in them that a coyote didn't make, and the blood was already too thick to run out. In fact, there was a dead coyote, but no bullet holes in her either. Didn't see any empty casings except one real old shotgun shell."

"So why don't you think they died of thirst?"

"You could push the spears to move them aside, so I don't think they would have held the cows ten minutes if they had really wanted out. Wouldn't they have tried to get out or up the banks if there wasn't any water left? I could see tracks going down in, but I didn't see any tracks going out up the banks, and if some could get out at the lower end, then they all could have."

"So this relates to your e-mail. You think they ate some poisonous weeds and died? Why didn't anybody else think of that?"

"There is almost nothing growing down in that wash. It totally blew out several years ago. The sides are straight up and down, and the bottom is mostly loose rock and gravel. The water runs under the rock except in a couple places. That's why the cows go down in it, not for food. A couple wet spots in the channel are the only water for a mile. Actually I planted cottonwoods in there last spring, and they ate those. There weren't any poisonous weeds."

"You didn't see the spears when you were planting?"

"No. I would have had to walk right through them. I had some volunteers with me. We planted everywhere we could find moist soil, that stretch included. We went from the top to the mouth."

"Do you think one of your volunteers went back later?"

"Not on your life. They were high school kids and a teacher. By the end of the day, they definitely thought I was crazy for taking them in there. None of them wanted to work that hard again."

"So what makes you think there might be a connection to Joshua?"

"Jerry Skinner, our local environmentalist, turned up dead in a canyon not too far away. He left a note about poison where some other sick cattle were rounded up. His death didn't make sense because he was too desert-smart, and supposedly he died of dehydration. Also, it didn't make sense that he had been out in that location alone without a vehicle parked nearby, but no vehicle was found."

"And you found a connection to Joshua?"

"Well, not directly, no. Like I said, this is a really weird, far-fetched idea."

"You've had some pretty far-out ideas in your past, Tom. Suppose you show me you have something real."

"OK. Let's say there are three incidents of cattle deaths. Those two are pretty close together in time and distance. The other one happened in Joseph Canyon at the south edge of Washington. From the condition of the cattle it happened a lot earlier, but I think it is related. Let's also presume the same person or persons who left our local enviro for dead participated in the earlier incident also."

"Did you find spears and traps in all those cases?"

"No, the only connection is dead or sick cattle."

"Not much of a connection, Tom."

"Right. In each case, the animals have no signs of violence except maybe symptoms that look like poisoning. The problem is that there is no obvious source of poison. Now, in two cases, there are some odd containers out of place. Both had this sticky residue that might turn out to be molasses, with bits of seeds and chaff in them. At the last spot there was some chokecherry cut down that one cow might have eaten, but I don't think that was the main problem. There were these odd roots lying around out on the rocks. I picked one up and took it to the office. I think it had molasses on it too."

"So you think there was a poison mixed in? Why would the cows eat roots instead of grass?"

"I think the seeds and roots were poisonous. The molasses smell might have attracted them. There was hardly anything to eat where the roots were left, only a little water to help attract them to the trap. At Joseph Canyon, the cattle came down off this incredibly steep slope that had a lot of grass, but there wasn't much feed on the gravel bar either."

"How far away can they smell molasses?"

"Probably not far. Most likely somebody set the trap and then either cut the fences or got above the livestock and chased them down the slope to the right spot on the creek."

"Like in the wash." Rita recognized that Tom was connecting patterns. "What kind of poison are they using?"

Tom sighed, "There is another tenuous connection. I think the perpetrators were experimenting, trying to figure out what worked best. I think they were improving the methods. At Joseph Canyon they damn near had to kill themselves carrying buckets of feed into the canyon from the bottom, then probably near killed themselves chasing the cows down the slopes. If one came in from below to set the trap, and the other one stayed above, the animals would stop right where they wanted them. They could have walked out together down the canyon to a vehicle. The cows wouldn't climb back out if there were something to eat.

"Where Skinner left the note," said Tom passing her the wine bottle, "they put real light-weight containers cut from milk jugs next to the only water in a two-mile radius, then cut fences and chased some animals or let them drift down toward water. In Willow Creek and Owl Spring they set out roots next to the water on top of the rocks. They didn't even use any containers and they cut down the material to make spears from a local source."

Rita drained the wine bottle into her cup. "It makes sense to cut down weight and make it simple, but if the cases are all connected, then why not figure out the best poison first and do them all the same?"

"Volume of poison is a problem. There must be a learning curve about what works best, plus where to find a large enough source of poison material. Up in Joseph Canyon all the seed left in the buckets was from some sort of legume with three leaflets. I got one to sprout in a flowerpot. There is a lot of golden banner growing in that country, especially along the river flats. It would be pretty easy to collect a lot of seedpods and extract the seeds in summer. We don't know when it happened for sure, but a couple cows may have floated out with the spring flood. At any rate, the golden banner seeds are poisonous.

"At Cow Creek there was a mix of different seeds in those milk jugs, but I would guess they were poisonous legumes like lupine and locoweed. There was an umbel seed that might have been poison hemlock, some larkspur capsules and seeds, and something else that might have been black henbane. Then there was grass seed with an ergot fungus. They don't all grow together and would have to be collected over a longer time, starting in spring and going on through summer. The symptoms the cowboy reported are about right, and none would be automatically deadly without heat and stress."

Tom said less certainly about the last case, "Down in the spear-trap, the animals must have died quickly. In fact, Troy said he noticed it too. He said it looked like they just dropped. Their legs were collapsed under the bodies. Maybe there was a little bloody froth dried on the nose. The symptoms fit with the roots I found. And, if a coyote ate the guts with some of that root inside, it would die quickly too." He walked to his truck and brought back an open book and a flashlight.

Rita looked at the illustration, "*Cicuta douglasii.* You want to translate?"

"The common name is water hemlock," said Tom. "Notice the cross-membranes in the swollen part of the root. It's about the deadliest plant that grows in the U.S. It's not very common. I've never found it in the wild yet, only around irrigation ditches in farms."

"Why wouldn't it grow naturally down in a wash then?"

"I don't know. I've simply never found it in the desert where I've worked. There's lots of poison hemlock, but that is less toxic, and the roots don't have the cross-membranes. There was nothing like either one growing there."

"So, it looks like circumstantial evidence that someone was deliberately trying to poison cattle. If Skinner was involved, why did he leave a note about poison?"

"Good question, Rita. I don't know. Maybe he wasn't directly involved, and it was a warning to the cowboys. Maybe he was confused and frightened. Maybe he was hoping someone would find the note and then find him, or maybe he was just plain confused by sickness and lost it."

"You don't think he ran out of water? He ate something he knew was poison?"

Tom hedged, "Well, beyond that point, it really gets into rumors and speculation. It would be better to avoid clouding the issue."

"How do you come a thousand miles down to Joshua Freeborn? What makes you think he was involved?"

Encouraged that Rita was asking in a serious voice, Tom said, "Well, I was having a conversation about meeting strangers for hiking or biking trips, and someone said something about Internet predators. That sounds crazier than it was. I, uh...." Tom suddenly remembered he was speaking to a law enforcement officer and realized it wouldn't be a good idea to admit he had broken into Skinner's house. "I found some information about Skinner, websites he liked to visit, chat-groups and e-mail contacts, things like that. I checked some activist group sites that specialize in resource issues, especially grazing. I cross-checked lists of names for duplicates. There were quite a few, but I found Jerry Skinner's name and also Joshua Freeborn at a lot of the same sites. Jerry and Joshua had been exchanging messages directly."

Rita reminded him, "This was the e-mail you mentioned."

"Oh, yeah, I told you about that, didn't I? So I went to the library and sent Joshua a note mentioning one of the old wilderness study areas in his back yard, Cross Canyon. I made out like I was interested in making an issue of the oil wells down there. I asked him if it was still as badly overgrazed as it used to be. He answered the next day and suggested I might contact him if and when I decided to visit."

"None of that makes him a cattle-poisoner," Rita said skeptically. "Actually, Tom, it sounds pretty flimsy. Nobody would even consider that circumstantial evidence. If you don't even know that Skinner was directly involved, why jump to the conclusion that Joshua was?"

Tom was used to being told his ideas were stupid, but this time it really stung. "Remember when I gave your office the tip on the Toyota with the camper that turned out to be a refrigerated walk-in cooler, a mobile meat-packing operation involved in commercial game poaching? Do you know how I figured that out?"

"So I owe you. No, I knew you were lying when you said you saw somebody put a carcass in that truck. My boss believed you and got the warrant. It's a good thing they confessed, and it never went to trial. You never told me the real story."

"It started with two beer cans and some cigarettes." Tom grinned. "The cans were two miles apart. The cigarettes were torn up and never smoked. Now about Joshua, I've just got a wild feeling."

"Bullshit!" Rita exploded. "Only a fool would try to get a warrant on that."

"Yeah, I know. It doesn't work. I'm playing long shots the whole way. I'm still hoping Randy might turn up other mass cattle deaths that might make the poisoning theory more obvious, maybe fill in a pattern."

"Tom, why would someone from here target cattle in your area?"

"Only to keep it far enough away to avoid suspicion." He saw the look of disbelief on her face. "I know. It's dumb. So maybe I'll do some fossil hunting this week and scope his place out from a distance."

"What are you going to look for, a smoking gun?"

"I don't know. I need to look. Maybe something will ring a bell. It is stupid!" Tom's voice faded.

Rita drained her wine and headed for the tent. "I'm tired enough to sleep."

Tom put Scrub in the back of the truck again, leaving her with a full bowl of water. He had to step over Rogue to get into the tent.

When Tom slid into his bag, she reached out and squeezed his hand. "Looking for fossils would be fun too. Let's do that tomorrow."

*

They were up with the first hint of light. Tom started the coffee while Rita disappeared. He filled a couple bowls with dry cereal and sliced a banana on each. When Rita reappeared, Tom took that as his cue to wander off. After breakfast they loaded the gear and drove back to Colorado. Tom consulted an old topographic map on which he had carefully scribed property lines. Out of habit rather than convenience he parked on BLM, a short distance north of a block of undeveloped private land.

He loaded a spotting scope and tripod into his backpack before refilling his water bottles. Scrub was pacing in anticipation of a walk.

Rogue sat quietly, watching the activity. Rita took several apples, a block of cheese, and a couple bagels from the cooler and put them in her pack. When Tom pulled out two containers of yogurt, she took those too.

"You don't have to carry all the lunch stuff," he told her.

"I don't mind. Better that than it gets squished by that scope."

They hiked off the eastern edge of the mesa, crossing Hovenweep Canyon, skirting the edge of another mesa, crossing Yellowjacket Creek, and climbing the steep slope of Cannonball Mesa, a distance of four miles. They crossed a primitive road on the mesa top, prompting Tom to apologize, "We could have driven here if we had gone around through Cortez, but I didn't want to risk Freeborn spotting my truck before I go visit."

As he neared the south rim, Tom pulled out a map and spent a couple minutes pinpointing their location. "The rim goes east another mile or so from here. There are a couple houses down in the canyon along the way," he said, pointing at symbols on the map. If these don't look interesting, we can cross the canyon over to the next rim and scope a few more from there." Scrub took off after a scrawny cottontail, but Tom ignored her. Rogue never strayed more than a few yards from Rita.

"Um, Tom, do you happen to know which place is Joshua's, or did you intend to keep walking until you've looked at all the homesteads in McElmo?"

"I had trouble pinning down the exact location. It's somewhere in this two-mile stretch. Actually, I was hoping you might know which house was his. You did tell me you had stopped at his place once." Seeing her look of disbelief, he added "I have the address number, but don't expect to be able to see that from the rim. If need be, I can find it when I go to visit."

"What if I didn't come with you out here?"

Tom grinned. "You noticed that off-white clay outcrop below the sandstone in Yellowjacket Canyon? That stratum is exposed in spots all around the edge of these mesas. That's where I found the big palm fossil back in '82. It was about a foot long and four inches thick. I figured that would give me an excuse to explore."

"You're either dumber and luckier, or more devious than I gave you credit for." She pointed, "See that bend in the wash? Joshua's place is about a quarter mile farther on. It's down low in a break. You can't see it from here." She stepped back from the rim to avoid being visible from below and headed east.

Tom followed happily, thinking about how good she looked in shorts and a halter-top. The olive-brown of her skin reminded him to roll down his shirtsleeves against the fall sun, which was still intense. "I sure am glad the cedar-gnats are all gone. Last time I was out here one bit me on the inside of my eyelid. That was the only place I didn't have citronella oil smeared on."

"You wore that stuff once when you rode in my truck. I had to leave the windows open for a week afterwards."

"It was worth the stench. Don't tell me you wear shorts when the gnats are out, do you?"

"No, there wouldn't be anything left if I did. But I can't stand the smell of insect repellent." She approached the rim behind the cover of a clump of cliffrose. "I think this is about as close as we can get without walking down into the canyon." She watched Tom fasten the spotting scope to his tripod, noticing that the surfaces of both were wrapped with a dull brown paper tape.

Tom kept the tripod legs adjusted to a low height and crept forward, lying on his belly while setting the scope at the edge of the shrub. After a couple minutes he said, "It must be nice having a long growing season. It looks like a jungle down there." He rolled to the side, giving Rita a chance to look.

"Wow, that is quite the garden. He must have irrigation rights too. Looks like he has a bunch of trees started in back. It looks like half the garden is flowers. Maybe he has a real sweet side." She moved back again. "What did you think you were going to see?"

"I wanted to check out the landscape from a distance. Sometimes it helps to see things like this, almost like you were flying overhead." He adjusted the magnification. "Those are damn funny trees. They remind me of manioc. The leaves are huge. I haven't seen anything like it since Vietnam. That really is jungle vegetation."

"It gets over a hundred degrees down there, and it doesn't cool down at night like it does in the mountains. He probably could grow tropical stuff if he had enough water." Rita kept watch through Tom's binoculars. "I don't remember any of that growing there before. I think he ripped out a lawn to put in the garden. What next?"

Tom kept his eye to the scope. "There is something at the top of those plants. I think it's a flower spike."

Rita started eating an apple. "You going to stare at his garden all day? Did you notice his old truck around the side? Must be a 1968 or '69 Chevy, but it runs. Mostly I think he rides his bike unless he needs to haul something. I saw him pedaling through Cortez every now and then."

"Why don't you unpack lunch. That will give me a few more minutes to keep an eye on things." They quietly shared the food, but Tom kept his eye glued to the telescope while he ate. "The manioc in Vietnam had a long stem, but this looks different. This plant is twice as tall."

"Tell you what, Tom, you stay here and I'll go back to that break in the north rim. I'll climb down and look for fossils. I'll work my way to the mouth of Yellowjacket Canyon, and you can catch up when you're ready."

Tom recognized the impatience in her voice. "No, give me a minute to pack this thing. I'll come with you." If he had the time, he would have spent most of the day, but he didn't like feeling her frustration.

They pulled back from the rim and walked west. Eventually Tom led the way down a cut in the sandstone rim.

They trailed across a steep slope of eroding clay that changed from red to yellow, then a chalky-white. "Keep your eyes peeled for anything that looks odd now," he said to Rita. "I found that fossil washed out below this slope."

"How did you know it was a palm tree?"

"A professor at the community college in Farmington told me that's what it was. You could see the structure of the wood and the pores on the surface. I'm sorry I left it at the office when I moved. They probably threw it away."

At the bottom of the slope they found a few small pieces of petrified wood, but nothing either of them felt compelled to keep. They decided to walk to Levy's Store out on the main road before climbing back to the truck. Both dogs had taken the opportunity to cool off in the creek, but Scrub looked like she had taken a mud bath afterward. "Rogue looks nice and fluffy," he said. "You want to trade dogs?"

Rita laughed. "Scrub had to do something special for her complexion. She certainly seems quite pleased with herself."

"At least she doesn't smell too bad yet."

Levy's store looked like it might have been used for the stage set of "Gunsmoke." The siding was made of unpainted, rough-cut Ponderosa pine boards, weathered to a rich honey color and streaked with black. The roof over the plank porch was made of corrugated metal. Tom held the door for Rita. "You dogs wait outside. They don't need any mud in here."

An ancient-looking man appeared from a back room. He wore a soiled cowboy hat with a brim curled up on both sides and the crown battered. His fierce blue eyes were made more intimidating by the squinting concentration on his face. Castro Levy hadn't forcibly ejected a visitor in four years, but he kept a rifle on the wall behind the cash register in case he felt like telling someone to get the hell out of his store. "Didn't hear no car," he told them.

"We hiked in from the north. Thought a cold soda might taste pretty good right now." Tom felt relief that it was nearly twenty years since he last stopped by in his BLM pickup. Castro had made it clear then that he didn't want any young government dumb-ass on his property. He followed Castro's gaze to see Rita leaning over a freezer to pick out an ice-cream sandwich. Her shorts had risen nicely on her thighs. Keep him distracted, Tom thought. He took a root beer from a cooler and a vanilla sundae cup from the freezer while Rita paid for her ice cream. Castro was smiling and exchanging small talk with Rita. She was looking at the silver jewelry under the glass counter as Tom stepped up to pay.

"Two dollars, even." He squinted at Tom, took his five-dollar bill, and slipped out three ones in change. "Jake McPherson's been hanging out around Cross Canyon. You stay out of there, or he'll shoot your ass."

"Pardon? I don't think I know him."

"He ain't so bright, but that boy figured out it wasn't no coincidence when the sheriff chased you into Hovenweep and caught him red-handed digging that grave."

Memories came flooding back. The boy, Jake, had turned 43 a week before he was convicted of violating the Archeological Protection Act. Tom was mindful of the rifle hanging on the wall behind the cash register. "That was more than fifteen years ago. You don't think he would still remember what I look like, do you?"

"I can't see so good as I used to, but I recognized you, didn't I?" He looked at Rita and chortled, "He ought to cut that scraggly beard off, don't you think?" He looked back at Tom. "Course you got a little gray now, but you're still skinny as a stick. He'd recognize you all right. He spent a year in jail thinking about you. You ain't changed much."

"I probably wouldn't know if we sat down at the same table. Hope I don't run into him."

"Yeah, well, it's not like I know anything about Jake doing any more digging. Wouldn't surprise me if he was, though. Goddamn graverobber's got no respect for nothing. It just seems like a coincidence when you come walking in here with Miss Rita—the Law. And she's not exactly wearing a uniform now, is she?"

Rita was amused, but not surprised. Her last visit had been only three years before. The locals would remember a female game cop. "I'm on a break before the next big season starts. We're only out to hike, not chase any pot hunters."

"Hmmpf." Castro opened one blue eye wide and glared at her. He pointed at Tom, "That boy ain't half as innocent as he looks. He finds trouble, not even trying."

Tom shifted his weight and thought of heading for the door. Castro sized him up once more. "All right, if it ain't Jake, what brings you back here? You get a lead on them survivalists dealing dope?" Seeing Tom's eyebrows rise, he added "If that's it, you can pack up and go home. Miss Rita checked 'em out before. I figure Freeborn and his bunch got their own little peyote church, but there ain't enough to go around. Nobody's selling down in this canyon."

"Is Freeborn somebody I should watch out for, too?"

"Maybe, or maybe not. Depends on what you're up to. He moved here after you left. No reason he should have it in for you. His kind just like to be left alone."

Rita asked to look at a set of turquoise earrings. Castro put them on top of the case. "Those are from one of the Begay girls over by Aneth. She does some real nice work." He glanced back at Tom. "They say he's a witch."

Tom poured root beer into the vanilla sundae cup, concentrating on avoiding a spill. "Who's that?"

"The Navajo. They say Freeborn's a witch."

Tom figured the Navajo would say Castro was a witch if they knew he could read minds. "Why would they think that?"

"They say he sent a ghost-spirit after their horses. Killed a couple mares and drove that gray stud crazy so he ran through a fence. Got cut so bad they had to put him down."

"By any chance are those horses still coming across that state line fence north of here?"

Castro laughed. "Ain't nobody can fix that damn fence for long since you left. Only now some of the gates stay closed, and the horses don't go any farther than Yellowjacket Canyon."

"Why blame Freeborn? Must be other folks who don't like stray horses."

Castro shrugged. He took a check from Rita for the earrings and put it in an old cash register that looked more battered than his hat. "Who knows how a Navajo thinks? You ever see a horse that got into locoweed? I think the grazing must be causing a change. I seen more loco now than ever before. That's what I think killed 'em." He saw Tom looking closely into a framed set of stone arrowheads. "Don't you be snoopin' on me. None of them come off government land."

"No, don't worry. I'd bet you had them before there was a law about archeology. Rita, look at this one. It's called a bird point, but some of the archeologists say the Indians used them to hunt big game. They didn't make much of a wound, but the point would go in deep and keep working deeper until it cut through something vital, even if the shaft broke off." Tom shook his head. "I'd forgotten that. Sometimes the animal would run for miles, but the Indians would track them down."

Castro added, "I think they used poison on the arrowheads too."

"You mean like curare?" Rita asked. "Wasn't that only in South America?"

"Wasn't nothing that deadly up here, but they sure enough knew how to mix some poisons that would slow an animal down some, make 'em weak and sick so they'd head for shade and water. Probably made it out of something real common. A white man would never think about it."

Tom followed Rita out. He stuck his head back in the door and said to Castro, "If you remembered me and knew I worked for BLM, then how come you let me buy ice cream? You aren't getting soft in your old age, are you?"

"I can still throw your skinny ass off the porch, boy. Lucky for you Miss Rita was with you." Tom smiled and waved.

Tom joined Rita and they waded across the creek. As they climbed the slope toward Tom's truck, Rita, remembering the Latin name for locoweed, pointed at a low gray plant and asked, "Isn't this an *Astragalus*, Tom?"

"Yeah, but there isn't that much of it, and it belongs here. You notice how it lays flat on the ground and has those hairy fruit pods? That's the wooly-pod milkvetch. It's all over the west from Arizona to Oregon. I've never heard of an animal getting sick from eating that species." Tom pulled a canteen from his pack and passed it to Rita. "Look at that white outcrop across the canyon with the binoculars, would you?"

Rita got out the binoculars. "Look for what? I can't see any fossils from here."

"Look for what's not there. Do you remember seeing a dried-up plant with yellow-green stalks about a foot tall growing on the white clay when we came down from the mesa rim? Even more, do you remember the smell? It was almost bitter. That was the smell of a poisonous species, one that concentrates selenium from the soil."

"Oh, yes, I did notice that smell. So did the dogs. I saw Scrub sniffing one and then back off like she knew it was bad. Why would a horse eat that?"

"They will if they get hungry. Sometimes a horse will develop a taste for it, and really go after it, even when other feed is available. Scrub, on the other hand, is pretty smart about poison. She knows better than to chew on the iris in my yard."

"I don't see anything like it." She handed the binoculars to Tom.

He scanned the slopes. "No, I don't think it is here, just back closer to Joshua's place."

"What about what old man Levy said? Is it increasing because of overgrazing?"

"Maybe, but those clay outcrops are so barren that cows don't waste their time climbing on them. Overgrazing isn't an issue. Plus, this is the same soil, so if loco was increasing over there, we should at least see a few over here. The only other place I found a loco that smelled like that was at the base of Mesa Verde. It was growing on dark gray Mancos shale. But it might grow here if you brought the seeds over and planted them." Tom paused. "I remember a rancher in Mancos told me he lost a horse that ate it."

"Castro seems to think he's seen plenty. Do you think he knows what he's talking about?"

"He always had horses in the old days. He might not know the scientific name, but he knows what locoweed looks like, and I bet he knows which are poisonous and which aren't. Even my mother can point out all the pasture grasses by their common names, and she hasn't lived on a farm since World War II."

"Well if he does know, then it must be more common than you think. Maybe you missed seeing it."

Tom's pride was more piqued than he let on. He looked at his map again. "You could be right. The last I saw was near the mouth of Moccasin Canyon. There is a road access right down the canyon on the other side of the creek. It would be easy to plant and easy to harvest when the time comes. That's a long way from Levy's store. He's a tough old fart, but I bet he's over ninety now. If I were him, I would just go out for walks up this canyon. Then I wouldn't see much locoweed."

"So, maybe he walked over into Utah. Maybe he drives out in different directions." Rita was too used to thinking like a cop to buy into Tom's convenient speculation.

"Castro seemed certain that Joshua wasn't selling drugs. If he keeps an eye on him, he'd have to be careful. If he went more or less the way we did, he'd get the impression there was a lot of loco on the hills. I think that's because Joshua is growing it on BLM ground close to home. It makes for more garden space, plus it takes a particular soil with selenium for that species. Nobody else would notice. It looks too natural."

Rita shook her head, "You're really stretching."

"Yeah, I know it." Tom groaned. "Maybe when I visit Joshua, I'll drive to Moccasin Canyon and check something. I don't remember seeing a single seedpod on the plants. Hell, even if I'm remembering that right, it's only something else not in place."

They climbed a small chute between the sandstone slabs to get back on top of the mesa. Rita flushed an owl from an overhanging ledge, and it quickly disappeared around the rim. "Wow, did you see that? That was great! You don't see long-ears very often."

"Is that what it was? Weird seeing that in daylight. It was like a ghost!" They found the road and walked together. She reached out and held his hand as they walked. Tom was happy, but thoughtful. "You know what else was weird? Levy focusing on Joshua with that witch story. It was like he knew why I was here. That peyote crack was odd too." Scrub saw the truck and ran ahead. Rogue placidly walked by Rita's side.

Rita agreed, "He did seem to believe we were investigating something. You think he was trying to point a finger at Joshua?"

"It would be totally out of character to rat on another local, even a newcomer, but indirectly he sure made out like Joshua was evil. That's what a Navajo means when they call someone a witch." Tom laughed at himself and looked at Rita. "Levy knows that because he's lived here all his life. I know it because I read it in a murder mystery!"

Tom drove to where they had left Rita's truck. They had an early supper, and Rita packed her gear to leave. There were some long, quiet pauses in their conversations. Finally Rita sighed, "It's going to be a long trip back to Pagosa. I'd better get going." She gave him a kiss and a hug. "You take care of yourself. If you find anything serious about Joshua, you get out of there and get help." When she started the engine, Rogue jumped into the bed of Rita's truck. Rita waved as she left, rolling up the window to keep the dust out. To no one, she asked, “Why do you have to live a thousand miles away?”

Tom waved through the dust, “See you!” He watched the taillights disappear over the ridge. He sat in his lawn chair and opened a fresh beer. Scrub laid her head on her paws with a huge sigh and looked up at him with wide, worried eyes. “I know what you mean.” Tom felt about as sick-lonely as he had the day his ex-wife had walked out. He thought about that for awhile as he peeled the label off his beer.

As Scrub watched, he poured the beer on a saltbush. He unrolled his sleeping bag on a patch of sand. She lay beside him with one eye open. The coyotes kept their distance.

Chapter 9

Tom drove into Moab the next morning. He found a cheap motel with a room available before 11:00. Tom promised the clerk he would leave Scrub kenneled in the back of the truck and went in to shower. Then he returned to the motel office to get directions to the local library. He drove to the library, but all the public computers were in use. To waste time, he put Scrub on a leash and set out for a walk. A few blocks away he found one of the repulsive signs of societal decay he usually derided, an "Internet Café." After he took Scrub back to the truck, he returned and logged on as "Leptodactylon" while sipping an outrageously expensive cup of coffee.

There was a note from Randy Bergen confirming one more possible case of livestock poisoning, this one in the Alamosa District in southeast Colorado. Tom wrote in reply, "If that's our boy, then he has been busy. It's out of the loop I thought we had." He closed his reply with thanks and a request for Randy to track down some range staff contacts in New Mexico to look for signs of another possible path of destruction that might loop back to Joshua. He closed that e-mail account and logged in to his "tkreug824" account.

A scalding note from Mary Twil demanded he contact her by phone and suggested he might face obstruction of justice charges soon. He wrote her back a vague note about his trip, saying he had been on a vision quest during the past week and might have actually seen the Madonna. He also mentioned the Land Cruiser with "3HUGGR" license plates for sale at the Safeway in Baker and asked if it belonged to Skinner.

He mentioned to her the evidence left in the herbarium cabinet, suggesting that an agricultural laboratory could identify the material and check for toxins that could then be compared to tissue samples from the dead cattle. Since there was no clear connection to Skinner, she could treat the livestock sabotage as her own case. If she wanted to earn points from Sheriff Greenwood, she might give him the toxin test results and see if anything similar was found in Skinner. He assured her that he had no intention of working on the Skinner case and was instead doing research on a modern peyote religious cult.

A note from his sister in Florida said that people from BLM had been calling to find him. She demanded he stop listing her as next of kin unless he was really prepared to die soon. His mother was worried in spite of the fact that he had called to say he was going on a long camping trip. Tom wrote back that he had contacted the people at work and all was well. "Unfortunately," he wrote to his sister, "my bosses are bumbling idiots. They want me to bail them out on year-end reports, so they might keep calling now and then."

Finally, Tom sent a message to Joshua Freeborn, letting him know he would arrive in Colorado in a couple of days and was planning to hike the old wilderness study area in Cross Canyon to see if BLM had ever reduced the grazing. Tom suggested they meet in Dove Creek and asked Joshua to reply quickly.

With no plans for the day, Tom drove west to BLM land where Scrub could run loose. The dirt road was lined with Toyota trucks, Subaru station wagons, and expensive new SUVs, all with racks for bicycles and kayaks. It took a while to find a place that looked unoccupied. When he let Scrub out, she was instantly surrounded by a pack of overly friendly dogs, which set Scrub into her indignant defensive-aggressive mode. A group of cyclists in shiny, colorful synthetics rode by. Observing the tense situation, they called to the dogs, but three remained. Tom let the tailgate back down, but before Scrub could retreat, the Malamute jumped in. Scrub continued whirling in circles to defend her honor from the others. "Get the hell out of my truck, you dumb shit."

"Hey, that's my dog!" One of the bikers returned, angrily assuming Tom intended to kidnap the Malamute.

"Well, I sure don't want the thing. His breath is worse than Scrub's, and he looks like he would eat more. How about if you call him so I can get my dog back in the truck?" Scrub made a snarling lunge at the liver and gray shorthair dog that wouldn't get his nose out of her behind. Tom yelled at her to stop.

"Why don't you control your dog? She's obviously vicious and untrained." The voice from the face beneath the helmet and behind the thick green rims of the sunglasses was female, but the bulbous orange nose-piece on the glasses created the appearance of something alien.

"If these are your dogs, then why don't you take them out of here? We were minding our own business." Tom grasped the Malamute's collar and pulled him out. "Besides, if I put my nose in your ass, you'd probably take my head off too. Scrub, load up!" She ran around the third dog and jumped in. Tom lifted the tailgate quickly, catching the Malamute in the chin as he attempted to jump in again. It yelped as it fell on the bumper. Scrub decided to bark loudly and continuously.

"You bastard. You did that on purpose!" The alien let her expensive bike fall in the sand and stormed toward Tom with her fists clenched.

"Whoa! Hey!" Tom raised his hands. "I was trying to get my dog away from these mutts before we have a real dogfight. How was I to know your dog was stupid enough to put his head through my tailgate?"

"What's going on, Cindi?" Another alien appeared, also dropping a flashy bike in the dust. Tom was distracted by the thought that the two bikes in the dirt had a higher market value than his 8-year old truck.

"I caught this guy with Karst in his truck. Then his dog attacked Tommy."

"Excuse me," Tom interjected while pulling the shorthair "Tommy" down from the truck's scratched side. "You caught me pulling your dumb dog out of my truck so my dog could get in before she got gang-raped." Another cloud of dusty aliens streaked by, accompanied by three more dogs. The pack at hand raced off in pursuit. Scrub continued barking fiercely for no good reason.

"All right," the larger alien bristled, "you don't have to be foul-mouthed."

From the voice the new arrival was obviously male. "It comes with being reminded that I don't know who my daddy was," Tom grimaced and nodded toward the creature, Cindi. He smiled at the male, "Wow, nice watch. Does that thing make cappuccino?" Tom could see the lycra bulge and the biceps tense. He concentrated on finding a good pivot balance without appearing tense himself.

The male watched him for a moment, but then pulled at his mate's arm to get her away. "Come on. Ignore him." The words "anti-social creep" rose out of the mutter as they left. They resumed aerobic exercise in the cloud of dust raised by yet another flock of racing knobby-wheeled aliens.

Tom waited a few more minutes, seeing a wide swath of many bike trails interwoven among the juniper. Two more groups of bikes and dogs went by. He gave Scrub some water. "Let's go walk down a nice quiet alleyway in town."

✯

He found an East Indian restaurant where he ordered yellow-curried chicken and passed up the imported beer in favor of iced tea. After dinner he grabbed a book from the truck and retreated to a nearly empty lounge across the street from his motel, where he ordered a draft beer. He sat at a table with his back to the television and the two rednecks at the other side of the bar.

The recently published book touted itself as an "authoritative reference" on livestock poisoning plants. The author had compiled a lot of old information from other sources, some having the quality of folklore. There seemed to be little new information on lethal doses or chemical analysis. Tom opened a folded sheet of paper he had prepared with a series of columns and rows, and into it he added notes on plant species, chemical toxicity, and symptoms.

Tom looked up when someone bumped his shoulder, seeing a pleasant-looking woman smiling down at him in the dim light. "Oh, excuse me," Tom apologized and scooted his chair closer to his table. He went back to his book. Later, when he looked around, considering a second beer, he saw the woman sitting with the two rednecks and laughing in response to their animated conversation while they bought her drinks. Tom saw her give a look back his way. The lounge was otherwise empty. The large, widely spaced tables behind him looked oddly like they belonged in a cafeteria rather than a bar. He drained his mug, put the book under his arm, and left and walked across the street.

He took Scrub for a long walk in the dark. "You know, Scrub, I missed my cue. I think that was supposed to be a pick-up. If I'd known enough to start a conversation, I might have gotten laid tonight." They doubled back from a dead-end street. Scrub seemed to be listening tolerantly to Tom's monologue. "I'm not really antisocial. I just never picked up on how to be social. I never liked the game. Going to bars to pick up a stranger, now that's lonely! Guess I'm not that bad off yet."

Back at the motel he wrote a letter to a friend in Alaska, commiserating on the lousy weather that had closed in on Juneau, describing Monument Valley, the alien encounter outside Moab, even the incident in the bar. He decided it was not important to mention Rita. At 9:30 P.M., he was asleep.

At 6:00 A.M. the next morning, he checked out and ate breakfast in the restaurant next door. When the Internet café opened at 7:00, he went in. Joshua Freeborn wrote that Cross Canyon was grazed in early spring, not fall, so there was nothing to see. In Joshua's opinion the grazing pressure had been reduced, but the stream had no potential for fisheries. He suggested instead that Tom drop by to discuss tactics for challenging grazing in other locations. Perhaps they could cooperate to address both wilderness and fisheries issues. Tom thanked him for the invitation and promised to stop by in two days.

Next he logged on to his other e-mail account and asked Randy to call the Durango office and check to see if there had been any adjustments to the grazing in Cross Canyon in the last ten years. He added, "If you get back to me quickly, I promise to tell you about the young woman who bumped into my chair last night to pick me up! I will come back here by noon, 11:00 your time to check my e-mail. Thanks."

After Tom went grocery shopping, he went to the library and put his name on a reservation list for a computer. He sat at a table, rereading a favorite Isaac Asimov tale until noon. Randy had interesting news. The range conservationist at the Durango office reported no significant changes in the grazing permit. More importantly, the Reverend claimed that the Skinner case was definitely a murder investigation. The cops were questioning everyone who knew Skinner. Tom promised to buy a round at the bar when he returned.

*

Tom decided to go see Cross Canyon for himself and evaluate Joshua's opinion of the improved grazing conditions. Since Randy had contradicted the grazing reduction, Tom thought it likely that

Joshua was still just trying to direct his attention elsewhere. When he reached Dove Creek he consulted a map, then headed south out of town. About fifteen miles farther the road ended on the rim of Squaw Point. Since it was mid-afternoon, he decided to set up camp and have an early supper.

While making dinner, he heard the sound of a distant vehicle. Scrub was paying attention, which meant it was approaching. Looking up the rise of the mesa, he could see a truck winding through the trees. "Probably scouting the prospects for deer, Scrub. Maybe he'll share some venison. What do you think?" She growled. "It's a little early to get pissy. He might be a great guy. Nobody but a local would come out here, so he won't camp near us." She continued her low grumbling. Tom concentrated on cutting vegetables and saving his fingers until Scrub's low bark and louder growl caught his attention.

The truck stopped on a high point. Presumably, the driver could see Tom's truck as clearly as Tom could see his. A flash of reflected light probably meant the driver was using binoculars to check out the campsite. Scrub's growling became emphatic. "Good grief, calm down!" Tom told her. "At this distance, it wouldn't matter if he was looking through a rifle scope. Now that he's seen us, he probably won't even come out here." Sure enough, after a few minutes the truck turned around and left. "See? Just because you were being anti-social, he turned back. We never will get any of that venison."

After Tom finished eating, he read from a paperback titled Bless me, Ultima, a story about old-time Hispanic culture in New Mexico. He set it aside to think about young boys, innocent and unaware enough to find magic plausible. Their lives could be ruled from moment to moment by love or fear, never understanding the nature of the forces they encountered. "Considering the balance, Scrub, it's good to be older." She opened her eyes to see if this signaled a change in activity, but he simply picked up a sketchpad and watched the nearby landscape mature in the gathering twilight. He drew bits and pieces of it, as though peering between the muntins of a window, focusing in different directions and at different scales through each pane.

The next morning Tom put away the camp gear and loaded canteens and a little food into his pack. The canyon hadn't changed much in fifteen years. The pinyon-juniper was still very dense on the canyon slopes, and there wasn't much grass to be found. The stream banks were still largely denuded, despite the few old cottonwoods valiantly trying to send up sprouts from the roots. The greasewood shrubs down near the Utah border still looked like they were heavily browsed each year.

Stray cattle occasionally crashed through the trees ahead of them, staying out of sight. It didn't look like the trespass cattle situation had changed much over the years either. Scrub made a few tentative forays as if to chase the cattle, but decided it was too hot to work hard if Tom wasn't going to provide better back-up. She fell in behind him and was glad when they turned around, once again taking the lead. The map indicated it was about six miles back, but the vegetation prevented straight-line travel, and the winding canyon was deceptive. Judging their pace, Tom thought it was closer to eight.

Tom decided the trail he was following was too well trampled to be the result of a few cattle alone. Every step by man or beast would leave a clear track in the soft red dirt, but this trail was hard and compacted from repeated use. When he saw that it branched into Ruin Canyon, he called Scrub for a detour. Two miles later they found it led up out of the canyon to a vehicle track that connected to the Pleasant View Road. The end point of the trail was marked by a vehicle turn-around where horses were obviously loaded.

He trudged back down Ruin Canyon, stopping to refill two canteens at a small spring. He opened a pocket on his pack and withdrew the iodine solution he used to treat water. Scrub lay down in the small depression Tom had made to pool the water and lapped the muddy trickle that passed downstream.

A bit farther on, he noticed fresh exposed earth off the main trail. Pieces of pottery lay scattered around several test-pits. Then he found a larger hole with some excavated slabs of flat rock and a piece of bone partly exposed. "Uh-oh, this doesn't look good. Somebody is pot-hunting." He pushed Scrub back and carefully removed the bone from the loose dirt. He held it next to his forearm for comparison and then carefully reburied it. He looked around for other oddities, then led Scrub away. Whoever had been digging hadn't bothered to collect the potsherds, even though the painted pieces would have been worth close to a hundred dollars.

Watching carefully on his way back up Cross Canyon, he found a large mound that was being artfully excavated from a trench behind a screen of thick juniper. After a little more searching, he found plastic washpans, a folding shovel, and a sifting screen tucked beneath some oakbrush. "Looks like somebody might be coming back. I wonder if this is what Levy was warning me about."

It was dark before they got to the truck. Tom loaded Scrub in the back and got out a flashlight. He carefully inspected the dirt road, finally locating the point where the brushing-out of footsteps gave way to vehicle tire tracks. Tom doused the light and waited for his eyes to readjust. He got into the truck and said through the window into the back, "Scrub, I've got a bad feeling Jake McPherson knows I'm here now. Why else would anybody care if I saw their footprints near my truck? Maybe he plans to come back tonight. I don't feel like getting my ass shot off. Levy was serious." With lights off, he drove out to the highway.

At Dove Creek he turned on the lights and headed south on Highway 666. He turned off toward the Dolores River overlook and found an obscure track out into the oakbrush on BLM ground. He turned out his lights before easing slowly up the trail and removed the light bulb from the overhead lamp before opening the truck door. He set out a lawn chair in the dark and listened for approaching vehicles. Only one passed on the main road a quarter mile away. The scanning spotlight and eventual rifle shot in the distance indicated it was a local getting an early freezer full of deer meat. Scrub eagerly crunched a bowl of dried food, while Tom ate a cold bagel with cheese and sipped a beer.

He spread a tarp and his sleeping bag a few yards away in the thick brush. Although he pulled off his boots, Tom slept in his clothes with the bag unzipped, waking frequently to listen to the dried leaves rattle in the breeze. Twice he reached out to check the placement of his flashlight and the hefty geologist's rock hammer next to his boots. Scrub lay close beside him, rarely sleeping.

The next morning, Tom waited for the sky to turn gray before lighting the stove under his coffeepot. He filled his cup, re-packed the stove, and set the coffeepot on the front floor between other gear. He drove out to the highway. He watched for any vehicle that might be trailing him. Seeing no signs of pursuit, he parked at a motel in Cortez, where he sat in the truck and finished the coffee and ate cold granola while watching the street.

Satisfied at last that Jake had not followed, Tom proceeded to a pawn shop he remembered. He showed his Oregon driver's license and an old Colorado hunter education card, paid an extra fifty dollars to backdate the paperwork, and walked out with a pump shotgun. At K-Mart he bought a box of shells. In the parking lot, he loaded the magazine, but refrained from putting a round in the chamber. He laid the gun behind the seat under a jacket. He had thoughts of a high-speed chase and rolling gun battle.

Once headed west from town, Tom realized the folly of trying to outrun anyone. The locals were passing him regularly, going 70 on the twisting two-lane. "The problem here is that these damn fools aren't even in a hurry. Now, what would you do if Jake pulled up alongside with an AK-47 or something poking out of his window?" Tom had no answer to his own question. The pavement ended, replaced by a washboard gravel surface. Traffic and housing development thinned out again. His fears faded as he began to concentrate on Joshua Freeborn once again.

Tom turned on a familiar road marked with a BLM sign announcing Moccasin Canyon and Cannon Ball Mesa. After crossing Moccasin Creek, he took another trail west. A private land sign blocked the approach to Yellowjacket Creek, so he turned around and drove back a short distance before parking off the road. Scrub barked madly to be let out. Tom lowered the tailgate. "Come on. You're my excuse for being here if anybody asks."

Tom crossed the drainage and headed straight uphill for a patch of white clay. "Sure can smell the selenium." Tom looked closely at a dried stalk. "This is it." He crushed a piece of the stem and held it to his nose. "Phew! It couldn't be much else." Kneeling, he looked beneath the stem. He found dried leaves, but no seedpods. He looked directly down slope where leaf litter had collected against a shadscale. "Not a single pod."

Scrub wandered down to the bottom where some rabbit-brush held the hope of something to chase. Tom continued along the slope, stopping to look under the shadscale where fallen seedpods might have lodged. He pocketed a few small pieces of quartzite and one piece of petrified palm wood. Scrub's barking drew Tom's attention to a vehicle approaching. He headed back down hill toward the truck.

The dried red face looked suspiciously at him out of the truck window. Tom smiled and waved. When he was close enough to speak, Tom asked, "Are we OK? I thought from the map that we were on public land."

"Yeah. You lost?"

"No, not really. It seemed like a good place to let my dog out. She needed a break."

"Looking for arrowheads?"

"No, just collecting some quartz and petrified wood."

"Yeah? Find any?"

Tom emptied his pocket. "I got one little piece that might be palm wood. They used to grow here a few million years ago." He held it out, and red-face took it for a closer look. "The rest are some old river pebbles, I guess." He showed a handful of smooth round stones. Scrub sat down in the shade of the truck and panted.

"Dog's hot." Red handed back the petrified wood. "You ain't gonna find any arrowheads or pots. Dumb bastard from out on McElmo walked all over that slope last June. He spent so much time up there he must have found everything. Covered every goddamned inch. I watched him carrying a bag."

"I think it's illegal to collect that kind of stuff, but a little petrified wood is OK."

"Yeah. Dumb hobby, though. Stay off my private land." Red started his truck.

"No problem. I have a map," Tom assured him. "Did it look like a pack?"

Red looked confused "Huh?"

"The guy on the slope. What kind of bag did he have? Did it look like a backpack or something on a belt?"

"Naw, just a paper sack, grocery bag."

"Well, I guess he couldn't have carried many rocks in that."

"Nope. Told ya he was a dumb bastard." Red pulled away.

Scrub was happy to climb back in the truck. "Well, at least it wasn't Jake, was it?" Tom started the truck and headed out to find Joshua Freeborn. "Old Red will probably call me a dumb bastard too, next time he bothers to talk to somebody."

Chapter 10

Joshua Freeborn's house was set below the road on the historic floodplain of McElmo Creek behind the old sheepherder corrals that were the remnants of the original homestead. The old cabin had fallen apart before Tom was born, but he remembered having seen some rotted old timbers where Joshua now had a large pole barn. Tom guessed the house was about ten years old. It was elevated from the ground, built on large, sunken poles. The barn looked newer. He could see the fenced garden extending back toward the deep gully where the creek had cut down during the 1930s.

He parked next to an old step-side Chevy half-ton. Scrub started barking immediately, demanding to be let out. Tom turned off the engine and waited. A figure in an olive T-shirt and military camouflage pants emerged from the garden and stepped through a gate. Tom opened his door.

"Hi, I'm Tom Kreuger. Are you Joshua?"

"Yeah. Looks like you found the place."

Joshua had a short crew cut that also looked military. He was tanned, tall, and muscular, not an ounce of fat. The T-shirt fit tightly over huge shoulders and biceps. Tom figured him for a weightlifter, yet he appeared to move gracefully. Maybe he was a swimmer instead, Tom thought.

Tom felt like he was being measured in turn. "You must have measured the mileage from the pavement. It was right on. Not like you have a bunch of neighbors to confuse things either. Nice place. Did you build it?"

"The house was here. I built the barn." Joshua looked at the truck where Scrub was still barking. "I guess you could let your dog out if it stays close."

"Thanks. She's usually pretty well-behaved, but she makes a lot of noise."

"That's why I don't have animals or neighbors."

Tom opened the tailgate, and Scrub jumped out. She quietly inspected the fence before taking a leak in the driveway. As she approached Joshua, she watched for a hand extended in friendship that was never offered. She sniffed his pant leg briefly, then wandered slowly around the yard.

"Aussie, isn't she?" Joshua asked.

"Yeah. I had a real sweetheart before her that gave me a good impression, so when she died, I got this one. They're an intelligent breed, but this one is more independent. The other one would do anything to please. Scrub just does what pleases her."

"Seems calm enough now." Joshua led the way up the porch steps. "Come on up and sit. Would you like some lemonade?"

"Yes, thanks." The porch looked out over the back yard. When Joshua brought out a pitcher and plastic glasses, Tom remarked, "From the looks of that garden, you must grow your own lemons." Scrub quietly lay down near the porch steps.

"Don't let the heat fool you. It's too cold in the winter." Joshua pulled two chairs out from under the table, sat down, and propped his feet up on the other chair.

Tom noticed the worn heels on Joshua's expensive, brand name running shoes. "I used to be a runner. Those look like good shoes. You run?"

"I do the Iron Man triathlon in Durango every year."

"Swimming and biking too! That's impressive. The only time I ever trained for a half marathon, I stepped on a nail the week before the race, put it right through my foot. So much for that."

Joshua sipped his lemonade and watched Tom over his glass. "So when exactly were you in Colorado before?"

"Back in the late 70's, up until '85," Tom considered how much truth to mix into his tale. "Then I moved down to Arizona for a few years, and then up to Oregon."

"Why did you leave Durango? Why Arizona? It's hot enough here."

Tom created a plausible lie, difficult to check. "I was working construction, then things slowed down. The guy I worked for went broke, so I found a job in Phoenix. They were building huge subdivisions until the banks started going broke."

Joshua took a sip of his lemonade. "I've worked on landscaping jobs down there during the winter to pick up some cash. They grow some interesting tropical stuff in Phoenix. So what made you an environmental activist? Building subdivisions doesn't exactly sound like something a tree-hugger would do."

"Oh, I don't know about that," said Tom. "You get sick enough of something, you might slip in a monkey-wrench here and there. Actually construction work is pretty flexible. Seems like you get laid off or the boss didn't line up enough work, so you've got time to go off hiking for a few days in the wilderness. Plus, I like to move around, see different parts of the country."

"What's so exciting about wilderness? It's just being out in the woods, isn't it? Seems to me those areas are all packed with people trying to get away from the cities."

"Exactly! That's the problem. There isn't enough to get away from other people. The feds don't know how to manage it right even when they designate it "wilderness," and the last undeveloped places that ought to be wilderness are being trashed by special interests like oil companies and ranchers. Do you know that there were twelve wilderness study areas on BLM land right in this corner of the state back in 1982? They all met the criteria for designation. Do you know how many BLM recommended? Just one! The only reason they let that one get by was because it was all rock, and nobody could even get a bulldozer in there. There was no oil, no gas, no uranium, and no coal. Hell, even the ranchers couldn't get any cows in there without floating them down the river."

"So? We've still got lots of rough, remote country here, even without wilderness designation. What's so important about that now?"

Tom sensed Joshua was trying to find a pure motive for hard-core activism. "Look, Man, I was out in this country a lot back then. You can't believe how much it has changed. There are so many new roads, there isn't a single place you can't get to in less than an hour of walking. Do you ever go looking for Anasazi pottery?" Tom stopped his breathing to listen.

"Nah. No interest in it."

"Well it's a good thing, because you wouldn't find much. Every time an oil exploration road went in, people used it to carry out every piece they could find. We've destroyed hundreds of places like Mesa Verde and Hovenweep. I'd bet there were over two hundred ruins in Cross Canyon alone."

"You're saying that Cross Canyon was one of the twelve? Man, this is the new millenium! What do you want to do about it now? You want my help or advice or what?" Joshua smiled in bemusement. "What's so spiritual about some old garbage from a dead civilization? We're going to die someday. In the future people will be looking in our garbage dumps, trying to figure out what we thought was so cool about cars."

Tom could see Joshua delighted in playing devil's advocate in person as well as in web page treatises. "It's a piece of the whole, Joshua. I came out here once with a hot-shot ecologist-professor. He spent the whole day gushing about what a beautiful wilderness it was, right out there a few miles." Tom waved in the direction of the canyon rims. "Me, I was kicking cow turds and looking at how there weren't any cottonwoods or willows left down in the creeks. By the end of the day I was ready to kick the guy's ass for being so blind to what was going on. He wasn't an ecologist, he was a tourist looking at the mountains in the distance."

"So now you want to be an activist and do something 'meaningful' about it?" Joshua said with a sneer.

"I've been an activist for years," Tom boasted.

"How would anybody know?"

"From what you've written, Joshua, you and I have similar philosophies. I met some folks down in Arizona. They were all talking about things they might do. Some were involved in Earth First, even got hauled into the big FBI fishnet when some power lines got sabotaged. They were stupid. If you want to be effective, you don't want anybody to know."

Joshua cocked his head and looked at Tom with a new interest. "So what is it you want to do? What do you want from me?"

"I'm not saying I want to do anything. I used to hike around here, so I thought I'd go back to a few places and check things out, see if the BLM and Forest Service are still screwing things up. Maybe I'll write them a letter to complain. Maybe not."

"That doesn't sound like much. I'm not interested."

Tom thought Joshua sounded interested. "Exactly. I don't expect you to be interested. On the other hand, like you suggested to those Germans on the net, what folks can do is cooperate in public education. Maybe if you know of a problem involving wilderness and grazing, you might invite me out to look at it. I might know about some trout or salmon spawning streams with problems. That seems to be your issue, so I might ask you to take a look at it. Or, say I come down to Colorado to hike. Say I wanted a ride from point A to point B. Maybe you might give me a lift. That way I could hike a whole mountain chain and get back to my truck. Maybe I could do the same for you in Oregon or northern Idaho." Tom smiled and waved his hand, "Maybe we'll all figure out ways to be more effective in the things we want to do."

Joshua considered for a moment, making Tom think he had overplayed his hand. "Did you just figure this out recently?" Joshua asked him. "You must have seen there are a lot of organizations on the web that do trips and a lot of ride share or travel exchange offers, even overseas."

"Yeah, well, I've been a loner for a long time. I'm also a lot older than you." Tom grimaced. "I never thought much of computers before. Now I'm starting to see how they can be useful making contacts with other folks who have similar interests."

"If you knew the people in Tucson who got busted for the power line fiasco, then you know how dangerous it can be to have the wrong kind of contacts," said Joshua. "Maybe you're better off staying a loner."

Tom detected something slightly odd with that statement, perhaps a slight change in inflection. "Luckily, I never hung out with them. Of the two I met, one lived in Phoenix and his buddy was from Prescott. They tried to recruit me once. The guy in Phoenix ran into me after the dragnet. He was looking for a job in construction because the Forest Service wouldn't hire him even though the charges were dropped."

"You didn't know Foreman when he was in Tucson?"

"I read about him in High Country News just because he was the head of Earth First. Never met him. I thought he was up in Flagstaff."

"Yeah, maybe that's right," said Joshua, sipping his lemonade. "It was almost before my time, I probably got it wrong. Seems like a dilemma though, if you're gonna do stuff like that. What if somebody gets stupid or gets nervous and decides to turn you in?"

Tom shrugged. "It's a risk, but it can be done. Best if the right hand doesn't know what the left hand is doing. If I give you a ride, and you're not carrying any evidence, there isn't much to tell. If you arrange your drop-off and pick-up points far enough away, nothing can be proved. You can walk ten miles a day in the toughest terrain anywhere, twice that, if it's easy." Tom smiled, "A clean-cut looking guy like you could wash up, change into fresh clothes, and hitch a ride with a total stranger. Good way to get to a city for a pick-up by your contact. He really doesn't have to know where you've been for sure."

Joshua looked skeptical. "Theoretically speaking, if a guy was going to monkey-wrench a power line, he'd have a hard time doing it alone or doing it without carrying around some evidence that someone else would have to see."

"Planning makes a difference. If you cache the tools you need to work and take your time, there isn't much you can't do alone. The trick is getting around without someone being able to trace when and where you've been. If you use cash sparingly, live on the streets like a nobody, or disappear in the woods for a month at a time, you can be pretty hard to track."

"Cops look for patterns, and if you're going to cross state lines, the FBI isn't stupid. How do you minimize those risks?"

"OK," said Tom leaning forward. "Let's say you don't already know this kind of stuff, but I think you do. Your editorial on the stupidity of eco-saboteurs was right on. Let's take patterns first. You have to change your methods constantly. Once I've got a good method figured out, I stop using it for a while. Figure out something else that gets the same results. If the cops catch on, quit using that method altogether. Take on different kinds of targets. Don't mess around in your home territory. Use different tactics in different places. Don't get too attached to one spot. If somebody might place you near the action, use a time delay."

"Never mind all that," Joshua interrupted. "Anybody smart can figure backwards how to avoid a mistake. How do you keep the cops from figuring out how you did something? That's a more interesting problem."

"Well, you can't always count on it, but the best way is to make it look like something else," said Tom, backtracking for the moment. "I mean you can always keep the effect small, so somebody gets pissed-off, but it's not worth the hassle to call the cops. But to change something, you've got to have an economic effect. Make it too costly for the other guy to keep doing whatever it is that you don't like."

"Yeah, we're thinking the same on that, but how do you break the bank and keep the cops from figuring out how you got in the vault?"

"Lots of ways. You make something look like an accident, like when a part falls off a machine and the whole thing gets wrecked. Sometimes you can make it look like a natural event, like a big rock fall, or a reservoir that drained when an animal dug a hole in the dam." Tom drained his glass. "What's really fun though is to make it look like you did one kind of thing, but the real method is too subtle. Then the cops never figure it out because they're looking at the wrong evidence."

Joshua laughed, "If a guy could do that, he'd be a genius. Maybe someday we'll trade stories." He refilled Tom's glass. "I still think sooner or later it boils down to trust. Say someone drops you off and picks you up later. He knows where you've been more or less. When something weird happens, he knows you did it. If you've got to trust him, you might as well get him involved so he goes to jail with you."

"Too much risk, unless you know for a fact he's as committed to action as you are."

"The problem working with dilettantes is that you can't keep them from thinking. There isn't any way to avoid problems in the long run." Joshua stared hard at Tom. "What do you do when the son-of-a-bitch gets too nosy? Say he follows you and sees what you're doing. Then he gets nervous and threatens to turn you in."

Tom shrugged. "Nobody lives forever. If you betray someone in a bad business, you ought to expect to die sooner than later. Something I learned in Vietnam, Joshua. To survive in a jungle, you've got to be quiet, and when the shit hits the fan, you've got to be very serious. If people know you're crazy at the start, they tend to leave you alone."

Joshua looked smug. "Talk is cheap. I've known a lot of tough guys who make threats, but they don't always do that well in a fight. You don't look big enough to scare anybody."

"I don't," agreed Tom. "Threats are stupid. If somebody warns you and you believe him, that's all the reason you need to take him out first. Why wait for him to come to you? On the other hand, why ask for a fight you don't need? I haven't killed anybody in thirty years, but if the time comes again, I probably won't feel guilty about it."

"Well, you've got some interesting philosophy. Sure, why don't we keep in touch? I might come up your way some day. Maybe if you plan a trip, you could send me a note. Only it would be better if we didn't crap in each other's back yard. I'd feel better if you forget Cross Canyon. It's too close for comfort."

"Depends on how well the job is concealed. It's been about sixteen years since that oil well went dry in McLean Basin. Did anybody ever figure that one out?"

"You dried up a well?" Joshua looked doubtful.

"Natural event." Tom gave Joshua a smug smile. "Then the drill stem got stuck twice before they gave up trying to get it to flow again. The gyppo driller went broke."

Joshua looked thoughtful. "You might be good, but I don't want attention drawn out this way. There are enough nosy people as it is."

"Why don't you point out a trouble spot where you wouldn't mind seeing some action? It might take me a year or so to set something up, but you could evaluate my tactics." Tom laid out his bait, "Maybe you could take on a target in my area. Then we can see if we want to try closer cooperation."

"Hmm, give me some time to think about that. I'll get back to you in a couple of weeks." Joshua rose. "Where'd your dog go?"

Tom looked in the corner, then under the table. Sure enough, Scrub was missing. "How the hell did she sneak off so quietly? I saw her lie down right there." He whistled and called. "Damn! Is there any water in the creek? She probably went for a swim. If you had a cow, she would be rolling in fresh manure."

"We better find her if you want her back. I've got some rat poison lying out in places. Dogs are nothing but trouble." Joshua was pissed. "I wouldn't have one. They always screw something up or draw attention."

Tom followed Joshua off the porch. Tom looked under the house and called. "No luck. She must have gone out back. I'd bet on the creek."

Joshua hesitated, then opened the gate near the side of the pole barn. "Come on then. She probably wouldn't come to me. Most dogs don't like me either."

Tom startled briefly when he saw a deer standing beside the barn, until he realized it was only an archery target. As he walked through the garden, he noticed a few tomato vines, one zucchini, and a patch of corn. The rest appeared to be flowers of various sorts, mostly dried or dormant, some of which were only vaguely familiar. A lot had been cut back or topped. A couple raised beds were empty, the soil thoroughly worked up. An irrigation ditch was lined with tall, dried stalks. The tops had been cut off those also. "You get deer bothering your garden?" Joshua didn't answer. On the far side of the corn, Tom stopped for a close look at the taller plants. "Looks like you're a master gardener, but I can't believe you grow manioc. I've never seen any in the U. S. Where did you get it?"

Joshua looked uncomfortable. "Uh, I guess I got it from a specialty catalog. Come on, we'd better find your dog." He continued past the garden, through a stand of native greasewood and wild rye toward the edge of the gully.

The creek was barely flowing, as dark as the soil of the banks. Tom whistled and called again. "How much ground do you own back here? She might have gone chasing a jackrabbit."

Joshua turned and marched back toward the barn. "Dog out of control could cause a lot of trouble. You take it with you when you dry up oil wells?" He was definitely pissed.

"Nah, not unless I'm pretending to be hunting birds. She's not much good at that either, but women in the park stop to talk to her. That's her main use."

As Joshua went through the gate, he heard a muffled bark. "What the hell?" Around the side of the barn Joshua found a fresh hole under the skirting.

Tom had dropped back from Joshua and walked the other way around the barn. Homemade solar panels outside the skirting appeared to pipe hot air under the barn.

Joshua exploded. "Hey, your goddamned dog dug under the barn!" There were a couple more barks, then the sound of movement inside.

Tom put his head over the fence to look at Joshua, "I think she's inside now. Probably decided to chase a rat. Maybe there's a hole in the floor?" Tom tried the back door. It was unlocked, and he entered. Joshua opened the front door and turned on the lights. Scrub looked over her shoulder at them, then charged forward into a stack of cans, barking furiously. The cans tumbled, but nothing spilled out of the tight lids. Joshua cursed again, and Tom grabbed her collar. "Yeah, she's got a rat cornered in there somewhere."

Joshua inspected the large hole in the floor under a huge food dehydrator where Scrub had clawed her way in. "Goddamn it! She knocked the hot-air duct apart to get in here. Now I'm gonna have to crawl under the floor to fix it."

A fabric tube hung limply from the base of the dehydrator. From there, Tom guessed, it connected to the solar panels. Above, the dehydrator was connected by ductwork to a chemist's vent hood. Directly beneath the vent hood was an electric stove. Tom thought the venting system was major overkill for a normal kitchen and canning work area. The chemist's vent was an expensive piece of safety equipment, out of place unless Joshua was handling toxic materials.

The back wall was full of stacked cans on the floor and shelves. Luckily, the glass jars were well up out of Scrub's impact zone. A wooden workbench was cluttered with paper sacks full of drying plant parts, screens and sieves, and several chemist mortar and pestle sets of different sizes, as well as what looked like an Indian grinding stone. A refrigerator hummed next to a utility sink. Several mesh bags full of roots were hanging among the rafters. A pantry wheel hung near the stove, cluttered with battered old pans and utensils.

"Man, I'm sorry for the mess. Let me put the dog outside and help you clean up."

Joshua looked darkly at Tom. "No. I have everything organized my own way. I'll put it back."

Tom put Scrub out the door. "Well, I am sorry. Scrub probably thought she was doing a good thing. She gets a biscuit every time she catches a ground squirrel out of my yard." He gestured toward the dehydrator. "Guess it's harvest time. You make herbal remedies?"

Reluctantly, Joshua answered as he moved, directing Tom outside ahead of him, "Yeah, I take some to the food co-op, teas and spices and what-not. It gives me a little extra cash."

"I knew a girl once who told me she and her friends ate skunk cabbage. She was cute, but I wasn't ready to go all natural-like, just because I had the hots for her." Tom turned to go out, but stopped at the door when he saw a lathe and small table-saw and a bench with a carver's vise. "Hey now, that's something I can relate to. I do some woodworking myself. What kind of things you make?" He picked up a short narrow piece of wood from a box by the lathe to inspect it.

Joshua frowned. "Odds and ends, I guess, mostly just shelves and benches. Come on, I've got to head to town pretty soon. Better put your dog in your truck before she gets into something again."

"Sure." Tom swiped his hand across the base of the lathe. "I never have learned to use a lathe; it's kind of a specialized tool. You make bowls?"

"No, I picked it up in a garage sale. I haven't learned how to use it yet." Joshua turned out the light before Tom was out the door.

Tom whistled, and this time Scrub appeared immediately. "Well, I should let you get on with business." Scrub recognized they were done visiting and jumped into the back of the truck, watching out the window as Tom closed the tailgate. "Let me know when you find something you might want an outsider to look at. I'll do likewise. You don't have a problem if I mess around up near Paradox or Grand Junction, do you?"

Joshua looked at the dusty cab of Tom's pickup. "Hmm? Oh, no. No problem up there," he said awkwardly.

After starting the engine, Tom leaned out the window and said, "You don't happen to collect rocks or petrified wood, do you?" Joshua shook his head, still lost in thought. "Well, it's probably a dumb hobby. I thought you might know a place around here where there might be something interesting. Maybe I'll camp out for a while before I head back north." Joshua looked at him hard. "I'll be all sweetness and innocence, don't worry," said Tom with a smile. "With this stupid dog along, it's only a scouting trip."

As he pulled out onto the road, Tom opened the sliding window behind him. "You want a little air-conditioning?" Scrub stuck her head through the window, dripping saliva on Tom's shoulder. Tom relaxed the fingers of his left hand while dropping the shavings removed from the lathe bed into the palm of his right hand. He sniffed them and held his hand up to Scrub's nose. "Now, why would he lie about a simple thing like using his lathe? These sure smell like fresh oak shavings to me. What do you think?" She sniffed, and licked tentatively at one of the morsels.

"By the way, while you were wasting time chasing packrats, I found the source of that ergot. Joshua cut all the seed stalks off his Basin wildrye back by the creek. A lot of folks in the Middle Ages died from ergot in their rye. Let's head back to Cortez, shall we?"

Before long Tom noticed a dust plume signifying a following vehicle going as slow as he was. Miles farther he turned in to a road near Sand Canyon. As he eased the truck through a cattleguard, he saw Joshua's ancient Chevy as it first slowed, then accelerated to speed by. Scrub was watching out the back, but refrained from barking. "He got into a hurry right there, didn't he? Maybe he figured he couldn't keep track of us without being spotted."

The parking area at the Sand Canyon trailhead was packed with eight vehicles. Five had multiple bike racks. Two had large plastic kennels. Dreading lycra-clad aliens, Tom did a three-point turn and headed back to Cortez. Accelerating to 65 and leaning into the curves, Tom never did catch sight of Joshua's old Chevy. "Looks to me like he normally drives a lot faster than when he was following us, trying to stay behind."

Chapter 11

Other than adopting the local custom of speeding, Joshua Freeborn was a careful man. In fact, he would not even speed outside of his home territory in southwest Colorado. He was justifiably proud of his intelligence, his wide range of knowledge, and his ability to do methodical research. He already had a plan to check Tom's cover story.

Years before, as William Carter, he was hired after law school by a Tallahassee firm specializing in corporate and tax law. They represented a number of small companies involved in shipping, waste management, recycling, and construction in the southern half of Florida. The executive boards and controlling partners of the companies included a relatively short list of investors. Most served several of the corporate entities. Approximately a third of them had prior indictments for various forms of racketeering, but only two had spent more than a year in prison.

The law firm tracked state and federal permits, fended off inspectors, and negotiated the fines and terms of remediation for major and minor infractions. They also did taxes and complicated financial transfers between their clients. The clients, as William Carter soon discovered, had a lot of profits that would never be fully explained.

Never, unless someone dug under the parking lots they constructed, and could prove where the unlabeled barrels of toxic waste had originated. William distinguished himself with hard work, creative advice, and adept, discrete handling of payoffs to various state officials. It was a good set-up, profitable for the lawyers as well. The risks were usually handled skillfully.

Unfortunately for the managers of the shipping company, they hired several drivers with connections to Cuban drug rings. Unknown to the managers, the drivers occasionally added undocumented cargo to their loads. An investigation following an accident in Miami uncovered all the corporate ties and led to the improper indictment of the shipping company owners for laundering drug profits they knew nothing about.

As a minor player who cooperated with the investigators, William Carter was allowed to plea bargain. He was disbarred, but never did jail time. His diversion of over $600,000 in corporate funds to a safe-deposit box was never uncovered. He informally assisted the public defender for three of the drivers. Two died in apparent drug gang hits the day after getting out on bail. Nobody figured out that Joshua had assisted them into the hereafter. The third remained in jail until he was deported. Carter stayed in Miami for two years, living a poor and honest life. Then he legally changed his name to Joshua Freeborn and disappeared. He established investment accounts in Bahamas and carried a pound of uncut cocaine from a storage unit formerly rented by the murdered truck drivers.

He purchased the property in McElmo Canyon using a trust fund established by his "father" in Santa Fe. The trust fund periodically deposited reasonable sums of money in his local bank account, obviating the need for gainful employment. For two years he dealt small quantities of cocaine to the affluent youth of Durango until the supply ran out. By the time the cops got around to making inquiries, the drugs were gone. The cash was carefully packaged and stored in several remote, hidden locations along with supplies of canned and dried food, ammunition, and a selection of superior weaponry.

It took Joshua a while to establish a sense of community and purpose. His natural allies came to be the fringe of local libertarians, survivalists, and later a few radical environmentalists scattered around a four state area. His neighbors were mostly long-term residents with extended family ties in the county. They were largely suspicious, unfriendly, contemptuous of Joshua's apparent education, and prone to slanderous rumors. They wanted no change in their way of life.

Joshua did not mind the enforced privacy of his remote location and sullen neighbors. His only real dissatisfaction was the nuisance dust from the unpaved gravel road in front of his house. He had tried to convince the county road department to pave the road or at least do something to control the dust. The canyon residents thought he was crazy to push for an improvement district that would cost them money. The man who ran the road department was the brother-in-law of one of Joshua's neighbors, and he refused to waste money on dust control. Moreover, he called Joshua a fool for buying a place on a gravel road if he couldn't handle the dust.

It was resentment of local politics and the control of the old, dying ranch and agricultural community that eventually caused him to gravitate to the complaints of the environmental movement. It was the disrespect and disinterest that prompted him to seek ways to strike back at the entrenched interests. Monkey-wrenching provided an outlet for his pride. He combined his new interests in weaponry and survival skills with the intellectual challenge of thwarting authority.

Joshua skirted around the south of Cortez and hit Highway 160 at the eastern edge of town. He didn't slow down until he reached the south side of Durango. He left his truck at a park by the river, and walked two blocks to the federal building. At the information desk he asked the uniformed attendant to speak to someone in the oil and gas leasing section of BLM.

Before the clerk could dial an extension, a second woman announced "Oh, don't bother, Jeanette, I'll take him there. I was going up anyway." The lacquered blonde had admired Joshua's large biceps and trim waist when she saw him approach. "Hi, I'm Martha," she said, needlessly giving the name emblazoned on her nametag. "I'm the Public Information Officer for the Forest Service and BLM." Joshua smiled and held the door to the hall open for her, half-bowing with a sweeping gesture of his arm. She giggled, "Well, I do appreciate a man with old-fashioned manners." She looked back to see if he was watching as she swiveled down the hall. "They're on the next floor." She guided him into the elevator, brushing against his arm as she punched the button. "Are you with one of the oil companies?"

"Actually, I'm an investor," he lied. "I'm considering buying several leases, and I need to ask some specific questions about some previous exploration and development."

"Oh, well, I'm sure we can help you." She smiled up at him, suddenly at a loss for words.

Joshua was glad he had grabbed a clean shirt and pair of jeans before pursuing Tom down the road. This vacuous woman was already making the elevator seem slow, but he could imagine her staring at his military fatigues and perhaps remembering more about him than he wanted. She led him around the corner to a large, open room cluttered with divider panels where she brought him to an officious looking man in his mid-forties.

"Charles, this gentleman would like to buy some oil and gas leases." She opened her eyes wide at Joshua. "You didn't tell me your name, so I can't introduce you."

"Oh, sorry. I'm James Carter. Thanks for your help." He turned to Charles.

"Uh, Mr. Carter, we don't sell leases. Those are bid out from the Denver Office. If you want information on the next opportunity to bid on open leases, we can get that for you."

"Actually, Charles, I knew that. I wanted to get some specific information on the production of a couple of lease tracts over next to Utah."

"We can't release that kind of information to you. It's proprietary."

"I understand. However, I'm trying to confirm some very specific information that shouldn't be proprietary. I'm told one of the wells collapsed and went dry. The driller who tried to reopen it supposedly wasn't competent. This was about fifteen or more years ago, out in McLean Basin. There should be some record of the dates on those drilling permits and the name of the operator."

"Yeah, we can probably give you that," said Charles. "You got the lease number?"

"No, actually I left the sales brief in Santa Fe. Surely you can check a map or a database and come up with the file for McLean Basin," Joshua tried to sound like an executive who expected better service.

Charles sniffed. He was used to businessmen in casual attire, but he was considering asking his assistant to handle this. Joshua's blue jeans were cues to underling status in his book. "Could be a lot of wells out in that area. Who are you with?"

"Carter Investments. It's my firm. I like to look at my acquisitions in the field before I decide to buy." Joshua gave him a firm and confident smile, looking into the back of his eyes. "I'm sure you'll find the well is part of one large lease. They should all be listed on the lease, but the production stoppage and the additional drilling permits will identify the one I'm talking about."

Charles grunted. He turned to the computer on his desk and tapped the keyboard. Joshua saw a map with lease numbers reflected in Charles' glasses. Charles said, "Could be one of a couple leases. It's going to take me a minute to figure out where the boundaries match with the basin. You don't have the name of the drilling company either?"

Joshua sat in a chair well back from the desk and crossed his legs casually. "No, he was described as a "gyppo driller," not a good reference."

Charles didn't look up as he tapped some more. "Lots of small-time contractors don't know what they are doing, really. It takes a good mining engineer to keep an operation straight." He inflated his chest, looking like a bird fluffing feathers. "Here we go. The well stopped production seventeen years ago. The drilling operation started late the next fall, got an extension after a problem, and got shut down in the early winter because of heavy rains. They came back the next spring, but they never completed drilling. Pulled out in late June. One Way Drilling Company."

Joshua asked, "Is that a joke? One way? You mean they only drill down?"

Charles sniffed again. "I remember this guy. The logo was a hand with a pointing finger. Believe it or not, the clown who owned it was getting contracts through church affiliation. That was 'One Way'—as in Christ's way. They had a big sect church over in Colorado Springs."

"What a way to do business," Joshua scoffed. "Why didn't they hire somebody else and drill again? Wasn't it a pretty good well up until it collapsed?"

Charles seemed to forget that was treading on the edge of proprietary information. "Yeah, it looks like it. Probably the driller convinced them it couldn't be done without taking a chance on some big losses. He had a theory that an intruded stratum had buckled, and it would jam the drill stem every time. Pure horseshit. It's all sedimentary and metamorphic strata out there."

Joshua laughed. "That's what I thought when I heard that. Well, I've taken enough of your time. Can you possibly print out a map with the location on it so I can go see for myself?"

"Sure. Are you a geologist? You know how to evaluate a site for potential?"

"No, I hire an expert for that. I want to look at the logistics, get a feel for the local environment. Speaking of which, is there any history of environmentalist opposition out there?"

Charles laughed, "No, all the granola types live here in Durango. The people in Cortez are all hard-headed working class. They like anything that produces jobs."

"Good. I guess what I heard was that there used to be some environmentalists that kept a watch on oil development. Maybe it had something to do with wilderness." Joshua pursed his lips and looked upward, as if trying to stretch his memory. "Ever hear of a guy by the name of Tom Kreuger? Seems they mentioned that name."

"Kreuger? Oh, yes. I remember him. He was the wildlife biologist when I first got here, but he moved a year later. He was an environmentalist flake all right, but nobody ever said he fought about oil wells. He did his job, but you could tell he was a granola-eater."

"Wildlife biologist? You mean for BLM?" Joshua was stunned.

"Yeah, here in this office." Charles misinterpreted Joshua's look of shock. "Oh, we had a bunch of touchy-feely types back then, but they've all moved on now. I don't think you have to worry. From what I remember, he was a tree-hugger. He used to foam at the mouth about the Forest Service. I guess he hated cows too. Used to fight with the range cons a lot."

"Any idea where he is now?" Joshua asked.

"Seems like he went to Arizona, but I never paid any attention to him, and I never heard any more about him." Charles looked puzzled. "Really, we don't get much static from enviros about oil and gas. It's a done deal now, although the new administration might let us increase the well density."

Joshua suddenly brightened. "Well, thanks for your help. If you ever get to Santa Fe, look me up."

He went down the stairwell, muttering as he opened the door, "What's that bastard up to?"

Chapter 12

Tom parked under a Siberian elm two blocks from the Cortez public library. He opened the side-window of the truck canopy to give Scrub some cross-ventilation and poured water into her bowl. "I'll be back in a little while to take you for a walk." He brushed chaff out of the long hair behind her ears. "We can tell you were crawling under the barn, can't we? I hope you didn't pick up any fleas from that rat's nest." He picked more chaff out of her tail. "Nice seedpod you have here, Scrub." He turned it over in his hand a couple times.

He opened the cab of the truck and removed a hand-lens from his pack. Then he rummaged behind the seat to find a book and opened it to compare the illustrations to the seedpod. Scrub pushed her head through the window and watched. Tom held out the book where she could see. "It's not off those old locust trees, so let's look at lupines." He thumbed through the pages. Holding the pod fragment over the book, he pried the valves apart. A single small seed fell between the pages. "This pod is too narrow to be a lupine." He looked at his hand-written table of plant names and poisons. He carefully placed the fragments and seed on a tissue on the dashboard and flipped the pages forward. He gave Scrub a knowing look and showed her the illustration.

"Now, I like golden banner. First off, you haven't been anywhere near one since Joseph Canyon. Second, it doesn't grow naturally anywhere near Joshua's place, especially not under the dehydrator." He held his notepaper in front of her. "See that? It says quinolizidine alkaloids. Not bad, eh? Bet you can't pronounce that! Now, check those symptoms. Arched back! Just like the cows in Joseph Canyon. See any other things on the list with that symptom?" Scrub puffed her lip and looked at him quizzically. "Damn, don't you wish you could read?" He laughed and shook her head, flopping her ears. Carefully folding the tissue with the seed, he placed it inside an envelope and then between the pages of the book.

He went into the library and asked at the front desk to use a computer. The young, overweight woman behind the counter continued stamping books. "You have to sign your name on the list for a reservation."

Tom missed the direction of her nod. "Excuse me; I don't see the reservation list."

She sighed without looking up and waved with her hand. "Oh, thank you," he said. Tom looked at the reservation list, turned it two pages forward to the correct date, and signed on the blank page for the time between 2 and 3 PM. It was already two o'clock. "These over here?" he nodded toward three computers against the wall.

"Those are for kids, so I can keep an eye on what sites they go to." She gave another vague nod. "In there."

Tom found an alcove with three out-dated computers, sat down, and logged on.

Over his back he heard, "You signed for computer one. That's computer three."

The site was loading slowly. Tom walked back to the desk, drew a line through his name, and wrote it two lines lower opposite number 3. He raised his eyebrows and tilted his head at her in a parody of one of Scrub's puzzled looks. She glowered at him, "You make a mess of my book, you can go somewhere else next time."

He returned to the computer and checked his "tkreug824" e-mail. His sister said she had told that dumb boss of his that she had disowned Tom as a brother, and if he called her back once more, he'd better hire a lawyer. She told the woman claiming to be a cop to come visit Florida with a search warrant, only be prepared to pull it from her ass when she wanted to show it to the judge. Tom mailed her back to assure her that she had done exactly right, and that he loved her and was proud of her for telling them off.

Without replying, Tom deleted a note from Vince asking him to call the office. The two notes from Mary Twil were angrier and less fretful than Vince's note. "Yes," the 3HUGGR plate had been Skinner's. "No," she would not pay a lab to identify the seed material, and most definitely, if anybody took tissue samples from dead cows, that was a job suitable for Tom. The second note simply stated there were no abnormal food items in Skinner's stomach, nor any identifiable toxins in his blood.

Tom set up a new e-mail account and forwarded Mary's notes to that address. He promised he would try to call her at home in the late evening or early morning within the next few days, but he would break off communication if she did not keep his new e-mail address away from Vince.

"Find out if the whittled splinter in Skinner's back was a small piece of oak, not chokecherry," he told her. "The type of wood can be identified by a wood technology expert, possibly somebody working for the Forest Service. All they need is a thin cross-section of the wood under a microscope and a comparative photograph of the grain. It matters because oak is an open-grained wood capable of absorbing and releasing liquids. In Skinner's case, you might think toxic liquid."

He continued, "Yes, I understand they didn't find an identifiable toxin, so try this. Let's guess the splinter was shaped like a very small arrowhead. If that is right, then check the body tissue around it for an 'irritant resin' made from crushed iris roots, specifically *Iris missouriensis*, common wild iris. Possibly the Indians used it to poison their arrows. Symptoms include vomiting and bloody diarrhea, which would contribute to death by dehydration. As I remember, there was no toilet paper in Skinner's pack, but there was a trowel. Odds are, he ran out of toilet paper along the way."

Realizing he was coming across as too involved, he added, "However, since I am not working on that case, I don't care. Research on the peyote cult is going well, but progress is likely to be slow. The cult members are suspicious and reluctant to trust outsiders. It could be they also experiment with jimsonweed, which has a potentially deadly alkaloid toxin."

Another train of thought occurred to him. "As for your cattle death cases, something here reinforces the theory that the Joseph Canyon incident was caused by golden banner, *Thermopsis montanus*. If you want to solve that case, you should at least send those seeds to a lab for confirmation. Be sure to tell Vince what you think it is before you send it off. That way, word will get around about what a genius you are. In the evidence bag from Cow Creek, the seed mix had some pieces of evergreen shrub leaves. Instead of rhododendron, I now think it might be oleander. That's a shrub used for landscaping in Phoenix. The books say it is poisonous to livestock. Hold off testing that material. I may know where to find some samples for comparison."

He concluded the long note, "Last thing, please call a poison control office and ask what the lethal dose might be for ricin in livestock. How would you identify the symptoms? Unfortunately the literature assumes cows only eat things that grow out there naturally. Also ask how much ricin is in castor bean leaves as well as the seeds. See if they know if a cow will eat the leaves without concealing the flavor with something like molasses."

Before logging off, Tom checked his "Leptodactylon" account. Randy had sent an electronic file, which was a veterinarian autopsy report. Tom studied the part about stomach contents carefully. He replied, "The cattle autopsy sounds like our boy's work, although it has a bizarre twist. It could be monofluoroacetate. Ask your friend to go look closely for any spillage of yellow-colored grain at that site. Best bet is a hard, flat surface, like rock, near a water source. The color is from a dye that was probably not visible in the stomach remains. I think I've seen some whole oats or wheat stored in a jar that looked like that lately. Warn him not to touch or eat it if he finds any."

"It's hard to believe this is only Thursday," he continued typing. "I expect to go look a little more closely at some plant materials this weekend. If you don't get another message from me by late Monday, tell Mary Twil I'm in the Rincon area of the Mountain Ute Reservation or north between the canyons up to Dove Creek. You never know, I might be in trouble. At that point, a helpful law enforcement contact would be Rita Cooper, out of the Durango office of Colorado Division of Wildlife. She at least knows the country."

Tom waved at the librarian on his way out. "Thanks. Sorry if I messed up your record book. I'll do better next time, now that I know the system."

She glared at him without speaking. Tom felt her eyes piercing his back as he went out the door.

Tom stopped at a Safeway to stock up on groceries. Near the door, he found a pay phone and called Rita. As expected, he got her answering machine. "Rita, this is Tom. I wanted to say thanks for coming out to hike. I had a great time. Maybe we can do this again next year, although we might want to go somewhere else." He paused and considered what else to say. The answering machine interpreted the silence as the end of the message, beeped at him, and hung up. "Shit. I hate answering machines!"

He inserted another dollar of change and tried again. This time he spoke without pause. "Rita, Tom again. I'm going to get samples from Joshua to compare with what I found in Oregon. It looks like he's collecting poisonous seeds. A neighbor saw him at the locoweed site with a paper sack. I think the manioc is actually castor bean, which is really deadly. He also has a target deer behind the barn, and there might be some bird-point arrowheads buried in it. I think he poisoned those, too." Remembering the message to Randy, he said, "If someone calls after Monday to track me down, please call back quickly." The phone beeped and disconnected. "Oh hell!"

He opened the back of the truck and pushed Scrub out of the way so he could load the groceries into the cooler and an old plastic milk-crate. "You would think I could have come up with something original. Next year! How the hell can you compete with time and distance? She's going to think I'm an idiot." Scrub was unsympathetic. "Get your nose out of there. You open that box of crackers, and you may find yourself herding sheep on the Ute Reservation. IF anybody would have you."

A sign caught his eye on the way driving through town. Tom wheeled around the block and parked in the shade of a building. Scrub immediately started barking to be let out again. He could still hear her barking when he went inside the store half a block away.

"Can I help you?" The salesman was dressed in a suit, but looked like he was still in middle school.

Tom considered asking for the boy's dad, but he realized it was his own problem. "I'd like to get a cell-phone." At least the phone would solve his problem of contacting Mary Twil if he needed help, he thought.

"What kind of service option do you want?"

"Uh, I guess I don't know. Actually I live in Oregon, so I need something that will work from there, but I want to be able to call while I'm here on vacation."

The boy smiled patiently. "We're a national service, so our phones will work anywhere. We can set you up with regional roaming access, one rate for all calls in eight states."

"Yeah, that sounds fine. Will that work for Utah and New Mexico, too?" Tom thought this was going to be easy. He relaxed.

"Well, if you want it to work for Oregon, you get Washington, Idaho, Montana, Wyoming, Colorado, Utah, and Nevada, but not

California, Arizona, or New Mexico." He saw Tom's confusion. "I mean you can still call from those states, but it's a higher rate."

"Oh, I guess that's OK. I won't be spending that much time there anyway. How much?" Tom started looking at the array of "free" candy colored plastic phones.

"We have a great deal on extended anytime minutes, fourteen hundred minutes for only fifty-nine dollars a month, one year minimum contract." The clerk handed Tom a pen.

"You mean calling somebody for...." Tom did some rough math. "That's over twenty hours! Who in the hell spends twenty hours on the phone in a year, let alone a month?"

"You don't have to use them all," said the clerk peevishly, sensing a low rate sale.

"How about something with six hours or less?" Tom resented spending money on a frivolous luxury, even an insurance policy.

The clerk sighed, "We have a three hundred minute plan for $39.95. Are you going to use the phone? We find that once people find out how convenient it is, they always run over their limit. I wouldn't advise anyone to get less than five hundred minutes. It's only an extra seven dollars."

"I'd have to call a friend while I was in the bathroom and discuss bowel movements. That could be interesting." Tom observed the clerk blanch. "But kind of sick, don't you think? Really, I'd rather not use the phone unless I have to. I only want it in case of an emergency."

The clerk nodded and looked a bit dazed. "Um, we do have a contract for emergency service only. You have to buy the phone, and then you can use it if you break down on the road or something. The per-minute rates are high, but you only pay if you use it. Sometimes people buy those for their wife or kids."

Tom smiled to ease his pain. "That's more my style. Randy says I act like an old lady most of the time anyway."

The clerk got out another form. "It's ninety-nine dollars for the phone and $49.95 for a one year contract." He saw Tom's mouth set. "No monthly fees. The phone is yours. If you want to renew the contract in a year, it costs another $49.95."

Tom grunted, "All right. It's probably a necessary evil right now." He pulled out his checkbook.

The clerk tried to look over Tom's hand at the check. "Um, did you say you live out of town?"

"Yeah, up in Oregon."

"Do you have a credit card instead?"

"No, I'm a conscientious objector. A check won't work? I do have a driver's license." Tom raised his eyebrows. "Safeway took my check."

The clerk sighed, "The grocery stores do that. We'd have to wait for the bank to clear the check." The clerk was not apologetic. "If you'd like to come back to pick up the phone in a few days. Or, if you have cash...."

Tom mentally counted the cash in his wallet, deducting the likely cost of gas and thinking it would cost four bucks to use an ATM. "Well, thanks anyway. I probably won't need it." He walked to the door, turning to look at the clerk. "There is a price for idealism."

Before pulling back on the road, Tom opened the sliding window and adjusted a fan vent to blow on Scrub's face. "Thank God we're not too old-fashioned for air-conditioning, eh? How come every time I talk about ideals people look at me like I'm stupid? You don't have a credit card, Scrub, and you're smarter than most humans. Damn it, if I didn't have to pay bills through the mail, I wouldn't have a checkbook either." Tom stopped at a gas station to top off the tank, then headed south toward Shiprock. About 15 miles past Towaoc, he turned west, and later, north on Route 41 to a series of gravel roads and dirt tracks leading through the Mountain Ute Reservation back toward McElmo Canyon.

Tom stopped twice to consult his map to find the old trail he wanted. Without lights, he pitched camp under a juniper and ate a cold supper of crackers and Brie. The wine was pleasantly smooth. Afterwards he sat in the lawn chair with his sleeping bag wrapped around him to ward off the chill. The stars filled the clear sky, fading only slightly when the thin slice of moon rose over the horizon.

Chapter 13

Randy Bergen was unusually quiet and thoughtful at Barney's Pub on Thursday evening. He sat at the bar, well away from the stage where Jesse Jackson was setting up drums for a late show. Jesse observed Randy smoking, a sign that he was in a bad mood. Jesse had also seen Randy withdraw from conversation with Bill Christen rather abruptly. Jesse decided to snoop a little and wandered over to the shuffleboard game. "How's it going, Bill?"

"Couldn't be better. I'm winning at shuffleboard, the Mets beat the Braves last night, and if Cleveland beats 'em tomorrow, I'm gonna be twenty bucks richer." Bill hooted, "Look at that! My partner is unbeatable! I could go home right now, and we'd still win."

"How come Randy isn't over here giving you some competition?" Jesse nodded toward the end of the bar.

"Ah, who knows what his problem is? I think he's missing his asshole buddy." Bill took his position, decided to do the "moonwalk," then slapped a shot without aiming. It slid clear of the scoring lane. "Oh well, I told you, I could get nothing and we'd still win." Jesse was already halfway across the bar.

"Hey, Randy, I thought you gave up smoking."

"Yeah, mostly, anyway." Randy stubbed out his second of the night. "You gonna be loud again tonight? I got a headache."

"Drums are made to be loud," Jesse grinned and raised his hands. "That's why I started playing, to drive my old man crazy." He looked at Randy staring into the ashtray. "What's Tom up to? He didn't come in for beer and grease night."

Randy threw him a disbelieving look. "You know he left town last week."

"Oh, of course. But I thought you might have some idea what he's doing, why he's not back yet." It was hard to speak in a conspiratorial voice that could be heard above the din.

"Well shit, Reverend, join the crowd. Every asshole in the BLM thinks so, and Mary Twil was breathing down my neck this afternoon like I was covering up for him." Randy groaned. "She's threatening to tell the sheriff I'm obstructing justice."

Jesse laughed. "And you are, aren't you?"

"I don't know diddly." Randy lit another cigarette. "All I know is that fool is somewhere playing detective and sending back enough information to get Mary into a lather."

"So, he knows something about the killing? Or the cattle-killing, or both?" Jesse watched Randy's eyes and whistled. "Oh, dear. Does he need an alibi? I mean for the cows? I don't think he would have...." He saw Randy's impatience and broke off.

"He thinks he knows how they did it, the cows. He's hiding out, having fun. That's all I know." Randy was fuming.

"So why worry? Did you leave some tracks they can trace back to you?" Jesse paused. "You must be helping him. Tom wouldn't risk contacting you otherwise if he wanted to stay out of sight."

"He's got me doing his damn research, finding more poisoned cows. I was looking at my e-mail when Alice came in. She might have seen a message from Tom before I deleted it. If she saw enough, she might figure it out." Randy explained, "They only back up our computers later in the evening. The rules say we can't delete anything until after they notify us the back up is done. The system in Portland might have a record of transmitting the message."

"How long before they tap your phone?"

"It ain't my goddamn phone I'm worried about."

"Then watch out, because they can record everything you do on your computer."

"You think I don't know that? I think the timing worked out pretty good because Tom probably got all the goddamn information he needs before they wised up, so he may not contact me again." Randy thought about that. "But if Alice talks, then I'm still gonna have a shit-load of trouble."

"You know where he's at?"

"I checked a map. Somewhere within a couple hundred square miles. Maybe. Maybe for a couple of days," Randy snorted. "He ain't even going to look at the places I found for him. He's a hundred miles from the nearest one. I don't know what the hell he's doing."

"Do they want him bad enough to do a manhunt?"

"What do they call them now? A person of interest, that's what he is, yes, a person of interest. They've got the questions, and he has the answers. Only he's not ready to give them everything they want yet."

"You could be out of it, Randy. You could tell them what you know and walk away. If they want him bad enough, they can go look for him."

"Yeah, only I'm from West Texas, Reverend. I believe in loyalty. There's a price to be paid for idealism." He left his new pack of cigarettes on the bar and walked out.

Chapter 14

Tom woke from a dream of being hog-tied in a dark room. He readjusted the head of the mummy bag and found Scrub stretched across his legs for warmth. She looked at him accusingly. "You're a dog. That's why you have a fur coat. Would you mind getting off my legs?" He raised his knees, forcing her up. There was barely enough light to walk without running into branches. Although his camp was not visible to any habitation, he decided not to light the stove for coffee. There was a thin layer of ice in his canteen.

In the duffel behind the seat he found wool gloves. He loaded the spotting scope into his pack and added food and canteens. He snapped on Scrub's leash and led her north to a vantage point on the rim. Scrub objected to being tied to a cliffrose until Tom told her to lie down. He crawled to the rim a few feet away. He carefully made sure the morning sun would not strike the lens of the spotting scope.

Half an hour later, he saw a wisp of smoke from Joshua's stovepipe. "Not much smoke. Either he's burning a few scraps or he has a pellet stove. I don't think he has the time or interest to gather firewood." Tom rolled onto his other side to give his aching hip respite from the cold sandstone.

An hour later, the temperature had risen with the morning sun. He peeled off his wool gloves and fleece jacket and put them in his pack. Tom saw Joshua emerge from the house to collect a utility cart from the barn and push it into the garden area. He pulled out the dried, bleached stalks from the edge of the irrigation ditch and carried them in bundles to a trash pile. Next he efficiently chopped down the "manioc" with a brush-hook machete and carefully took what Tom presumed to be seeds from the tops and placed them in a small box. Joshua then chopped the stalks into short lengths and piled them with the dried waste at the back of the garden.

"I guess that answers the question about whether or not the leaves are poisonous enough. He didn't bother to save them." Tom ate a snack and finished his first canteen of water. Casually glancing through binoculars, he saw that Joshua was busily raking and gathering dried stalks from the flowerbeds. "Hard worker, old Josh. Doesn't drink enough water though." Tom poured water into a plastic bag that he held for Scrub. "Bet he has kidney stones before he's forty."

A plume of smoke drew Tom back to the rim. He saw Joshua had set the waste pile on fire. "There goes the conspicuous evidence. Those tall stalks on the ditch were poison hemlock. Not the one with the real serious root, but still poisonous if you get enough. Bet we could find a few seeds on the ditch bank." Tom looked to see if Scrub was paying attention. "He didn't dig up the manioc roots either. Kind of dumb if you intend to use them for food. I'll bet a chemist could find some ricin in those roots." Scrub was bored. She rolled onto her side and exhaled heavily.

Tom munched a bagel as he watched Joshua continue to work through the early afternoon. "He must have eaten a big breakfast." The garden was looking much neater, as Joshua worked between the beds and tended the smoking fire. Joshua then wheeled the cart into the barn and disappeared. "Nobody is going to complain about the flowers he has left either. Who would ever suspect a bed of iris?"

Tom left the rim for no more than three minutes. He fed Scrub and gave her more water. There was no more visible activity until nearly 5 P.M. When a shadow alerted Tom to smoke emerging from the vent on the roof, he picked up the scope. "OK, he's cooking something. There was no wood stove in the barn." Scrub raised her head and sniffed. Finding nothing of interest in the air, she lowered her head again.

As soft breeze stirred, signaling the cold night yet to come, darkness crept around them and the ground cooled. Tom saw a light appear, flooding the ground on the opposite side of the barn. Then the light went out. Another appeared as Joshua entered the house. Tom watched Joshua move about the kitchen, then settle in front of the television with a can of beer and a tray of food. "Why don't we call it a day, Scrub?" He removed her leash. She stayed close at his heels.

Again, he ate a cold meal of bread, cheese, and raw vegetables dipped in salsa and polished off the bottle of wine. He set up the tent and placed a foil-faced "Space Blanket" on the floor for Scrub. "These fifty degree temperature swings at night are hell on old bones, aren't they?" he said to Scrub. "The sad thing is you're already older than me, and I feel old as dirt. Well, with luck, he'll go into town tomorrow or Sunday. Otherwise, I might have to go down there in the dark. I do not want to do that, but we need to get this finished soon before he thinks about moving the rest of the evidence." Scrub lay down heavily, grunting her assent. She watched him zip the tent and carry his sleeping bag a short distance under the trees. He spoke softly to reassure her when the coyotes howled later. He wore a wool cap that allowed him to leave his head outside the sleeping bag and his hearing unobstructed. Neither one of them slept more than a few minutes at a time.

Saturday morning, still in the dark, Tom loaded water into the solar shower bag and propped it on the hood of the truck to gather sunlight. He ate cold granola with colder milk and looked longingly at the coffeepot. Before leaving, he packed the tent and tied Scrub to a branch with a bucket of water and two-day ration of food within reach.

He packed food and water supplies, but he left the telescope behind. After gently calling to Scrub to stay and be quiet, he set off. She whined and barked softly a couple of times, but she settled down before he had gone far. Before the sun rose over the eastern horizon he was at the north rim, where he noted approvingly that Joshua was already active inside the house. He looked at his watch. "Better get up a little earlier tomorrow." He shivered in the breeze. The sun's meager orange rays quickly submerged in gray scudding clouds.

This time Tom spread a foam pad for insulation. He arranged his pack and a water bottle within reach, then settled to watch through binoculars. At 7:30 A.M., Joshua entered the barn. Soon Tom saw heat waves distorting air currents over the exhaust vent. The air warmed enough for Tom to take off his jacket and stuff it in his pack. At 11:30 Joshua emerged, carrying two large rectangular cans to the other side of the house, out of sight. Joshua reappeared on a bicycle with pannier bags and turned east out of the driveway.

"Hot damn! Saturday is shopping day. I'd rather be lucky than smart any day." Tom spoke, forgetting that Scrub was not present to hear. "A bike is slower than a truck, even if you look like Nietzsche's superman." He watched Joshua pedal out of sight toward Cortez. He rolled the foam pad and tied it to his pack. To stay out of sight of the road, he descended into a canyon from the east rim. He followed the dry wash out into the channel of McElmo Creek, intermittently wading and walking on dry mud back toward Joshua's property. The detour took time, and he realized that Joshua's house and barn were out of his sight as well. There was no way to be certain the place would be unoccupied when he got there.

He climbed a deer trail up the steep gully side, cautiously peering over the edge a short distance from Joshua's fence line. He could see Joshua's old Chevy in the driveway, but no bike or other vehicle. A car passed going west on the road. "Greasewood doesn't make very good cover," he reminded himself. Then he ran hunched between the brush, crossing over onto Joshua's land where the fence gave way to the eroding gully bank. He crept to the edge of the open garden, then dashed across to the barn. The back door was locked from the inside. "This is not entirely surprising," he muttered.

Momentarily delayed, Tom went over and ran his fingers over the surface of the target deer. Its body was designed with a replaceable fiber core. From the tight grouping of puncture marks, Tom deduced that Joshua was a good shot, but for some reason he preferred to shoot his prey behind the rib cage. Prying the core out and probing with his knife, Tom was unable to find an imbedded arrowhead. He examined the rear flank, and as he probed from inside the cavity, he found something inconsistently hard. He carefully cut to retrieve a small wooden point. To his satisfaction it was meticulously carved, complete with backward pointing barbs. He reinserted the body core.

Tom presumed the barn's front door was also locked, so he followed Scrub's example and pried loose a section of the foundation skirting. Suddenly he heard a clattering noise that alerted him to someone nearby. "Oh shit!" He wriggled through the opening into the crawl space. He then reached back and smoothed the dirt and pulled the skirting tight. He peered out through the crack but saw nothing. Tom checked his watch for the first time since descending the canyon rim. He had been too slow and cautious, but there was no way Joshua could have made it all the way to Cortez and back.

He heard a bump and steps that indicated that someone had entered the front door and was crossing the room. Then a hollow thud that sounded like something dropped on the floor or table. More thumping and clattering came from the end of the room. Tom crawled close enough to hear a thin "shssh-clack, shssh-clack" noise, then more footsteps followed by the distinct click of a deadbolt in the door. As steps crunched away across the driveway, Tom crawled to a crack, where he saw Joshua mount his bike and head out, this time turning west. "Stay away a little longer this time, Asshole. Nearly gave me a heart attack."

Tom crawled toward the duct under the dehydrator and waited for his eyes to adjust to the total darkness. A sudden thump and scratching noise set his heart racing. The skirting pulled back from his entryway causing daylight to spill inward. A dark form, momentarily blocking the light, leapt in with a scrabbling noise. Tom pointed his knife outward as the dark form rushed toward and past him, stinking of mud. It collided hard with the coiled fabric duct from the solar heating panels, spilling in more light as it leapt through the floorboards. "Why do I keep this dog?" Tom followed, pushing his pack through the opening before squeezing his shoulders to get through. "Stop! For God's sake, stop!"

He pulled Scrub from the clattering pile of cans and forced her to lie down. When she complied, he stood, listening carefully. "Stay! Don't move." After peeking out the window, he began inspecting. The oven was still warm. Baking pans were piled in a utility sink.

Scrub whined and crawled toward the pile of cans again. "No! You stay, dammit." Tom saw a spatula lying in the sink. He picked it up and held one of the pans. When he scraped the spatula on the surface of the pan, he produced a reasonable imitation of the "shssh" noise. When he tapped its edge on the pan, it produced a poor gong tone. He looked around. "The pannier cans, eh?" He then tapped the spatula against the can, approving the sound. Inside the can was a plastic bag filled with cookies. Using Joshua's rubber gloves, he placed a single cookie into a spare plastic bag from his own pack, then resealed the can.

Scrub made quiet, muttering noises and inched forward again. "Would you lay off the goddamn mice?" He pulled her back and inspected the cans himself. The faded labeling indicated ancient army surplus. The floor was surprisingly clean, with no nest debris or droppings to indicate a packrat or mouse had been there. Tom watched his whining dog, whose gaze was riveted at the nearest can. He picked up the rectangular can and held the label to the light while Scrub sat quietly, drooling on the floor. "OK, so you get the credit for finding his molasses. I'm not going to tell anybody you read the label, though." Tom assessed the cans after stacking them back in order. "Looks like he buys his molasses in bulk, doesn't it?" He set the last can down. "Molasses cookies."

He rapidly put small samples from various containers into a series of small envelopes. Since most of Joshua's containers were unlabeled, Tom wrote notes on each envelope, inventing a system to relocate the source for each sample. He tried very hard to maintain the order of jars and cans on the shelves and to leave cabinet doors as he found them.

He used Joshua's stepladder to climb up and open one of the string bags in the rafters to take out a lump of root he recognized as water hemlock. When Tom climbed down, he held it out to show Scrub. The root went into a paper bag, then inside a plastic bag. He also wrapped the seed envelopes in plastic and stuffed them all into his pack. He replaced Joshua's rubber gloves on the utility sink. Then he took a series of photographs around the barn, the darkness causing the flash to trigger each time.

Tom selected a piece of oak from a box next to the lathe. They were all about a foot long and half an inch thick and wide. He examined the lathe for a moment, then the carving bench. The floor was clean, but the shop vacuum was mostly full of wood shavings. Tom checked the tool drawers and found an assortment of expensive hand tools made for precision work. "Nothing but the best for our boy. That garage sale lathe was made in Germany. Cost about four thousand bucks."

The back door was fastened with a deadbolt, same as the front. He looked out the window again. "All right. Let's go out the way we came." Scrub dashed between his legs and down the hole. Tom eased through, tucking the fabric pipe straight from the bottom of the dehydrator and checking to make sure the edges all fit within the hole. He attempted to refasten the heating duct from below. He gave up when it fell the third time. "Screw it. Let's get the hell out of here." Again, he brushed the scuffmarks from the soil around the skirting and pushed the loose nails back with the butt of his pocketknife.

Tom unclipped the gnawed piece of rope from Scrub's collar and put it in his pack. Together they dashed across the garden and through the brush to the creek. Near the fence Tom cut a branch from a rabbitbrush, and swept their tracks back to the deer trail and down into the creek. Scrub was happy to stay in the water as she followed Tom.

Daylight was fading as Tom arrived back at camp. He removed Scrub's gnawed tether from the tree, emptied the bucket as soon as Scrub was done drinking, and packed the last of his camping gear into the truck. Scrub settled into the sand nearby to watch. Tom opened the tailgate.

"What do you say we get going now, and I give you some extra food later to make up for it? If Josh checks the barn, it won't take him long to figure out the dehydrator system got knocked down again. He might start looking for us. Load up."

Chapter 15

Joshua did not collect artifacts, but he found Indian lore and history useful. He thought about their communications and travel routes and their use of the land. In his explorations he had occasionally found cave shelters and granaries that the archeologists had apparently never discovered. Rather than dig for valuables, he concealed the sites, even planting grass and brush to screen them from view. At two perfectly preserved rock granaries, Joshua had found pottery filled with ancient dried corn. He concealed these sites because of their present usefulness as hiding places for himself and for his equipment rather than a sense of preservation.

Joshua left home Saturday morning and pedaled to Risley Canyon, hiding the bike and hiking to one of the granaries. The ancient corn had been buried elsewhere. Now the pots held Joshua's biscuits. The year before they had held part of his bulky seed collection. He took the new biscuits out of the plastic bags, calculating correctly that the pottery would breathe sufficiently to dry the biscuits without spoilage. It was a quick chore, and he carried the empty cans back to his bike.

With no plastic or other modern evidence, anyone uncovering the secret might presume he had found an ancient cookie jar. Joshua smiled, thinking a pot hunter might even sample the sweet-smelling goods, in which case he would probably die before getting far enough to tell what he had found. With luck Joshua would hear about it and cover up the evidence before the site was discovered a second time.

Joshua headed back on his bike, crossing the ridge and coasting down into Moccasin Canyon. A truck was coming north raising a huge cloud of dust. Joshua waited for the truck to pass.

Instead, Bill Remy pulled up and stopped beside the bike, rolling down his window. "You lookin' for arrowheads again?" he said with a grin.

"No, just gathering some late pinyon nuts and wolfberries." Joshua smiled back innocently, waiting to see what his lowbrow neighbor might have to offer.

"Find any?"

"A few. The squirrels got most of the good nuts this year." Joshua didn't offer to show what was in his pack.

"Competition's getting tough these days. Even the goddamned tourists are coming out here to hunt pots. Must've cleaned out the country up around Hovenweep."

Joshua knew Remy considered him an outsider, like any other immigrant within the last thirty years. He wished he could see Remy's grin turn sour after eating one of his biscuits. "Yeah, lots of tourists coming through these days."

"Saw a dumb bastard from Oregon climbing that same hill you picked over last spring," Remy pointed, "looking under every bush like he was hunting Easter eggs. Said he was hunting rocks."

"Oregon, huh?" Joshua's interest picked up. "That's a long way to come for rocks. You know the guy?"

"Naw. Climbs like a goddamn goat. Got a sunburnt neck like mine. Green truck. Talked like he'd been out in this country before. Showed me his goddamn rocks. No shit!" He guffawed. Remy took a pull from an open can of beer. "Showed me his goddamn rocks. Like I'm a dumb-ass to believe that."

Joshua wondered if Remy had seen Tom's truck in his driveway. "I think I met the guy. He said he used to live in Durango and come out here now and then. Name's Kreuger. Ring a bell?"

"Nope." Remy said. "You want to know about somebody in this country, talk to Castro Levy."

Joshua shrugged, "No reason."

Remy revved his truck and put it in reverse. "Not unless he's on your ass. Could be a fed looking for pot hunters." He wheeled around and sped down the canyon, leaving Joshua in a cloud of dust.

Joshua frowned and considered the possibilities. "Why the hell would he be up on that hill?" The coincidence bothered him. When he returned home, Joshua was in a hurry, taking time to clean up a little more evidence, but not bothering to check the computer that stored images from the security cameras expertly hidden around the premises. Nor did he look back as he left again, or he might have seen Scrub dashing through the garden, hot on Tom's scent.

Castro Levy, who happened to be stacking a fresh delivery of ice-cream sandwiches in the freezer when Joshua arrived on his bike, looked out the door toward the crunching gravel. "Ain't this a week for old acquaintances?" he muttered. Joshua pulled open the screen door. "Glory be. What brings you in, Freeborn?"

Joshua waved his hand. "Ran out of beer. Thought I'd work off a few calories riding down here so I could drink a little more tonight." He headed for the coolers, sensing Castro's suppressed hostility. He presumed some part of the drug rumors reaching the cops originated from Castro. Picking out a couple twelve-packs, he set them on the counter. "You don't mind taking my money, do you?"

"Just so long as the damn government takes it back without a fuss." Castro decided he wasn't going to carry on a useless grudge.

"Guess it's been a while since I've stopped in. Not very neighborly."

"Four years, more or less. Twenty bucks, the Governor's cut is figured in." Castro did not believe people changed habits without purpose. He waited to discover Joshua's real motive for coming to the store.

Joshua made a show of digging through his pockets. "Saw an old friend of yours yesterday. Well, at least he said he used to work around here, so you probably knew him. Fellow by the name of Tom Kreuger, worked for the BLM."

"Couldn't be no friend of mine then."

"Said he used to be a wildlife biologist here. Said he was collecting rocks, though maybe it was pots and arrowheads." Joshua persisted. "You know anything about him?"

"I recollect the name. Met him once when he was new. Talked to me about getting a public easement through my place. Came back a few years later and said he hoped I'd never do that. Ran his ass out both times. Where'd you see him?"

Joshua knew Castro rarely left the store, so he guessed there was little chance he had observed Tom's visit. "He was climbing around Moccasin Canyon, not too far east of here. Bill Remy saw him there too, thought he was collecting artifacts."

Castro shrugged, wondering why Tom was wasting time when he damn well knew Jake McPherson was over in Cross Canyon, a good ways north. "Could be, I suppose." Then, thinking he might keep Joshua from drawing attention where it wasn't needed, he said, "Seemed like a do-gooder to me. Kind of simple-minded too. Probably if he told you he was collecting rock, that's just about it."

"Maybe." Joshua gave Castro a knowing look. "I checked him out with the BLM office. They thought he was a closet environmentalist. One of them even said he thought the guy had sabotaged an oil well up near McLean Basin. Said Kreuger might have wrecked a drill rig when they tried to reopen the well. Ever hear anything about that?"

Castro figured if Joshua was so interested, then Tom must have been snooping in Joshua's business. "Somebody was blowing smoke. I don't know why that old well went dry, but only one drill rig ever went bust out here. The biggest bunch of drunkards and screw-ups you've ever seen ran it. They didn't need any help to wreck their rig. Did it twice. Stuck a whole lot of drill stem down in that rock."

Joshua thought if the crew had been a bunch of misfits, that would have made it easier to sabotage the rig. "Well, he didn't seem simple-minded to me, more like he was pretty smart. I couldn't figure out why he would be there unless he was spying on Bill Remy. Maybe he was too smart. Struck me as a liar."

"Struck me as an educated fool," Castro parried. "Knew every kind of lizard and bird and plant there was. Didn't get along with people that well. He's probably retired by now. Got nothing better to do than come back and pick up rocks."

"Retired? He seemed way too young for that." Joshua was puzzled. "I guess he was sun-dried, but not that old."

Castro realized he had said too much. "Government folks can retire after thirty years. Depends on how much military time he had. I met him about twenty years ago." He shrugged as he closed the cash register. "Couldn't really tell how old he was then either 'cept he was a whole lot younger than me."

"You've got a good memory," Joshua looked hard at Castro. He carried his beer out to the bike and loaded a twelve-pack into each side of the panniers. He pedaled slowly homeward, concentrating inward and barely watching the road. Half a mile from home, he shook his head and picked up the pace. "So he knows plants. He saw the garden. What else?"

He rode to his back deck. He carried the beer up, set the packages on the table, and stood looking out over the garden where the waste pile was still smoldering. "It was mostly dried out and dead, not much recognizable." He drank a lukewarm beer, then carried another to the barn. He unlocked the door and stood looking around the dark interior. "Looks innocent enough. Just a kitchen for canning and drying produce from a big garden." He looked up at the bundles of drying roots. "I could hang those in the granary, maybe do a lot of processing tomorrow and take the rest of the seeds." Joshua felt glum and uncertain. He checked the back door, finding it undisturbed. "Shit. Maybe I ought to work late. Get it all out of here by morning."

He turned on the lights and closed the door. Crossing to the sink, he picked up the baking pans and laid them on the worktable. He retrieved a huge mixing bowl from the sink and carried it to the pantry shelves. In addition to gluten and flour, he loaded a selection of jars of dried seeds into it. As he stooped for a can of molasses, he felt something crunch on the floor under his foot.

Fastidious by nature, Joshua moved his foot to pick up the debris, but he found a clump of dry mud rather than the crumbs he had expected. Looking at an angle, he could see a smear of mud with a partial paw print. "That goddamn dog." He got a broom, dustpan, and a sponge, and bent low to clean the floor thoroughly. He rehung the broom and dustpan on their wall hooks.

When he checked the dehydrator, he found the fresh material had not dried. The digital thermometer showed the peak heat had occurred at 2:10 P.M. It was hardly above room temperature now. When he put his hand over the vent in the bottom, he felt little airflow. "Crap!" He lifted the duct from the floor and, as expected, found the duct from the solar panels had fallen again. "I hate dogs." As he stood, he banged his head on the edge of the dehydrator stand and cursed again. He brushed the dust of dried mud from his knees. "I'll kill his goddamn dog if I ever get a chance."

He went and got the sponge again, then stood at the sink and looked back. He could feel his pulse rising. "I fastened that damn thing yesterday, and I didn't have to brush off my knees." He examined every object in the barn carefully, seeing nothing out of place and nothing missing. "I would have noticed that mud yesterday," he said to himself.

He went quickly to the house, where he entered a series of three passwords into his computer. "I should have asked Charles to look up Tom's name to see if he still worked for the government." He logged on to the Internet and did a quick search that turned up a match for Thomas Kreuger, Department of Interior employee, presently working in Baker City, Oregon.

Joshua felt his spirits sinking, as he fast-framed in reverse through the five-second-interval security camera images for Saturday. Dismay turned to cold anger when he saw Tom and Scrub leaving through the garden. "Moves pretty fast for a goddamn retiree." After he noted the time signature on the image, he shut down the computer. In the hallway he palmed a wall panel that released a hidden catch. Joshua opened a padded sling pack and checked the semi-automatic rifle to see that it had a round in the chamber. Then he slung the pack with the rifle in it over his shoulder. Quickly, he was out the door at a full run.

From the photos, Joshua saw that Tom was headed toward the southeast corner of his property, but he ran to the wash bluff near the west fence line where he started watching for tracks and loose dirt at the wash bottom as he headed east. When he found no sign, he turned north along his east fence line and moments later arrived back at the back edge of the garden. Baffled, he looked back to the south. "Son-of-a-bitch swept his tracks." Joshua leapt over the fence and resumed his search along the wash bank.

He spotted the deer trail down into the wash and recognized clods of dirt dislodged on the wash floor below, but he saw no tracks. "If a deer or cow had knocked that dirt loose, Tommy, there would have been tracks." Joshua resumed running along the bank, watching for telltale signs of Tom's exit. He saw spots where either Tom or the wallowing dog had splashed water along the way. He nearly missed the branch of rabbitbrush with its broken end concealed, jammed into the bank. Joshua smiled appreciatively, "Nice touch, Tommy. It almost looks real."

At the mouth of the side canyon Joshua dropped down into the wash. He found smears of fresh mud on the otherwise dry rocks. A little farther he found clear tracks in the sand headed up the slope. Joshua knew the primitive roads on the mesas intersected near the head of the drainage. From there it either went northeast back toward a crossing at McElmo Creek, or south into the interior of the Mountain Ute Reservation. Joshua removed the rifle from the sling pack and ran straight for the intersection, easily maintaining a strong, pumping jog uphill.

Joshua heard the vehicle engine echoing off the canyon rim. He was less than half a mile from the road intersection and, despite the fact that he was wearing boots, covered the distance in three minutes. He arrived in time to see the settling dust disappear into the juniper to the south. He heard the truck accelerate over the next ridge and caught a glimpse of a taillight through a break in the trees.

If Tom had turned north, Joshua would have had a clear shot at him over open ground, with Tom exposed on the near side of the truck. Joshua knew the juniper that blocked his line of fire extended south for another mile, but he decided to follow to the top of the next ridge anyway. He saw lights glowing through the stunted trees in the distance. Finally, the engine noise subsided. In the gathering darkness Joshua started walking back home across the mesa, knowing he could drop directly from the rim down toward his yard. The darkness did not hinder or bother him.

He was plotting his next moves, planning a sleepless night moving evidence out to his second secret granary a few miles across the state line. He did not know how much time he would have, possibly as little as an hour, but likely more. He judged correctly that Tom was retreating either to evaluate what he had found, or to reach a location where he could contact the law. The sound of a vehicle interrupted this reverie.

From the south rim of the mesa he saw a truck bouncing on the rough primitive trail through the valley below. From the configuration of the lights Joshua concluded it was a small pickup, probably Tom's Ford. "He's headed to the creek crossing, back to Levy's!"

Castro had spied on him and had probably tipped the cops about drugs. Joshua figured there was no reason for Tom to come snooping unless someone had tipped him that there was something suspicious going on. Castro had contacts with the Navajo, who had their own suspicions. Maybe Castro had put two and two together and called in an unofficial investigator, someone who knew all about plants.

By an awful coincidence it turned out to be someone from BLM in eastern Oregon. It was unlikely, but somebody there might have figured out the unorthodox cattle poisonings. If Tom got back with what he had seen, other people might start asking questions. "Levy was covering for him, trying to mislead me. They're in this together." Joshua had already made a decision to kill Tom and hide his body. Now he decided he was at war with other conspirators as well.

Joshua raced across the top of the mesa, landing only on the balls of his feet to avoid tripping in the darkness. He picked his way more carefully down the slope to the wash, lowering himself by his hands from the twenty-foot embankment before dropping into the creek. He scrambled up the opposite side. A red fox froze under a low bush, watching Joshua streak by before silently skulking away.

Chapter 16

Tom engaged the four-wheel drive to cross the creek, prompted by the memory of spending hours digging out a co-worker's macho Jeep pickup from the same muddy crossing years before. After making it to the north side without difficulty, he got out to unlock the hubs. Before heading into Utah, he decided to risk imposing on Castro Levy's good will.

At Levy's store he let Scrub out and removed two five-gallon jugs and his pack from the truck. He knocked on the screen door to announce himself to the invisible owner in the back living quarters. "Mr. Levy," said Tom loudly, "would it be possible to get some water to refill my camp supply?"

"There's a short hose on a bib off the side of the porch." Levy appeared, pulling his suspenders up.

"Thanks." Tom carried his jugs over to the side and filled a canteen from the pack first. Levy followed and stood on the edge of the porch to watch. Tom decided it might be polite to make small talk. "It might take me a couple more days to get home. Thought I'd need some water tomorrow, especially if I want to use my shower."

"You figure Joshua Freeborn and Jake are digging ruins together?"

"Uh, no." Tom hesitated. "I guess I wasn't thinking about that. Are they?"

"If they ain't, then why the hell are you messing around with Freeborn? I told you his kind don't like to be messed with, and you got him about two shades of pissed-off." Levy sounded disgusted.

"What makes you think he's pissed at me?" Tom thought this was too quick for Levy to have heard about his return trip to Joshua's barn.

"He knows you've been hanging out in Moccasin Canyon. Thinks maybe you've been spying on Bill Remy, maybe even spying on him." Levy smiled knowingly, but with his back to the light, his smile was wasted on Tom.

"Would Bill Remy happen to have a dark-colored truck and a bright red neck? Maybe he lives down near the mouth of Moccasin? Has a lot of big veins on his nose so it looks like he might drink a lot too?"

"That sounds about right."

"Um, I wanted to ask...when you said you noticed a lot of locoweed growing lately, were you talking about those clay slopes above Moccasin Canyon?"

"What the hell?" Levy was flabbergasted. "What in the hell is that about?"

"When Rita and I were here earlier, you said something about noticing a lot more loco than ever before. There's some growing on those white clay deposits." Tom thought carefully before daring to continue. "When you mentioned Joshua and the Navajo horses, it made me wonder if you thought he might be connected to the increase of locoweed. It could be it doesn't occur there naturally. Maybe someone is growing it intentionally."

"That's about the stupidest thing I've ever heard of," Levy exploded. "Nobody grows goddamn locoweed. You're wasting time looking at plants and collecting rocks, which is so stupid that nobody, not Bill Remy, and sure as hell not Joshua Freeborn is crazy enough to think that's what you're really doing, only it is!" Levy flapped his hands excitedly. "What the hell is Miss Rita doing hanging out with a fool like you?"

"Well, sorry," said Tom defensively, "I didn't think collecting a few rocks would cause any harm. I even showed Bill the rocks. Found a piece of petrified wood." Scrub came to see what all the shouting was about.

"The only harm was getting folks suspicious and asking questions," Levy said with bitter disgust. "It won't be long and Jake will know you're in the neighborhood looking for him again. You won't even catch wind of him."

"Really, I did not come here to look for Jake. From what you said, I'd just as soon avoid him." A truck pulled into the driveway. "I'd rather not risk getting shot at." As Tom finished his denial, Levy turned away.

Levy looked back over his shoulder, "And I ain't that goddamned dumb either." He spun and slammed into the wall. His hands grasped at the rough planking as he fell backwards.

Tom saw the flash from the pickup window at the same time he watched Levy fall. The pop of the rifle registered only after he had started forward into the light to help. "Oh, shit!" He dove off the porch and almost landed on Scrub. The bullet that hit the dirt between them sent a spray of dust into Tom's eyes. He rolled over and ran blindly away from the building. He squatted in the brush and put his hand on Scrub to hold her still.

Tom heard Levy's voice and a third shot, then silence. A shadow slipped around the porch, crouching in the darkness and examining the ground as though looking for blood. Tom kept holding Scrub's collar. Then he slipped it off and held the tags between his fingers to silence them. The shadowy figure passed through a shaft of light. The head was oddly bulky. The figure proceeded slowly, head down, out of the direct light, advancing along Tom's path. "Tracking!" Tom thought. "Night-vision goggles! He's tracking me in the dark." He threw the collar off to the side, where it jingled and reflected a little light from the tags.

Another shot rang out and the figure charged toward the empty collar. Tom dashed off in the opposite direction, keeping his torso low, followed by Scrub. The spines of the greasewood tore at Tom's face and arms, but he kept to the low ground where it was thickest, because the long slopes up to the ridgetops were too sparsely covered. He ran at full speed north toward familiar ground. He crossed Yellowjacket Creek and made his way through the thick tamarisk on its banks.

He passed through a jumble of boulders, but felt slight comfort from the barrier of rock at his back, that protected him from the bullets. He paused to catch his breath, knowing that Joshua would need to go slower to follow his tracks with the night-vision goggles. Focusing on the drainage above, Tom muttered, "On the other hand, we don't have much choice but to take some risks." Again he ran full speed up the sandy creek bottom with Scrub close behind until he reached a small patch of willow at a seep.

Listening, Tom could hear the echoing sound of footsteps approaching up the drainage. Joshua was moving faster than Tom had hoped. Tom figured Joshua would come up the bottom where the cover was thickest, yet he would keep an eye on the slopes in case Tom tried to break out of the canyon. Tom left the sandy wash, stepping on clumps of grass as he doubled back. He crouched in the brush and reached out for the dog. Feeling guilty, Tom whispered, "Scrub, there's a rabbit up there!" Scrub looked confused. "Rabbit! Up there." He pointed. "Go get it. There." The urgency of his whispering finally convinced her, and she ran off.

Tom waited a few seconds, then duck-walked behind the brush as quickly as he could toward Joshua. When the brush thinned, he lay in the sand only yards from the streambed, between clumps of alkali sacaton grass that were barely taller than his prostrate form.

Suddenly, Joshua loomed ten feet away, back lit by pale moonlight, with his rifle held at ready. He lifted the rifle slightly, took aim, and fired. Tom heard the bullet ricochet from the rocks on the canyon slopes. Tom saw Joshua run toward his dog. Tom realized he had been holding his breath. He lifted his head slightly and watched Joshua pass through the screen of willow sixty yards to the north. Another shot fired, and Tom could hear him curse and keep running.

Tom ran back south toward Levy's store in a crouch until he had once again passed through the boulders, then straightened and ran for all he was worth. He might have heard a faint confused bark, but his own ragged breathing and pounding heart drowned out all noise except the sound of the brush slashing at his body. As he sloshed back across the creek, he heard a splash at his back.

"Oh, Scrub! Sweet Jesus! Come on, let's go." He was certain that Joshua would quickly realize the dog had followed Tom. Tom counted steps to develop a rhythm and take his mind off the rising pain in his side. Seeing the lights of the Levy's windows ahead, Tom lengthened his stride.

He burst around the side of the store and grabbed his pack where it had dropped next to the faucet. He stopped briefly and saw the small hole in Levy's forehead and the pool of blood in which the head rested. Tom ran to his truck, opened the door, and shoved Scrub in.

He started the engine and fiercely spun in reverse around Joshua's truck. As he dropped the truck out of gear, he reached behind the seat for his shotgun. The possibility of a gunfight was not in his interest because he had no delusions of winning that battle. He hopped out, took aim at the rear tire of Joshua's truck, and put a large hole in the sidewall. An answering shot cracked past his ear. Tom leapt back in his truck and wheeled out on the county road, instinctively turning right instead of left. A bullet crashed through the passenger window and out the windshield. Tom ducked and swerved, but kept the truck on the road. He felt rather than heard another couple of bullets slam into the back of the truck.

Tom turned on the headlights when he was convinced they were out of firing range. "Where the hell do we find a cop, or at least somebody with a phone?" Scrub sat on the front seat looking worriedly out at the night and trying to keep her balance as Tom skidded around the curves. Suddenly the headlights showed the maw of McElmo wash where there should have been more road. Scrub rolled off the seat and beneath the dashboard in disarray as Tom overcorrected and corrected the slide again. "Damn! OK, we're OK. Slow down, Dummy."

He slowed the truck. "Scrub, stay down. Just stay down there on the floor." He pulled his pack out of her way and set it on the seat, then laid the shotgun flat on the seat also. "Make yourself some room. Push that crap out of the way." Scrub whined and lay panting heavily. "We're OK," he reassured her. "He can't travel fast with a flat like that." Tom passed a turn toward Aneth, sweeping around the curve to the north instead. He vaguely remembered a loop road connection that would go back toward Pleasant View.

Moments later, the shadow Tom thought he had imagined seeing behind him rammed the back of his Ford, nearly breaking his neck. His first reaction was to put on the brakes, but that caused a second impact. Then he sped up, watching the mirror for the truck to attempt to pull alongside. "Oh Christ, Levy, did you leave the keys in your damn truck?" The bright light in the mirror nearly blinded him.

The remaining headlight on Levy's truck alternately flashed on and off. Then Levy's truck slammed into Tom's Ford again. Tom lost control as the sharp impact spun his truck to the side and it rolled over once.

Joshua regained control of his own vehicle, slammed on the brakes, and raced back with his rifle at the ready. He found Tom's truck stalled, the right front wheel disabled, and the passenger door open. The windshield was gone. There was a clutter of scattered books, papers, and assorted clothing, but no body. As Joshua ran back to Levy's truck for his night-vision goggles, he failed to notice the shotgun lying in the dust where the truck had rolled.

Chapter 17

Mary Twil had not been waiting idly for Tom to contact her again. Early Friday morning she had made contacts with the FBI to seek their assistance in tracking down the origin of Tom's e-mail to her. They had patronizingly brushed her off after asking a few questions, reminding her that it was not their job to look for potential witnesses. On the other hand, if she were prepared to charge Tom with traveling across state lines to commit a felony, perhaps they would put the case in the system to be prioritized. They reminded her that they were very busy.

When Alice Straw called, Mary was feeling impatient herself. "Alice, this sounds a little vague. You saw Randy yesterday with a strange e-mail, but you don't know what it was about because you didn't really get a chance to read it, and you don't know who it was from because it was a strange name on the address line. Now, why do you think it had something to do with Tom?"

"It wasn't just a strange name, it was 'Leptodactylon.' That's the scientific name for a plant—prickly phlox." Alice explained. "Who else would come up with a goofy name like that?"

Mary's antennae went up. "Good point. But you don't have any idea what the message was about or where it came from?"

"No, he closed it too fast. Not where it came from either, but later I saw Randy looking in the dictionary. He was talking to himself, saying 'What the hell is monofluoroacetate?'"

"Sounds like something in toothpaste."

"Yeah, maybe, or maybe sodium monofluoroacetate." Alice added, "That's a poison. The military tested it for warfare, then it was used for coyote bait, but the EPA banned it back in the Nixon era."

"Can you still get it, though?"

"Not the coyote bait, not unless you have a research permit," said Alice. "In some places they use it to manufacture poison grain for prairie dogs."

"So, does it kill people or cows?"

"Yes, but it takes a big dose. It takes about nine ounces of grain to kill a cow—maybe not so much for a human—but the dose is based on body weight. It's pretty ironic that humans and vultures are the two most resistant species."

"Not something you could put on an arrow then, not like curare?"

"No, I don't think so," said Alice. "Maybe for coyotes, they are real susceptible."

"What else do you know about it?"

Alice searched her memory. "Well, it's odorless and colorless. It kills by cutting off nutrients to the cells, kind of like starvation, only quicker. An animal can die with a full stomach. If they get too small of a dose to kill them outright, it might kill enough cells in the organs to cause kidney or liver failure. Oh, yeah, and it doesn't leave any detectable traces either, so it's hard to tell what killed the animal."

"Where did you learn about this stuff, Alice?"

"I looked it up once after Tom got off on a diatribe about subsidized animal control. He told me a rancher in New Mexico was so dumb that he dumped sacks of poisoned grain out on his prairie dog town, but he still had livestock in the pasture. He lost a prize bull and two cows, then turned around and sued the county for giving him the poison." Alice chuckled. "Tom knew the judge. He said the judge told the county they were stupid for giving out poison to untrained nincompoops and said the rancher was negligent for not reading the instructions. He split the costs between them."

"So it can be used to poison cattle. Alice, what was the date on the e-mail? When did you see it?"

"Randy was reading it yesterday afternoon, about four o'clock or so, but I didn't see when the e-mail was sent. Like I said, he closed it right after I came in." Alice hesitated. "Mary, I really don't know it was from Tom, and I don't want to get Randy in trouble. It simply seemed strange. Randy's not a bad guy, but if Tom told him to keep something secret, he might enjoy pulling the wool over everybody's eyes."

"I don't know how you can work next to him, Alice. The guy's a demented lecher."

"He sure talks big anyway," said Alice with a laugh. "I think he likes women in uniform, Mary. Watch out."

"Yes, I will. I know how to get a look at that e-mail without getting near enough to touch. It's probably nothing, but if Tom is sending Randy information on this investigation, I'll put his butt through a wringer. Um, Alice have you said anything to Vince about this? Maybe he should lean on Randy a little, see if he can help us contact Tom."

"I will if you think I should. Mary, has Tom broken any laws?"

"Not that I know of. Only I don't think he would tell me if he did." Mary hung up the phone and went down the hall to find the computer system administrator.

⁂

Vince looked a bit hurt when Alice suggested that Tom and Randy might be exchanging messages. "Do you really think so? I mean, those guys always give each other a hard time. Don't you think Tom would contact me first if he needed help?"

"Well, maybe, but your background is archeology, and Mary thinks Tom might contact Randy if he wanted information about range stuff. She thinks he's trying to figure out the cattle sabotage."

"Oh, yes, I see. Umm, then he doesn't want to talk about his problems? I think he might need help."

"Problems? Vince, do you think he's involved with the sabotage?"

"Oh, no! I didn't mean that. I just, uh well, he talked to me a little bit about some personal problems. I can't discuss them, you know. Um, it's just that he kind of has some personal problems."

"Oh. Well, that's probably why he hasn't called you, Vince. I don't think Tom would talk seriously about his personal problems. Besides, I bet Tom would be the last one to know if he was in trouble, let alone admit it."

"Uh, maybe he's just shy with you, Alice. I was finally getting him to open up. I mean he really started to talk to me about things. It was kind of a surprise."

"Hmm, I guess it would be a surprise," Alice nodded wide-eyed. "Well, I'd better go do some real work. Let Mary Twil know if you have any luck."

"Uh, thanks, Alice. I'll have to give this some thought, uh, how to approach this."

*

After Alice left, Vince wasted no time. He looked through the neatly organized piles of paper carefully sorted into eight different trays. He found the memo he was looking for, then carried it over to Randy's cubicle. "Hey, Randy, you got a minute? Um, uh, maybe you could give me some help."

"Sure, Vince. I can't figure out how to get this new user-friendly data program to print a simple report out anyway. What took me five minutes last year just took two hours, and I still don't have anything to show for it. You can't slow me down much today."

"Um, oh, uh, I was going to ask you how that was going. I thought the state office said it was going to be a piece of cake to switch over from the old system."

"Well, I called the asshole who wrote the program, and he can't get it to print my report either. Yesterday, we sent out bills with the wrong dates and seasons because that didn't work. We had to cross out what it said and write in the changes by hand. Alice had to go find a calculator to add up the right bill because the computer wouldn't take our changes."

"Oh, uh, that doesn't sound so good."

Randy bit his tongue. "What you got, Vince?"

"Uh, this memo came in asking for the year-end reports for the wildlife program. Umm, well, Tom's not here. Uh, maybe you could help me."

"You want me to do Tom's work?" Randy tilted his head incredulously. "Vince, I got my own bucket of shit to shovel for the year-end. Deadline's Monday, remember? I've got to get this stupid program to print out ten reports today or else Alice and I both stay in Monday and sort the records by hand."

"Uh, oh, no, I didn't mean you should do the report, I just thought maybe you could give me some ideas on what we should report." Vince shuffled uncomfortably. "Gosh, it sure would help if we could get in touch with Tom. Um, I mean if I had his phone number or something, I could just talk to him for a minute and I bet he could tell me what to report. Um, you know, for units of accomplishment."

Vince squirmed under Randy's stare. "Um, well, I had an e-mail address for him away from the office, but now I get an error message that says the computer can't find his address."

"Bastard probably didn't pay his bill and they cut off his account. Here, give me that." Randy took the memo. "Oh, hell, this is easy, Vince, you don't need Tom. See here, they tell you what your target numbers were. You just tell them you did ten percent more and got it all done with less money. Ahead of schedule and under budget, that's us!"

"Uh, are you sure? I mean, what if they check it against last year's report?"

"They can't! They changed the whole reporting system each year for the past ten years, Vince. That's the beauty of the goddamned government. No two reports are ever the same. Just tell them whatever they want to hear."

"Uh, do you think that's what Tom would do?"

"He's still collecting a paycheck, ain't he? You got the idea? I gotta get these reports done, Vince, or I'm gonna put my goddamned foot through the computer screen and go have a cigarette."

*

Back in his own office space, Vince dialed Mary Twil's number. "Oh, um, hi, Mary, this is Vince. How are you?"

"Just fine, Vince. I'm sitting on my thumbs waiting for the computer router system files to come through. Is this a social call, or do you have something for me?"

"Um, Mary, I'm not so sure that Randy knows how to get ahold of Tom. I talked to him, uh, Randy, and he didn't seem to know much. Um, he thought maybe Tom's e-mail account got cancelled because he didn't pay the bills."

"Vince, Hotmail is a free service. They only close an account if you haven't used it in a month. He just sent me...oh, never mind. Did you ask him about that e-mail Alice saw?"

"Uh, no. That would kind of get her in the middle. I was pretty subtle, you know. If he had some way of contacting Tom, I bet he would have told me."

"Well, that message isn't in his mail basket now. He must have deleted it."

"Oh, uh, don't they back up all the files each night? Um, really, Mary, I don't think he would be in touch with Tom. Randy is really busy now. He's going crazy trying to get some reports done."

"Vince, do you know how much crap Randy has in his e-mail file? He hasn't deleted a single message in six years, not until now. He has them all sorted and archived, even the trashy jokes people send."

✯

Twenty-eight hours later Mary Twil, tired, frustrated, and in uniform, sat down across the table from Randy, who had an empty shot glass and half a beer in front of him. Another empty glass and crumpled napkin showed that someone had recently left the table.

"Oh, now, ain't you the answer to my prayers. Sit down, Mary, let me have Emma bring you a beer." Randy waved toward the bar. When he caught Emma's eye, he raised his glass and two fingers. "You aren't still on duty, are you? It is Saturday night, after all."

"You been in here for a while, Randy? I tried to reach you at home." Mary's smile was predatory.

Like a shark, Randy thought. "You have to get in here early to find a seat far enough away from the speakers." He gestured toward the band on the stage.

Emma arrived and raised her eyebrows at Mary as she set one beer in front of Randy. "Is this one for you?" she said to Mary.

"Yes," said Mary. "That looks good." She smiled more genuinely. Emma set the second beer down with a clean napkin, sweeping up the empties and a five from the table in front of Randy.

"You actually going to let me pay for that?" Randy challenged. "What ever happened to women's lib?"

"Even your friends say you aren't good for much," Mary shot back. "I might as well tap you for a beer while I have the chance. Get any good e-mail lately?" As she sipped her beer, she watched his face.

"Well, I got a hot tip on a good porno site. I was thinking of trying my hand at making movies." Randy grinned. "That wouldn't be why you called me at home, would it?"

"It wouldn't. Somebody's complaining about you violating policy. Seems you've been deleting e-mail before it gets backed up."

Randy stayed cool. "Hell of a thing to complain about. Dave's been yelling at me to delete some of my stuff for weeks now. Says I'm going to bring the whole system down. He's getting some kind of error messages on the server."

"Not old stuff, just a dozen or so new messages in and out during the last week."

"If you know I deleted some stuff, then it sounds like you got some kind of backup record then. What's the problem?"

"I think you know. The router system reports numbers, computer addresses as numbers. I've got three people tracking down those addresses. I'll bet we find some messages from you on those people's computers. I'll bet we find copies of the messages they sent you." Mary's throat was already raw from the thick smoke.

Randy shrugged. "Not anything to get excited about. Just some unofficial chit-chat with my range buddies."

"Most of them were addresses inside the BLM system. One wasn't. Where did that one go?"

"Oh, could be I know which one you mean. Some clown started spamming me. Sent me some things that were just plain totally inappropriate for the workplace, so I got rid of them quick. Didn't want anybody to file a lawsuit against me. I told the guy to stop or I'd sic the cops on him. Seems like it worked. No more messages."

"Randy, you don't know what inappropriate means, but you will if I find out you're hiding something about Tom. Do you know where he is?"

"Hard to understand that guy. He talks crazy all the time, you know. One day he's in the city getting picked up by babes in a bar, the next he's out in the wilderness communing with God and seeing visions of the Madonna. I swear, that's the kind of crap he talks."

Mary heard honest laughter and knew she was hearing partial truths. "What city? What wilderness?"

Randy shrugged again. He finished his beer before answering. "He never says. When he tells you where he's gonna go, he could be anywhere, hundreds of miles from where you think."

"You're hiding something. You'd better reconsider." As she waited a moment, she saw he was not going to panic. Probably the messages she could trace would have no reference to Tom, only ambiguous clues. It was the direct messages that mattered. "Did he tell you he was in trouble?"

"Somebody get pregnant?" Randy looked wide-eyed, attempting innocence.

"Randy, he's out there alone, investigating a dangerous criminal. I could use his help. He could use some back-up. Do you want to risk him getting killed?"

Randy dropped his act. "It is my well-reasoned opinion that he has gone off with a bunch of plant books to study possible livestock poisoning by weeds in various remote places west of the Rocky Mountains, maybe even east of them. We're talking Washington, Oregon, Idaho, Wyoming, Colorado, Utah, New Mexico, and maybe even Arizona and California. The odds of him getting kicked in the head by a sick cow are not that good. The odds of his breaking a leg or running out of water on a long hike are better." Randy signaled for another beer, only one this time. His voice was boozy, but firm, "He likes the risk of traveling alone in the wilderness. That's his choice, not mine."

Mary looked angry. "Did he tell you he's looking for a murderer?"

Randy suddenly felt very uncertain. This was more serious than he had imagined. "I wouldn't have any idea about that. How could he? This shit is practically scattered all over the globe."

"What shit, Randy?"

"Weeds. Things that make cows sick."

"Did you figure out what monofluoroacetate was?"

Randy turned white. "No. Probably some chemical in a plant." How much had Alice seen in that damn note?

"I'll be talking to you again. Don't go anywhere without telling Vince or me exactly where and how we can get in touch." Mary left, turning to look at him once before going out the door. He smiled and waved, his false bravado returning.

Bill Christen returned to the table along with Emma and Randy's fresh brew. "What was that all about? She looked pissed." Emma stood longer than necessary to collect her money.

"She called me at home. I stood her up," Randy lied. "After all, she is a married woman."

"When did you develop this new moral outlook on life, Sweetie?" said Emma with a laugh.

"Why do you think I'm drinking so hard tonight, Darlin'? Being an honest gentleman is going to kill me."

Bill sat down and watched Emma walk back to the bar. "I'd sooner believe you turned queer."

Randy raised his fresh glass to Bill in a toast. "Life ain't all bad. Mary owes me a beer now. One of these days I'll collect."

Chapter 18

When Tom kicked open the door, he and Scrub bailed out and up through the pinyon-juniper in a hurry. He bemoaned his luck at losing the shotgun. In the dense woodland, it would have given him an advantage in ambush. "As long as Scrub didn't give away my position." Looking at the tired, frightened animal following close in his steps, he realized it would not have been a good idea to attempt an ambush anyway. It would have been necessary to sit absolutely still and to allow Joshua to approach closely.

"I don't have a plan, Scrub. We have to keep moving and hope he thinks we still have the shotgun." They continued along a ridge to the top of the mesa. Tom's heart settled into a more normal pace. He was thankful he had the presence of mind to grab his pack. He pulled out a compass to check his bearings. The luminescent dial glowed faintly with the crescent moon overhead. When he looked behind, Tom noticed the moonlight highlighted their tracks in the soft red dust, and he realized that Joshua would not even need his night vision goggles to track them. "Go away," he said to the moon. He walked as rapidly as possible without crashing through branches. Tom was counting on the trees to screen them from Joshua until he was close enough to hear his approach.

Tom got out his canteen and sipped from it without stopping. He considered his meager knowledge of the nearby topography on the Utah side of the state line. It was not a good situation for playing hide-and-seek. The way the road twisted, he knew they were within a couple miles of the border, maybe closer. If he headed east, they might even come out near Levy's store. Tom knew there was a Park Service outpost somewhere to the north, but he had never visited Hovenweep and felt uncertain he could find it without a map.

Twenty minutes after they left the wreck, they arrived at the eastern edge of the mesa. Tom could see the lights of Levy's store a mile away. "There's a lot of open ground and poor cover between here and there, Scrub," Tom whispered. "I don't like it. He's got to be close behind." Thinking the odds were not even good that Levy owned a phone, Tom opted to turn north, staying in the trees and backing away from the mesa edge. The trees soon opened to a long straight corridor. A power line crackled static overhead. As he peered in both directions, he debated whether or not it was safe to cross.

When Scrub leaned against his leg, Tom felt a strange raggedness in her breathing, then realized she was growling so softly he couldn't hear it through the static. He slowly crouched down beside her and followed the line of her stare. He was afraid she might begin barking, so he put his head next to hers and whispered, "Shh, quiet." Tom could see nothing but the dark forms of the trees. A deer flushed thirty yards to their right, bounding across the hundred-foot width of the corridor and disappearing into the trees again. Scrub huffed, but didn't bark. "Just a deer. Quiet now."

As he began rising to go, he caught a glimpse of pale light reflecting off plastic or metal another forty yards beyond where the deer had reentered the woods. He froze and looked down. Scrub was still focused there, still growling, feet braced with her weight thrown against Tom's leg. He eased down again and backed away from the clearing slowly, guiding Scrub with his hands.

They headed west, then skirted around a large brushy clearing, staying in a narrow band of trees that ended at the power line again a half mile away from where they had been. They crossed and ran through a mixture of brush and old, bulldozed skeletons of junipers, 1960s relics of the Kennedy administration. When another patch of trees loomed, Tom halted in their shadows to watch the open ground behind for movement.

"He took a risk trying to outsmart us, Scrub. Ran ahead and staked out the power line where he could see across the canyon to Levy's and still catch us if we crossed the corridor. Now he has to figure out if we are waiting to ambush him or if we ran in another direction. He has to go back to find our tracks." Tom finished his canteen. Scrub watched enviously. "We'll find you a mudhole somewhere along the way soon." He slipped the canteen back into his pack, tightened the straps, and started a steady jog northward.

They intersected a canyon trending west to east and scaled down the slope and across the bottom. Tom picked his way through the rubble of sandstone and brush around a point and then went northward again into another large canyon. They dashed across that one and up a long, gentle, brush-covered slope. They continued east until they hit the state line fence and reentered Colorado.

Tom knew he was about a mile north of the camp where he and Rita had stayed a week before and fully three miles from Levy's store. "Joshua could be headed back to Levy's place himself," Tom muttered. "Or he could come running up behind us in five seconds." Scrub groaned, and lay down to rest. "Well, we have to stick to cover, and we need water. Let's go." They crossed the ridge and descended a short distance to the canyon rim before moving rapidly northward again.

Three miles farther on they passed through a fence and followed a trail below the rim to a large alcove in the sandstone. A spring flowed from the overhanging rock and splashed into a small pool at its base. The spring had been one of Tom's favorite places when he had worked in Colorado. A partial wall of mortared sandstone and a pile of rubble from an Anasazi ruin sat at the back of the alcove. Barely visible in the now dark sky above, a western hackberry tree grew where some wise ancient one had planted it to provide shade. As far as Tom knew, there were only two trees of that species in Colorado. The Anasazi had brought them up from Arizona, where the tree grew naturally. Tom felt like he was home. Scrub lay down in the pool, lapping and rolling at the same time. Tom held his canteen to the rivulet draining down the rock. When it was full, he treated it with iodine solution, carefully measuring three caps into the canteen. "How come you never get giardia?" he said to Scrub, but he didn't attempt to quiet her noisy splashing.

He thought they had made good time, but he didn't know for sure because his watch was broken. His arm was seriously bruised and sore, probably from the roll-over. He sat down and leaned his back against the rock, drawing the pack near. The foam pad, though now shredded at the edges, was still tied to the outside. He unrolled it and used it for a backrest. He took his fleece jacket out of the pack, and when he put it on, he found it warmly comforting against the night chill and his evaporating sweat.

Tom examined the oak stick he had removed from Joshua's barn and idly carved at its end with his knife. Scrub left the pool of water and for once shook off the excess without getting Tom wet. "I appreciate that," he said as she wandered over to lie at his feet. "Why would Joshua use a twelve inch piece of wood to carve an arrowhead the size of a bird-point?" He held it out for Scrub to examine. "These were in a box next to the lathe. There were oak shavings on the lathe. So maybe he was making something else, and the arrowheads were made from the scraps."

He judged that his canteen had cured for close to half an hour, so he drank, grimacing at the taste of the iodine. "How come you aren't freezing to death with wet fur?" he complained. Tom finished the canteen, refilled it and treated it with iodine again.

"Well, if Joshua does follow our tracks tonight, he could figure out we were headed here for water, so let's move on a bit." Tom checked Scrub's feet and found them scraped and cut, but not bleeding. He returned to the rim, and using the sandstone to maximum advantage, worked his way around a draw to the north, crossed Hackberry Canyon, and worked south again to a point where he could watch the spring from the shelter of thick trees. There he spread the foam pad again. Lying on his side, he tucked his musty, damp dog against his stomach to share warmth and sleep if possible.

✵

Joshua was quite familiar with the terrain on the Utah side of the border. Once he had retrieved his night-vision goggles, he followed just enough of Tom and Scrub's tracks to determine the direction they were going. He knew it would be tough following them far through the woodland without risking an ambush. A shotgun is a formidable weapon at close range. He also knew he had limited time to get back to Levy's store to move his own vehicle before some Sunday tourist discovered the whole mess.

He ran back to Levy's truck and wiped off his prints with a rag while he drove. He reached the power line corridor a mile from where it intersected the mesa's east rim. There, he abandoned the truck under the trees and ran silently, carrying his sling pack and rifle. It took six minutes to reach a point near the rim from where he could see across the entire broad canyon to Levy's store. He found a good position with his back to the trees on the northern side of the corridor and pulled out his night vision goggles again. He calmed his breathing with a few simple yoga exercises and waited.

When a deer flushed, Joshua was momentarily startled. He moved his head rapidly to focus the goggles, rifle at the ready. His first thought was that Tom had burst into the open in abject flight, but the deer gave him a reality check. It was probably fleeing ahead of the dog's scent. He figured Tom would plan on using the trees for a screen, waiting silently for Joshua to blunder into his position, head down, following their tracks.

He waited patiently for Tom to panic or decide to retreat. It would be a battle of nerves as well as wits. Joshua had to balance time for escape and covering his tracks against the chance to kill Tom. With Tom dead, he might gain days to disappear without losing the value of years of work. Possibly he might even have a chance to fool the local law and remain where he was, continuing more cautiously in the future.

As one hour, and then two passed, Joshua became agitated. He knew he had to find and kill Tom. He had to get his own truck out of Levy's driveway, change and hide the tire, and dispose of the rifle. To find Tom he would have to conduct a search of the woodlands, and that would make the odds much more even for Tom.

Joshua was chagrined. It rankled that Tom had outwitted him, doubling back to get his vehicle and weapon. Even the damn dog got away. He also knew it had been pure luck that Levy had left the keys in his truck, or Tom would have gotten away completely. It was approaching midnight. The moon was dropping below the horizon, and he had to act.

Joshua crawled across the opening to avoid showing a skyline profile. Then he began a slow stalk through the trees, keeping near the east rim to cut off Tom's flight in that direction. He divided his concentration—scan ahead, scan the ground, scan ahead again, and then move. Always he listened for the slightest noise. He noticed a small owl, mice, and once a rabbit. A coyote howled in the distance, but he didn't hear any evidence of the dog moving around. Finally, he found tracks at the rim where Tom had considered heading to the store. Slowly, painstakingly, but with growing urgency, he followed their tracks to the point where the deer had flushed. "Son-of-a-bitch!" he muttered, "Did he see me, or did he just chicken out?"

He resumed following the tracks, this time with less caution. He noticed the increased spacing of Tom's steps in the dust. The dog's tracks were superimposed on some of the boot tracks, meaning it was following behind. "Better behaved than I thought, maybe just tired. Too bad it didn't chase that damned deer." When he again reached the power line corridor, only a hundred yards from where he had parked the truck, Joshua knew he had wasted a lot of time worrying about an ambush. It was now two-thirty. He could see that Tom had broken into a run, landing heavily on his heels with a long stride.

"Hovenweep is only three miles north. He could be there by now. Hell, he could be in Dove Creek drinking a beer." He ran his fingers through his short hair. "I'm blown." Joshua decided he would follow and finish Tom if he could, then disappear into the canyons. He would live off the land for a month or two, then make some contacts and pull out. With the money he still had stashed in Bahamas, he could buy a new identity and start over. The property in McElmo would be a loss, but not an irrecoverable tragedy. The cops would probably dismiss the stuff in the barn as vegetarian fodder for a deranged loner.

Joshua ran north. Counting the three full clips in the pack, he still had enough ammunition to kill a small army. It didn't bother him to consider the possibility of taking out any number of federal employees at Hovenweep, but he would need to be efficient. He should reserve enough ammo to discourage close law enforcement pursuit. He had several caches of food, water, and ammunition within reach in the canyons if given enough time.

Even in the dark, Joshua covered a mile every eight minutes. He didn't bother to follow tracks. He ran in a straight line toward the outskirts of the park, then put the night goggles back on and paced the boundary looking for Tom's tracks. He nearly screamed in frustration when he failed to find any tracks. He calmed himself, muttering, "I did not miss his tracks. He did not come here." As Joshua walked south along the rim of Little Ruin Canyon, he tried to keep the bottom of the canyon in view, while also watching the open mesa to the west.

A large block of pinyon-juniper covered the mesa point between Little Ruin and Wickiup Canyon. Joshua coursed through it like a hunting dog, searching for tracks. He no longer expected to see Tom leap out with the shotgun. He was beginning to believe that Tom had really outsmarted him this time, doubling back in a long loop to Levy's store, or maybe Remy's place. Other than the park, they were the closest habitations. Thus, when he dropped into Wickiup Canyon and intersected Tom and Scrub's tracks going east, he cursed himself. "No more guessing!" He followed the tracks grudgingly, wishing he could figure out where Tom was headed and cut him off. When they turned north into Little Ruin Canyon, he groaned. "Goddamn it! How many times can I outsmart myself? He is going to the park, right up the damn canyon bottom!"

In two hundred yards, the tracks broke from the edge of the rocks and led eastward again. Joshua was dumbfounded and very, very angry. "Only two miles from the park, and he heads back to Colorado! I don't believe it." He considered leaving the tracks again, speculating that Tom might do another wide loop to enter the park from the north. He reminded himself that the tracks were cold. He had to know where they led. It was now after four in the morning, still dark.

✯

With night temperatures below freezing, Tom slept fitfully and woke well before dawn. He considered the possibility that Joshua had given up the chase. It seemed unlikely, since hiding the evidence of Levy's murder would do little good if Tom were alive to report it. More likely Joshua was moving slowly, assessing the risk of ambush. Tom was grateful for the illusion of strength he retained from his brief possession of the shotgun. He drank the remainder of the canteen while thinking about his next moves.

He saw no movement across the wash, and Scrub merely seemed impatient, so he crossed directly back to the spring. Tom refilled the canteen and again went through the ritual iodine treatment. Scrub waded into the pool to drink, but she refrained from taking a full bath. Tom climbed back to the rim. This time, he walked in the soft red dirt, making no effort to conceal his tracks.

The Pleasant View road was only a mile due north, but it was unlikely to be traveled until after dawn. Tom intended to flag down a motorist and beg them to flee to Dove Creek with him as a passenger, but the timing had to be right.

He circled the wash until he reached the place where they had earlier left the bedrock rim. He called Scrub to his side on the bedrock, clipped on her leash, and went half way back around the rim. He picked Scrub up and braced her against his chest with both arms. She was fifty-five pounds of lanky muscle and had no desire to be held. "Hold still," he warned her, tightening his grip. He carried her well into the trees, then tied her leash to a stout branch.

"Now stay, and for God's sake don't chew your leash." He removed a juniper branch, retraced his path to the rock, and slowly backed toward Scrub, carefully stepping over the tracks he wanted Joshua to follow, and ever-so delicately brushing out all other tracks, even blowing on the red dirt to conceal the traces of brushing. Scrub nervously paced and watched until Tom returned. Tom untied the leash and led her away. He waited until they had gone some distance before he unclipped her leash again.

Twice in the next mile, Tom made small loops back upon his own tracks, scuffing the duff under a tree each time to make it appear he had waited in ambush. The morning sun brought welcome warmth. Tom listened for the distant sound of an automobile, but when he heard none, he continued on a track roughly parallel to the county road, doubling back again to create another mock ambush site. Gradually he reduced the distance between himself and the road. At the pace he was moving, Tom estimated he would cover a mile every twenty minutes.

Joshua arrived at the spring in time to notice a slight dampness on the ground where Scrub had stood with her belly dripping. The air was dry, and there was no dew. "I'm close, Tommy, very close." His own tiredness left him. He paused to drink from the water flowing down the rock wall. The advantage conferred by his night-vision goggles was lost as the gray light appeared in the east, and he put them back into his sling pack. He followed Tom's tracks around the rim of the canyon in the dim light, but he failed to notice the faint brush marks where they crossed the trail.

When he reached the point where Tom and Scrub had lain through part of the night, the hackles rose on his neck. Joshua could see the spring where he himself had been only minutes before. "Son-of-a-bitch! If he had a rifle, he could have shot me." Joshua looked around and tried to evaluate the congestion of tracks that suggested Tom had been stayed at this spot for a while. When he concluded that Tom was not nearby, Joshua paced the site looking for the tracks that led off. However, the only tracks led to the rim and down and across to the spring.

Joshua followed the tracks to the spring. "He came back to get water. Did I miss his trail?" He concentrated on the boot prints, looking at the pattern of the lugs on the soles. He thought he could now see two sets of boot tracks on the trail to the rim besides his own, but he and the dog had both carelessly stepped on Tom's prints.

Above the spring, he found only one trail, so he hurriedly followed it out and around once more, watching for any tracks diverging until he arrived back at the point where Tom had slept.

"He stayed here part of the night. He went back to the spring," Joshua started a mantra to calm himself. "There was only one set of tracks coming around from the spring." Joshua considered how Tom had accomplished this trickery. "Those tracks were fresh, so he deliberately led me here. He must have walked on rock to get away. But he didn't cross his own tracks, so he followed the rim south." Joshua walked on the rock another hundred yards until it became broken, determining that there were no fresh traces, either down into the wash, or away from it. "You dumb-ass!" he cursed himself. "He went to the other side to get fresh water."

Joshua crossed directly to the other side. He found that the bedrock outcrops were patchy up to near the spring, but there were no fresh tracks in the dirt around them. Half-panicked, he followed Tom's tracks north for the third time. With the low sun angle now fully outlining the trail, he saw the faint brush marks and fresh dust brushed over crushed black lichens. Following them to where the clear tracks began again, he saw that Scrub had been tethered, pacing in a semi-circle. "Goddamn magician, covering up that dog's tracks." The long strides away indicated that Tom intended to re-gain some distance. The ruse had worked, and Joshua felt rage and hatred toward Tom for tricking him.

Joshua cradled his rifle in one arm and held the strap of the sling pack with his other hand. He ran to catch up. When he encountered the first of Tom's fake ambush set-ups, he sucked in his breath. "Christ, Tommy, you could have had me if you had waited a little longer. You know I'm coming, don't you?"

Joshua slowed his pace, keeping his frame low and ducking back and forth between trees. He kept a bit more distance, just close enough to see where the tracks led. Tom's tracks were also weaving between trees. It was tougher to move at a good pace and keep the trail in constant sight. Fifteen yards out from the track, Joshua ran straight into the second "ambush" position. He stopped and dropped dead still behind the tree.

Cold fear, then anger filled Joshua's mind. "Twice! Twice I come right in to an ambush if he had waited. I would have waited if I were you. I would have killed you." He stared at the dog's prancing, pacing tracks in the dust around the tree. "I hate that friggin' dog. Now it makes tracks." He turned to continue the pursuit, but stopped and wheeled back. "No. Careless! You let the goddamned dog walk around your ambush? This is bullshit." He charged after Tom's tracks, bellowing "You don't even have the goddamned gun, do you?"

Even after twenty-four hours without sleep, Joshua was still capable of athletic feats. Although his rage interfered with his breathing, he covered the next mile in seven minutes, pausing only long enough to confirm that Tom had not restrained the dog at the next "ambush" either. The tracks appeared quite fresh, restoring Joshua's confidence that he would soon catch up to his prey. He knew they would soon cross a road leading south to a ranch house. Joshua reasoned that was Tom's last hope because there was no other habitation for miles.

Joshua swept to the east, striking the road a little south of Tom's apparent path but he saw no tracks on the road and no fleeing figures across the broad opening of a grass seeding. He scanned the mesa carefully, examining the fallen piles of juniper that might provide concealment. When he saw the unbroken tree line to the north, he knew he had made another mistake. "He's sticking to the trees for cover." He cradled the rifle across his chest and resumed running northeast until he intercepted Tom's tracks again.

When he heard the whine of a vehicle on the Pleasant View road, he realized what that diversion had cost. In the distance, he saw Tom running hard away from him toward the approaching truck. Joshua tried to hold the wavering rifle steady and aimed high, anticipating the bullet's dropping trajectory. It was difficult keeping his aim centered on Tom's moving back. His first shot missed. He steadied himself again and aimed at the truck instead. His second shot had the desired effect.

Joshua saw the truck slide sideways and leave the road, raising a huge cloud of dust that obscured his vision of Tom. He heard the whine of the motor and shifting gears as the driver plowed through brush and around, back on to the road headed away. He figured he had at least disrupted Tom's escape. There was no way he could have made it to the lurching vehicle. Yet, when the dust thinned enough to see, there was no target.

Chapter 19

Rita wrote her last ticket at 5:30 Sunday morning. She confiscated two loaded rifles, a spotlight, and a bag with half an ounce of marijuana. As she followed the chastened sportsmen out of the forest toward Pagosa Springs, she radioed the fixed wing aircraft overhead that she was going home to get some sleep. Radio traffic settled as the dawn broke. The prime time for spotlight hunting had ended. The pilot needed rest too. Rita heard him contact each of the other patrols, telling them they were on their own.

Halfway to town her scanner caught the Montezuma County Sheriff's Dispatch reporting a shooting at Levy's store and sending a patrol out to investigate. She stopped at the Archuleta County Sheriff's office to drop off the confiscated evidence. By the time she filled out the paperwork, a deputy had reported an elderly white male, presumably Castro Levy, was dead at the scene and that apparently his truck had been disabled by a shotgun blast directed at the right rear tire.

By the time Rita got home, she was dead tired. She went to the refrigerator and stared at the mostly empty shelves. "I need a live-in cook." She settled for a quart of orange juice and an oatmeal cookie, drinking the juice straight from the jug. Rogue picked up his empty metal bowl, dropping it loudly on the floor to get her attention. "All right. You don't have to get pushy." She filled his bowl, wondering if it was worth it to make her own breakfast before going to bed. She made the choice to sleep. As she passed the phone, with its message light blinking, she decided to call the regional office in Durango.

"Millie, this is Rita. I'm at home now, going to catch up on three days of sleep."

"Thanks for letting me know, Sweetie. I always worry about you. You get yourself a good meal before you go back on duty too. Don't be eating those greasy hamburgers."

"Yeah, thanks. I need it. Say, did you hear that report of the shooting over in Montezuma?"

"Yes, some rafters stopped at Levy's store on the way to the San Juan River. It sounds like the old man had been dead for a while. Montezuma County Sheriff's crew are all over it now."

"Yeah. Would you keep tabs on what is happening over there? I may call you back after I've had some rest."

Millie said, "Don't you worry about it, Hon, you get your beauty sleep."

"OK, thanks. I need that too." Rita punched the message button and sat down to take off her boots.

She shook her head and smiled as she listened to Tom's voice. He was so like an awkward child at times, still unused to leaving messages on tape. When it cut him off, she wondered if he had tried a second time. She laughed when the second message started. Before it ended her mind was racing and she had forgotten about being tired. She said to her self, "Joshua's messing around with poison. Tom's going back to get samples. This sounds like trouble. What does he mean call back? Somebody trying to track him down?"

She dialed her regional office. "Millie, it's Rita again. Can you find a number for the BLM law agent there in Durango?"

"Sure thing, Honey. You might go through the sheriff's dispatch, too. He might be working today. Hold on." While she thumbed through a directory, Millie had another thought. "I heard another report out of Montezuma County. They found a wrecked truck a few miles across the border, with some bullet holes in the back. Whoever owned it disappeared. Oh, here's the number. You got a pencil?"

Rita wrote down the number. "What kind of truck, did they say?"

"A Ford Ranger. Oregon plates, but I didn't get the number. The phone started ringing right then."

"Oh, great. Look, it might be a coincidence, but I know someone from Oregon who was going to be in that area. Would you please call the Montezuma Sheriff and see if they've traced the plates? I'm going to try to make some contacts with BLM. If you hear anything else, please get back to me."

"Hmm, and I thought the tourist season was over."

The phone number indicated it was a cellular phone. Juan Mendez was at home, watching a taped version of Saturday's ball game. "Juan, I need to contact the BLM Ranger up in Baker, Oregon, to get some information about a friend who might be missing somewhere west of Cortez. She's a woman, but I don't remember her name. Would you have a phone number for her on a weekend?"

He gave Rita less than half his attention. "Lucky for you I've got my phone directory at home. Otherwise this would have to wait a while." He pulled his directory from a cluttered table. "Or-e-gone, right? What district?"

"He works in Baker City."

"No, there's no Baker District in Oregon. Maybe you mean California?"

"No, he really knows where he works, Juan. It's eastern Oregon, right next to Idaho."

"OK, Vale District looks right on the map. So, looks like Mary Twil is your number."

"Yes, that's it. I remember he mentioned that name."

Juan recited the number. "So, did your buddy get lost? Is he a hunter? Why don't you call Dean over in Cortez, or even the sheriff's office?"

"Somehow this all relates to a livestock case up in Oregon. I want to talk to Mary to find out what Tom didn't tell me."

"Your guy's a cop? What the hell is he doing down here?" Juan bristled with territoriality, "He's not working on BLM out there, is he? I didn't get no call about nothing on BLM."

"No, he's not a cop. I think he was doing some kind of background research, that's all." Rita thought about it. "Look, I'll give you a call back if I find out he's tripped over something criminal. He seemed to think somebody was growing poisonous plants on BLM land to create problems for livestock."

"What! That was what you were talking about. It sounds like a pretty stupid idea to me."

"Yeah, but I don't think he told me everything. Are you going to be home for a while?"

"Yeah, all day. If I go to the store, I've got my cell."

"Thanks, Juan."

The phone rang as soon as Rita hung up. "Hello."

"Miss Cooper?"

"Yes."

"This is Deputy Oswald, Cal Oswald, Montezuma County Sheriff's office?" He paused, the inflection of his voice made the statement sound like a question. "Millie Roberts said you asked about a truck wreck out our way, the one with Oregon plates?"

"Yes, I wondered if you had traced the owner's name."

"Do you know a Thomas Kara Kreuger?"

"Kara? His middle name is Kara?"

"I take it you know a Thomas Kreuger then?"

"Yes, if he's from Baker City, Oregon."

"His truck was abandoned?" Deputy Oswald spoke slowly. "Do you happen to know where he is right now?"

"No, I haven't seen him since last Sunday. He left a message on my phone three days ago."

"Is he armed?"

"I don't think so. I don't know. It doesn't sound like Tom."

"There were some holes in the back of his truck? Looked like bullet holes?"

"Not last Sunday." Rita was getting irritated. "Look, I'm a District Wildlife Manager. I called because I need to find Tom." She hesitated, "He was helping me on an investigation."

"Is he a cop?"

"No, he works for BLM, a specialist. He was doing some research on...well, research."

"He had a shotgun? Recent papers in the truck?"

"I don't know."

"You investigating something out here, Miss Cooper? You working with Dean Booth?"

"No, Dean is not involved. It's something more general."

"Any reason why Mr. Kreuger would blow a hole in Castro Levy's truck?"

"No. Hard to tell, but I think they liked each other. Kindred spirits in their way."

"Mr. Levy was not known to like any government employees. Did your Mr. Kreuger know that?"

"I heard them joking about it." Rita struggled to keep the annoyance out of her voice.

"When you last saw him, did Mr. Kreuger seem depressed, angry, or unstable in any way?"

"No."

"Your friend, Mr. Kreuger have a dog, a black dog?"

"Mostly black, yes."

"Does he have a beard, and wear a wide brim hat?"

Rita sighed, "Yes, a beard, sometimes a hat."

"Man fitting his description? He ran out of the trees to flag down a passing motorist this morning? Motorist says this man took a shot at him, blew out his windshield."

Rita was wondering why the last statement was not a question. Then the meaning sunk in. "Oh."

"Officer Cooper? Maybe you should come on over here? Help us locate your friend?"

"Yes, all right." Rita paused. "It will take me a few minutes before I can get started. The sheriff won't mind if I speed a bit coming over on the highway, will he?"

"No, not if you keep it under a hundred?"

When Rita hung up she felt like a rag doll. She dialed the number Juan had given her for Mary Twil. After the phone kicked over to voice mail, Rita left her own number and mentioned an emergency about Tom Kreuger. Then she stripped, took a shower, and found a clean uniform shirt. She took the cleanest pair of uniform pants from her overloaded hamper, tied her boots again, and drove through town. She stopped at a deli to get a full thermos of coffee and a chicken pita wrap.

On Highway 160 near Bayfield her cell phone rang. "Hello, this is Rita Cooper."

"Rita, this is Mary Twil. You left a message about Tom Kreuger?"

"Yes, Mary, I got a contact from Tom and think he might be in some serious trouble. I was hoping you could fill me in on some details. He told me he was assisting you on a livestock poisoning case."

"Like hell, he was!" Mary exploded. "I told that dumb shit to stay put and let me investigate things my way. Did you say you're in Colorado? He's in enough trouble up here. What's he doing now?"

"That's the best question I've heard today. Last week he was checking out a potential suspect's place. He actually set up a meeting to go see the guy. I knew about that. But this morning I found a message on my home phone with some real strange pieces of information.

He must have seen something that related to your case because he said he was going back to collect samples."

"Back, as in, going back uninvited," Mary said pointedly.

"That was my take on it. The suspect is not exactly Mr. Sociable."

"Well, he sent me a message that mentioned looking for samples. I thought he might have known where some stuff was growing. I'm not going to guess. Please don't tell me he got caught breaking and entering."

"Not that I know of," said Rita. "Something is going on. I don't know exactly what, but it looks real bad. We have one man shot to death. Tom's truck was found wrecked and abandoned with bullet holes in the back end. The officer said Tom had a shotgun, so maybe used it to shoot the dead man's truck. Also, someone looking like Tom and Scrub tried to flag down a motorist, who claims he was shot at."

"Oh, Jesus! He flipped out. Did he rape anybody yet?"

"Don't panic. The motorist said he saw Tom flagging him down, then a shot blew out his windshield. Don't you think the guy would have noticed a gun in his hands if he had one? He probably wouldn't have slowed down at all."

"Have you got an alternative explanation?"

"You might try to flag down a stranger if you needed help. Mary, I really don't think Tom is dangerous. On the other hand, Joshua Freeborn, the guy he was meeting, is an odd loner. I checked him out once on a report of possible drug dealing. When he associates with anyone at all, it's a group of survivalists who all live out in the boonies. If Tom found something serious, it's possible Joshua might do something drastic to cover it up."

"Rita, Tom is not a cop. He has no training. He actually told you he was going to check out a suspect? Did you warn him not to mess with this guy?"

"I warned him, all right, but he's a free man. He didn't say he was going to do anything illegal, just look around and see if he could spot any clues. He actually got an invitation to go talk to Joshua about some kind of environmentalist activity. I think sabotage."

"Oh boy. How did he track this Joshua down there?"

"Incomplete information. Something about a link to Jerry Skinner through environmental groups on the Internet. I suggest you get a warrant for Skinner's computer and see if you can find the same links."

"Been there, done that. It's password protected. The sheriff got a computer from Skinner's house. He's having a state police expert try to crack it. I don't think Tom could have figured that one out. He didn't mention finding any letters or anything like that?"

"Computer files, website addresses in history, things like chat-groups and e-mail, that's what he said." Rita felt a twinge. "They didn't happen to take fingerprints from the keyboard did they?"

"This is a small county. Sheriff's boys tried to guess the password before they handed it on to the state. Besides, I think Tom may have fingerprints and keyboards all figured out. We found one at the Baker office that had been wiped."

"At the office? Don't you all have your own passwords and a security tracking system? Tom would know that, wouldn't he?"

"Oh, yes, he would. He also has a cynical streak and likes to flaunt the system's weaknesses. He took the opportunity to make somebody else look like an idiot."

"Not a good way to make friends and influence people," said Rita.

"Especially when the idiot is your boss. So what else did he tell you, and how can I help?"

"OK, let me get back on track." Rita replayed the phone message in her mind. "Tom said Joshua was growing castor bean plants. At first he thought it was manioc, but he must have got a closer look."

"That would be the ricin. It's a chemical extract from the castor bean seed, and it's very deadly. It's in the whole plant, leaves and all, but mainly it's concentrated in the seeds. He asked me to check if it could be used on cattle. Have there been any poisonings there?"

"Not that anybody has reported. There might have been an accidental case with some horses. Tom thought there were related cases in a wider area around the region. His theory was that Joshua was going other places to do his dirty work, but he didn't want anything going on too close to home. He thought that was why Joshua agreed to meet him." Rita backtracked, "He was having somebody in BLM ask around for livestock poisoning cases and send him the details."

"Yes, I think I know who that would be. So he had some real evidence."

"No, not really. Not when I talked to him. He knew it was all circumstantial. That's why he was so determined to get a closer look."

"That's it?" Mary sounded perplexed.

"No, there was something about poisoned arrowheads, bird points. What was that about?"

"Bird points? Are those little wooden arrowheads?"

Now Rita was puzzled. "No, the Indians made them out of stone, something like chert or obsidian."

"But a bird point would be small, right?"

"Oh, yes. They're about half an inch long."

"Tom thinks oak would be more effective."

"What? More effective than stone? No way. Obsidian is sharp. It cuts like a razor."

Mary sighed. "More effective for delivering a shot of poison. Skinner died with a tiny wood arrowhead in his back. I don't know how Tom figured that out."

"He's very intuitive at times. Usually it relates to other people's business."

"Tell me about it. I think he cheats too, but he won't tell how he does it. Better not if he broke into Skinner's house." Mary changed tracks. "So, do the Indians use iris roots to make a poison?"

"Iris? Scrub! Tom said Scrub knew better than to eat his irises, so he thought they were bad, maybe poisonous. But I don't think the Indians used to have flower gardens."

"Does '*Iris missouriensis*' mean anything to you?"

"Oh, duh! Of course," said Rita. "It's the wild iris. It's very common in wet meadows.... Castro said the Indians made poison from common things."

"Castro? Are we talking Cuba now?" Mary's voice climbed a notch.

"No, Castro Levy. The dead man. The one who got shot."

"So he knew something too?"

"Maybe. He gave us an odd lead about the horse poisoning and locoweed. He said the Navajo thought Joshua was responsible for it. They called him a witch."

"Oooooh! That sounds on target, doesn't it? I read Hillerman's books, too."

"Oh, yeah—target. Tom said there was a target deer behind the barn, and it might have some arrowheads buried in it."

"That would be pretty damning evidence, Rita. It might tie buddy Joshua to a murder."

"I heard nothing about a murder," Rita complained. "He had to know Joshua was dangerous! And if Joshua has already murdered someone, then he might be willing to go for another."

"Yes, you might be right," Mary said softly. "Tom could be in some serious trouble. Do you have any idea where he might be right now?"

"Depends on how fast he's moving, and when he started. Also whether or not the motorist actually saw Tom and not somebody else. I'd say we could figure it out within a ten or twenty mile radius, thirty at the most. It's rough country, and he's probably on foot."

"Uh, I don't have a calculator handy, but wouldn't that be a large area?"

Rita thought about geometric formulas. "Roughly somewhere between sixty and a hundred-eighty square miles. We might get lucky. I'm on my way over to Cortez. The sheriff is looking for Tom. About ninety percent of that territory is BLM ground. Maybe you should contact Juan Mendez. He's the BLM cop in Durango. If you can pry him away from his television, maybe he could get a plane up in the air."

"I'll see what I can do." Mary was silent for a moment. "It sounds like you were in contact with Tom fairly recently. Did you actually see him or just talk to him on the phone?"

"We spent a couple days hiking together last weekend. He left the phone message on Thursday."

"You didn't meet him in a bar, by any chance, did you?"

"I know nothing about a bar," Rita said.

"I figured as much. You must be the Madonna."

"What? No resemblance, as far as I know. Where did this come from?"

"Just male horse-shit, never mind. Look, keep in touch, would you? Let me know if I can help. Maybe I can get approval to come down there."

"I don't think we have that much time, Mary."

✯

Forty minutes later Rita arrived at the Montezuma County Sheriff's office. The parking lot was half-empty, busy for a Sunday. She checked in at the front desk. "Deputy Oswald asked me to come over."

The woman behind the counter rolled her eyes. "I'll bet he did," she muttered as she punched three numbers on the phone. "Officer Cooper is out front. Yes." Her eyes were hooded as she looked up at Rita, "He'll be out in a couple minutes. Probably needs to stop in the men's room and comb his hair."

Rita looked at the attendant's nametag. "Rose, is there any chance they have a plane in the air looking for the guy who shot at that motorist this morning?"

"Not yet. There are a couple roadblocks out. The sheriff will be in around eleven. If they haven't found they guy by then, he'll probably authorize it."

Rita stood looking out the window as she waited. When Deputy Oswald appeared, she pointed and asked, "Where did they get that old brown Chevy on the tow truck?"

Oswald put his hand on her shoulder as he looked out the window, then cocked his head and leered at her. "That's the old man's truck your friend blasted with his shotgun. We brought it in for evidence."

Loud enough for Rose to hear, Rita said, "Then you'd better run the plates." Rita pointedly removed his hand from her shoulder. "If I were you, I'd also put out an APB for Levy's Dodge. It's a green, three-quarter ton." Oswald did a double take looking at the truck disappearing into the storage yard. "While you're at it," Rita added, "you might want to find out if anybody knows where Joshua Freeborn is right now. Don't approach him without back-up." She nodded at Rose's cup on the desk, "If I can get a cup of that coffee and you show me on a map where that motorist was shot at, I might be able to help you prevent somebody else from getting killed."

Taken aback, Deputy Oswald glared at her in disbelief, but he led the way down the hall. Rita shared a discreet smile with Rose, then followed. He showed her to the sheriff's private office. "There's a coffee pot and some extra cups in there. Have a seat. I'll be back in a minute." He went back to the dispatcher to have someone check vehicle registrations for Castro Levy and run the plates of the impounded Chevy.

"This is Deputy Jones," he nodded toward the young woman who followed him back into the office. "Jones, meet Rita Cooper, Colorado game and fish." He used the familiar name for the agency. "Deputy Jones is going to take notes. She'll start the tracking process if you can give us any new information pertinent to our investigation?" He settled himself into the sheriff's plush chair behind the desk and picked up a coffee cup. "Now what can you tell us about Thomas Kreuger?"

"He's a BLM wildlife biologist from Oregon. He came here about a week ago to research poisonous plants."

Oswald interrupted, "Yes, you said before he was a specialist doing research? Did the BLM people in Durango bring him down here?" He wondered if this might be something to cause embarrassment to BLM. The newspaper was fond of exciting the local anti-government fervor.

Knowing where that question could lead, Rita said, "No, he was taking some time off from work, doing some unofficial investigation into possible causes of livestock poisoning."

"Why here? I'm not aware of any reports of poisoned livestock in Montezuma County." He looked at Deputy Jones for confirmation. She shook her head to indicate she hadn't heard of any either.

Rita saw her opportunity to re-direct the interview, "Actually, Castro Levy told Tom that some Navajo horses may have been poisoned over by Yellowjacket Canyon. Castro said the Navajo thought Joshua Freeborn was responsible. He lives out in that neighborhood."

"Mr. Kreuger told you this?"

"I was there at the time. It was last Sunday. Stopped into Levy's store to get something cold."

"Oh, yes, I believe you said on the phone that he was investigating something for you?"

"Um, I said he was helping me. We were out looking for poisonous plants. I'm cooperating with a BLM law enforcement officer in Oregon on a very unofficial basis," said Rita revising her previous lie. "I had to get back to my job. Tom arranged to go visit Joshua Freeborn on his own."

"Joshua Freeborn. Is there some reason why we should be trying to find him? Are we going to find him dead, too?"

"Tom seemed to think he had found evidence to link Joshua with livestock poisoning in Oregon. It sounded circumstantial, but there might also be a link to a more serious crime, a murder."

Deputy Oswald decided it was time to strike. "Yes, the Baker County Sheriff would like to talk to your friend. The deputy I spoke with said it was a sure bet Mr. Kreuger was involved in a conspiracy. Now it looks like he blew out the back end of Mr. Levy's truck, shot Mr. Levy on his front porch, and put a bullet through his head to finish him off. Then he had a wreck during his escape and tried to hijack another vehicle."

Rita lost her patience with Oswald's style and didn't try to conceal it. "Help me here, Deputy. There's something I need to understand unless you're ready to take this case to court. You said Tom used a shotgun he had recently acquired to disable Joshua Freeborn's truck, not Levy's. Presumably this was so Levy couldn't escape. Then he shot Levy on the front porch and put a bullet through his head. Did he shoot Levy with the shotgun?"

"I can't share that information with you at this time, Ms. Cooper."

"Well, there had to be another gun involved. Let's presume it was two bullets then. One to stop him, and one to finish him off, no shotgun wound. Did you find any evidence that Tom had a rifle or pistol?"

"Levy had all kinds of guns. No telling what your friend might have taken."

"But you thought the truck was disabled to prevent Levy's escape, which means it was shot before Levy, right? Castro never even made it off the porch. The guns were inside—either with Levy, or Levy was going in to get one."

"I figure Kreuger got the drop on him," said Oswald. "Took his gun and shot him with it."

Rita turned to Deputy Jones. "If that were the case, both wounds would probably be from very close range. You can check that." She saw the young woman make a note. "Now, you presumed that the brown Chevy was Levy's truck. Let me guess that's because it was the only vehicle in the drive. Levy had a full sized, green Dodge, fairly recent model. So Joshua's truck was disabled in Levy's yard. That leaves reasonable doubt if Tom Kreuger was there alone."

Oswald objected, "Levy and Freeborn were neighbors. They might have swapped trucks for a day or so."

"Hmm, but you'll have to find Joshua to ask him, won't you? You do need to find Levy's truck. It would help to know when it disappeared. Then there were the bullet holes in the back of Tom's truck."

"Most likely it will be Levy's gun did that."

"While Tom was making his escape? Before or after Levy was dead on the porch?" Rita asked. Deputy Jones looked down at her notepad, scribbling furiously.

"So we don't have all the details yet," said Oswald somewhat defensively. "There might have been a gun battle. We don't know. Maybe Levy shot at him first. Tried to drive him off."

"If that's possible, then you want to check Levy's hands for gunpowder. I heard Tom's vehicle was a few miles into Utah. What caused the wreck? Any blood in the cab?"

Back in control, Oswald had no intention of imparting information. "Unfamiliar road at night, got in a hurry, who knows? What's his connection with Freeborn? Are they in a conspiracy together? Maybe he was implicating Freeborn to take suspicion off himself."

Rita cursed herself silently for being unable to think fast enough. Debating had never been her strong suit. "I told you what the connection with Joshua was about." She started thinking aloud. "So he wrecked. In Utah he wrecked at night. This morning early somebody found Levy. You guys sent a patrol out to check. Not long afterwards, somebody discovered the wreck. Then a while later he and his dog are reported at an apparent hijacking attempt. That was in Montezuma County again."

Rita closed her eyes, and thought hard. "He went west from Levy's place. Lost the truck, but didn't come back, or your cop or the ambulance driver would have seen him. Hours passed. So he went north on foot to the Pleasant View road, didn't he? It's not that far for him. Ran out of the trees waving his hands, but the motorist didn't see a gun until his windshield shattered. Then I'll bet he didn't look too close, either. Got the hell out of Dodge."

"Ms. Cooper, other than yourself, do you have any knowledge of persons or places where Mr. Kreuger might go for assistance?"

"Don't you have the roads blocked, Deputy? Only he's not going to be on a road because he has a man with a gun hot on his trail. That's the guy who shot the back of his truck and the other guy's windshield. Tom will go into the canyons, either north or south. He either has to outrun the guy or make him lose his trail. The rougher the better, more turns and side canyons, more stone and water to cover tracks, that's what he needs." Rita paused, "He'll go north toward Dove Creek. It's only twenty miles or so. Get a plane over Cross Canyon and all those side canyons."

"You sure he'll head that way? Lots of homes in the country if he goes half that distance east."

"Lots of open flat ground, too. Look at it this way, either he's running from a madman with a gun who already killed one man and nearly killed another—or he's running from you and he knows there will be cops on the roads."

"If he's innocent, then why not try to find a cop on the road?"

"Open flat ground. He's close to his mid-forties. Joshua is in his late-twenties. I saw him compete in the Iron Man triathlon last year. He looks like Schwartzenegger with long legs. Tom didn't have time to flag down a passing motorist because Joshua was close enough to shoot them. He's not going to run down an open road looking for one of a few cops randomly scattered out over the whole west half of the county."

Oswald looked at his watch. "Sheriff will be in before long. We'll take it up with him. You should hang out in the lounge. We'll call you if we need you to talk your friend in."

Chapter 20

Tom had been breathing too hard to hear the first bullet snap behind him. He was waving both arms as he ran, and saw the surprised face of the driver as a ring of fractured glass appeared around the hole caused by the second shot. The truck swerved wildly, left the road, and circled completely around Tom as the driver regained control and bounced back through the brush on to the road, headed in the opposite direction.

It was Tom's turn to curse. If only he had been moving faster, he could have been another half mile up the road ahead of Joshua. The driver was sure to report the attack, but it would take too long for the cops to investigate. In the meantime, Tom had no choice but to get far away as fast as he could. With his adrenaline fading, he settled into a strong pace, wishing his boots were as light as his running shoes. He ran across the upper reach of McLean Basin, with no plan left except to put as much rugged terrain between himself and Joshua as possible.

Tom figured he had less than a three-minute lead on Joshua. He was running fast, but had no hope he could outrun Joshua on flat ground. He crossed a primitive road at the top of the folded mesa, and twisted southwest down into Ruin Canyon. "Might as well keep the asshole guessing where we're going, Scrub." Although he slowed his pace, she was barely keeping up. Her tongue looked about a foot long.

They intercepted the horse trail at the bottom of Ruin Canyon, a short distance from where it climbed out to the road. They had been here only a few days earlier, but the thought barely registered. Tom concentrated on putting his feet down without twisting an ankle on rock. He counted paces, continually starting over at one hundred, never tallying the total. He succumbed to an endorphin-induced high, grinning stupidly as he dodged through the cobbles, shortening or lengthening stride as needed, bounding lightly from side to side. He almost laughed. Let Joshua come try to catch them.

Suddenly Tom tripped over an invisible cord that snared his foot, causing him to pitch forward as though diving into a pool of water. A thick branch hit him in the forehead as he crashed to the ground, driving a knee into stone. He heard a snap in his already bruised arm, and before he lost conciousness, imagined he could hear a clattering as though Scrub had knocked over another pantry full of molasses tins.

He woke with Scrub breathing in his face, sniffing worriedly. "Oh, go. Go." He pushed her away, rolling over and wiping blood from his eye. He looked up at the shadow of a man.

"Looks like you come back." The voice sounded cloudy.

Tom tried to push himself up, but winced at the pain and fell flat again. Scrub backed off growling.

"Tripped and fell," said the man laughing. "You sure did, didn't you?" He pulled at the trip-cord, causing more clattering of cans. "Heard you coming."

Tom could barely see the face under the straw cowboy hat. He saw a rifle. "Joshua?"

The figure kicked his injured knee. "You ought to remember my name, you son-of-a-bitch. It's Jake, Jake McPherson." Heavy running footfalls stumbled on rock on the trail up-canyon from them. Jake heard them coming and made a quick decision. He kicked Tom in the chest and knocked the wind out of him. He crouched and took aim toward the intruder. "Tried to do it again, didn't you?" He fired.

The bullet struck Joshua in the chest. He sank to his knees and fell forward, dropping his own rifle. Jake checked Tom, then scurried forward to kick Joshua's rifle out of reach. He turned Joshua over with his foot and saw blood bubbling from Joshua's mouth. Looking at the camouflage pants and green T-shirt, he giggled, "You're out of uniform, Soldier."

Joshua was confused. "Ambush, now?" He struggled as if to rise, with one arm pinned uselessly behind him in the pack.

"Yeah, that son-of-a-bitch led you right in to get me. Only I changed the ending this time. You're gonna die pretty quick." He walked back to Tom. "Maybe I ought to think about how to make you last a while longer than him. He kicked Tom in the stomach. Scrub leapt at Jake and fastened her teeth on his hamstring. "Ow! Goddamn!" He swung the rifle and thumped her in the ribs. She dropped and crouched, prepared to charge again. Tom rose on his good arm and pulled his knees under him. Jake staggered back and swore at the dog, "You hold it, goddamn you." He pointed the rifle at Scrub, then screamed in pain and fell forward into the sagebrush.

Tom tried to understand what was going on as he watched Jake thrashing in obvious agony in the brush. He saw a short, round stick protruding from Jake's lower back. Tom turned and saw Joshua drop a small crossbow, not much larger than a pistol. The sling pack lay open at his side. The light faded from Joshua's eyes, but they continued to watch.

Jake disentangled himself from the brush, crawling out on his hands and knees, still holding the rifle. With one hand, he found the neatly turned oak shaft protruding from above his left kidney. He tugged on it lightly, feeling it give. He groaned in pain as he pulled the bloody shaft out. The tip was slightly splintered, as if it had shattered. Jake rose and staggered toward Joshua's body. Angrily, he took aim and pumped two rounds into Joshua's inanimate face. By the time he thought about Tom again, he saw only tracks and a few drops of blood headed down canyon.

Tom was having a difficult time avoiding any rocks as he made his way slowly, stumbling and falling several times in the first half mile. With one eye swollen shut, his vision in the other wavered between being double and simply unfocused. Several times he attempted to adjust the glasses that he no longer had. He held his left arm against his stomach. Nothing could make his knee function properly. Speed was out of the question.

He tried to remember how far the burial that Jake had been excavating had been from the canyon junction. Maybe it was a mile and a half to Cross Canyon. From there it was about two miles to a dirt track that led out in different directions to other roads. Altogether it was about six or seven wandering miles to get to the county road where he was likely to find help. It was only four miles straight-line if he went over the mesa-tops, but Tom no longer trusted himself to find his way through the woodlands. There was no way he could make it up Cross Canyon to Dove Creek. Instead, he followed the course of the dry channel. He needed water. There would be another spring below.

When he finally found a spring, Tom realized he had entered Cross Canyon without recognizing it, and probably had gone farther than he thought. That was good. The bad part was that he wasn't sure how far he was from anywhere.

Scrub collapsed in the small pool and delightedly stirred the mud while she drank. Tom set the pack down, held the cap on the canteen with his teeth, and unscrewed the neck with his good hand. He filled it with muddy water. He set it down, and repeated the bottle-opening trick with his iodine solution. He dumped a small amount directly from the bottle into the canteen. He refastened the bottle top and retreated a distance into thick brush. A while later he checked his useless watch, forgetting that it didn't work. The sun was high above the cottonwoods. He drank the sickly stained water and fell asleep.

He dreamed he heard a plane fly over and that he signaled it down with the mirror in his pack. In his dream, it landed on a paved highway in New Mexico. He woke and looked around for a minute, then closed his eyes again. Scrub lay beside him, dozing as well.

When Tom woke, one eye was swollen shut, but his vision had cleared in the other. His left arm was swollen twice its normal size, but there was no sign of a bone badly out of place, so he used his handkerchief to make a sling and hold the arm to his chest. He finished the canteen of water. He oriented himself and headed back to the spring. As he stepped into the trail, a horse shied away and ran. Tom saw it was saddled and the reins had been tied up to the saddle horn. The rifle scabbard was empty. When he approached the spring, he heard a voice groan and curse, then the unmistakable sound of someone being violently sick. He saw Jake McPherson's body lying on the ground at the spring. Jake was laying with his face half in the pool of water. Tom watched the body, but saw no rifle and no movement until he was close enough to nudge Jake's boot.

Jake looked up at him and drew a pistol from his belt.

"Jake, stop!" Tom raised his hand. "You need help. I can help you."

"I'm not so sick I can't shoot you."

"Jake, there's something you need to know. That arrow was poisoned. Did you get the arrowhead out?"

"It didn't have an arrowhead. It was just a stick. It broke. I've got a splinter inside me still. I can feel it move sometimes. Hurts like hell."

"More likely it's a small arrowhead. He carved them on the end so they would break off. I dug one out of a target he used. He soaked them in poison."

"How do you know?"

Tom shrugged. "You're sick, aren't you? The symptoms are vomiting, diarrhea, and dehydration. You'll die soon if you don't get help. It happened to someone else."

"If you didn't get any farther than here in all this time, then how are you going to help?"

"Can you get up?"

"I don't think so. I'm too sick." As if to prove it, he choked and gagged again, spitting bile. "Goddamn. What kind of bastard cop puts a poison arrow on a crossbow."

"He wasn't a cop. He was a murderer. He was after me. We ran into you by accident."

"Bullshit. Just like when you got that cop to follow you into Hovenweep and catch me."

Tom shrugged again. "He was just a suspicious, nosy bastard, the way most cops are. It was your bad luck to be digging when we showed up. I didn't know you were there." Tom saw the look of disbelief on Jake's face. "Hey, I can't make you believe. You want help now, you've got to let me help you."

"How?"

"Truce. Toss the gun away. I take you to civilization, get you to a hospital. They can treat you."

"You going to carry me?" Jake spat and waved the pistol. "Maybe I ought to keep this and make sure you don't drop me."

Tom waited silently. Scrub sat watching.

"Ah, shit." Jake threw the pistol away.

"What happened to your rifle?"

"I left it back up the canyon after I got sick."

"OK." Tom pointed at the horse that had approached again. "Is that your mare?"

"Yeah, looks like she followed me. I couldn't get back in the saddle with this arrow in my gut. Nearly passed out trying."

"I think she would like some water. Do you think you could talk real sweet to her? Maybe get her to come to the water while I'm close enough to grab the reins?"

Tom figured out that with only one useful arm he couldn't get Jake up on the horse's back. Jake barely had the strength to stand once Tom propped him up against a tree. "This isn't going to work."

"Guess I should'a kept the gun."

"At least I'm trying. You could have shot me and made sure you would die here." He helped Jake to sit down. "Keep your head up so if you get sick again, you won't choke." Tom collected two large broken branches and fashioned a crude travois with a roll of strong cord he found in the saddlebags. "We're going to have to pull this behind the horse like a sled. It's going to be rough. I can't promise much." He piled pine boughs on the travois to provide some cushioning.

Jake belched more blood and bile. "Damn, maybe I should just stay here and die. Even if we get out, I'm gonna go to prison. Don't know which is worse."

"Now you think about prison? What about when you shot Freeborn? You thought he was a cop. How many people do you know who are walking around free after killing a cop?"

"Not too many, I guess."

Tom eased him on to the makeshift sled. "Yeah? You got caught once digging ruins and went to jail for it. So you go right back and do it again. Even if you get away with it for years, what makes you think you can always beat the odds? Seems pretty dumb to blame other people when you get caught."

"I take my chances."

"Is that right? Sound's like you still blame me for you getting caught the first time."

"Yeah, well." Jake thought about it. "It wasn't none of your business, what I was doing."

"Would it bother you if I dug up your grandmother and took her wedding ring?"

"That's different."

"Not really," Tom replied. "Most folks don't like the idea of grave-robbing." He left it at that. He tied the cord in a doubled loop from the sled to the saddle horn, then took the reins and led the horse down the creek.

Epilogue

Randy Bergen walked into Barney's Pub and regarded the early evening activity around him. "Well, if it ain't the Shadow!" he said loudly. "I heard you were gonna be back in town today."

Tom turned around from the tables he had just pulled together and bowed.

"Damn, I've never seen a bruise that ugly before!"

"Thank you, Randy, how did your mother train you to have such tact? Her being an only parent, it must have been quite a challenge. Why don't you help me pull these chairs back." He waved his arm in a cast. "Me being an invalid and all, you would think somebody would help, but the patrons here seem to be a rude, worthless lot."

Emma appeared with a pitcher of beer and a tray of glasses. She said to Tom, "You going to start picking on people already? You must be feeling all right."

Randy looked hopeful. "Are you buying? It looks like you're expecting company."

"Bill is here, the Reverend is here, Eddie is coming in to play to-night, have a seat. Hell, who knows, maybe even Vince might slip away from the wife and kids since he knows I'm back in town. I tried to get Mary Twil to stay over, but she says she doesn't hang out with the low-life crowd. I think her husband's suspicious of how I got this shiner."

Bill, who appeared with a mug in hand, grabbed a new glass and filled it from the pitcher. "Emma says we should toast to your health. So who kicked the shit out of you?"

"A boring tale. I was out for a nice morning run and met a branch on a tree."

"What kind of bullshit is that? I heard you got mixed up in some old man's murder and a car-jacking."

"Bill, are you listening to Fes spread slander again? Don't you know that guy never graduated from traffic control school?"

"I heard it on the news. Two guys were killed and you ride out on a horse with another guy who had an arrow in his gut. They killed each other and you got a wrecked truck full of bullet holes. Now how did that happen?"

"You know, you can go to L.A. for vacation and wind up in the middle of a gang war. People are crazy. It happens all over. Hell, it could happen here. I just happened to be in the wrong place at the wrong time, pure coincidence."

Bill looked at Randy for confirmation, "Look, BLM in Colorado sent out a goddamn plane specifically looking for you. I've got a friend in Grand Junction who says it's true. Are they gonna make you pay for that plane?"

"How can they? There I was, on vacation, out hiking in the desert, communing with God and nature. Other than the Madonna herself, I hadn't talked to another human being in two weeks." Tom nodded to the Reverend, who had just pulled out a chair and sat down, "Maybe an alien or two. I also admit I talk to my dog and to myself at times. Regardless, there I was, blissfully unaware that there was any problem in the whole world. I was never truly lost. I never asked anybody to come get me, and I even checked in with my mother to let her know where I was going and when I would be back. Actually, I even reappeared ahead of schedule, so nobody should have been looking for me."

"Some folks thought you might be out looking for eco-saboteurs linked those livestock losses out in Willow Creek," said Jesse. "Remember the argument with your boss?"

"I think everything about that was too vague and circumstantial. Nobody is ever going to prove how it happened or who did what."

"I've been hearing some new rumors," Jesse announced. "They say there might be a connection between Jerry Skinner's murder and one of those guys who died in Colorado, but they're keeping the details real secret for the moment." He looked at Tom. "You know anything about that?"

"I think Mary Twil has her own connection to the Madonna. I think she pulled some clues out of thin air and plans to share the credit with Sheriff Greenwood and the sheriff down in Montezuma County. Could be the reason the rumor mill ran dry is that Fester and his friends haven't heard the details.

Randy raised his eyebrows. "Speaking of the Madonna, how was she?"

"Religious experiences should not be discussed lightly in a house of bad character. Some day soon I hope to have another visitation."

Emma set down a large platter of cheese nachos. "Don't blame the house for the bad characters that walk in and out."

Tom scooped up a handful of cholesterol. "Ah, health and life! Bill, did I ever tell you my trade secret for picking up babes in bars?"

"Oh, yeah! I gotta hear the punch-line!"

"No, seriously, this even works in bars in Utah!"

"I know the answer then," Jesse chimed in. "You just sit down and read a book. Ignore everybody. Some woman's going to come and try to talk to you. Works every time."